Lord
of the
Pies

Also available by Nell Hampton

Kensington Palace Chef Mystery

Kale to the Queen

Lord of the Pies

A KENSINGTON PALACE CHEF MYSTERY

Nell Hampton

CROOKED
LANE

NEW YORK

Published in the United States by Crooked Lane Books, an imprint of The Quick Brown Fox & Company LLC.

Crooked Lane Books and its logo are trademarks of The Quick Brown Fox & Company LLC.

Library of Congress Catalog-in-Publication data available upon request.

ISBN (hardcover): 978-1-68331-559-9
ISBN (ePub): 978-1-68331-560-5
ISBN (ePDF): 978-1-68331-561-2

Cover illustration by Teresa Fasolino
Book design by Jennifer Canzone

Printed in the United States.

www.crookedlanebooks.com

Crooked Lane Books
34 West 27th St., 10th Floor
New York, NY 10001

First Edition: April 2018

10 9 8 7 6 5 4 3 2 1

This book is for the readers.
Thank you for being part of my life.

Chapter 1

"What are you doing in the kitchen so late?" Penelope "Penny" Nethercott asked as she walked into the room. Penny was dressed in a Topshop miniskirt and T-shirt. Her blonde hair was down around her shoulders and she wore bright blue and pink eye shadow to highlight her eyes and bubble-gum-pink lipstick.

"Where are you going all tarted up?" I asked as I frosted the chocolate digestive biscuit cake I had baked for the family's dessert tomorrow. "You look marvelous, by the way."

Penny smiled and stuck her finger in the frosting bowl for a taste. "The girls and I are going clubbing. Why don't you come with us?"

"It's Wednesday night. We work tomorrow."

"All the better," Penny said. "Come out and get crazy with us."

"Who are you going with?" I wiped my hands on a clean kitchen towel and studied the cake. It was a no-bake cake with chocolate ganache frosting. It was the Queen's favorite cake and one of the duke's favorites as well. The duchess asked that I make it at least once a week. I was getting very good at dessert.

The no-bake cake was new to me, but I was proud at how much the family loved my version.

"I'm going with Evie Green and Rachel Houser from Duchess Anne's household. They work in the offices."

"As much as I'd love to meet more people, I think I'm going to pass this time. The duchess has asked me to cater the bridal shower she is giving your sister on Saturday. I got her approval on the dessert lists and there are a few new recipes I want to perfect by Saturday."

I had been working for the Duke and Duchess of Cambridge at Kensington Palace in London for three months and still felt the need to prove myself as an American Chef in a Royal British Household. So far, the staff had gotten to know me as Carrie Ann Cole—the chef who gets on Head Chef Butterbottom's last nerve. As the upstart American who thinks she can cook for the future kings of England. That strange American girl from Chicago who found her assistant dead under a raised bed of kale. I really wanted them to think of me as the amazing personal chef to Will and Kate. I guess amazing is too strong. What I really wanted was to simply fit in. That was tough because I was an outsider.

Most of the employees were like Penny. They either went to school with the Royals or had generations of their family working and living in and around royal households.

It was a tall order for a Midwestern girl to be seen as anything other than an interloper.

"You worry too much. My sister and her friends will love everything you make," Penny said and came around to give me a hug. "They know you are my friend and therefore their friend."

"All the more reason to get everything just right."

"I have to admit, your choice of pies and tartlets for the shower is very unique."

"My thinking was that everyone expects cake for a wedding—but it's spring and something light and dainty like lemon, coconut, and cinnamon cream pie would be a wonderful surprise."

"I like that you've chosen a pie theme, starting with veggie tartlets and moving on to meat pies and then the desserts. It's a veritable pie-heaven party."

"Well, you did say your sister loves pies."

"And the guys will enjoy your hand pies," Penny said as she snitched one more taste of ganache frosting and headed toward the door.

"Guys? I didn't know there would be any men at the party."

"Oh, they won't be there," Penny said. "But they expect the girls to bring them leftovers."

"Then I'll make extra." I took a deep breath. "No pressure."

"No pressure," she blew me a kiss and left the kitchen.

I added some pink flower decorations to the cake, and when I thought it was good enough I covered it carefully and put it in the refrigerator. Chilling was the secret to the icebox no-bake cake that was a royal favorite.

I made myself a cup of tea. Careful to put milk in it, not cream. Here I'd been making tea what I thought was the English way by putting cream in first then pouring the tea. But someone had pointed out in public that if I really knew how to make tea the English way I would use milk, not cream.

Yes, I was a silly American. But as embarrassing as it was to be called out in public, I now made tea correctly.

In fact, I actually preferred milk to cream in my tea. The one thing I knew for sure was that I didn't like sugar in my tea or coffee. I guess that comes from living in Chicago. Sweet tea was more of a southern comfort.

The little private kitchen was quiet tonight—well, most nights. I liked the calm that came at the end of the day and the sleepy calm of the beginning of the day before the rest of the workers showed up at the palace.

I felt intensely blessed. A year ago, my girlfriend in New York had gotten sick and needed me to step in to cater an event for the Duke and Duchess of Cambridge's visit to the states. When that happened, I felt like I had hit the top of my dream list. Then afterward when the duchess asked to meet me, I was sure that it was the best night of my life.

Until three months later, when I got the call asking me to come work for the young couple. To inhabit one of the three kitchens in their Kensington Palace apartments and cook for the family and their guests was bigger than any other dream. Even if it meant the end of my relationship with my boyfriend.

While it was well known that the duchess liked to cook for her family herself, the growing number of obligations and public service events made hiring a personal chef a necessity.

In three short months, I, Carrie Ann Cole, from Chicago, Illinois moved to London and became a personal chef to the Duke and Duchess of Cambridge.

A movement in the window caught my eye. I gasped and looked again. It was dark out but there appeared to be a man looking in the kitchen window right at me. I stood and grabbed the kitchen phone and called security.

"Palace Security, this is Hawthorne Willis, what is your emergency?"

"Hi, yes, hello, a man was outside the window watching me," I said.

4

"I see," Hawthorne said. "Is this Miss Cole?"

"Yes, I'm in Apartment 1A's professional kitchen."

"Yes, Miss, we have identified your whereabouts from the phone line. You say someone is peering in your window?"

"Was," I studied the now empty window. "There was a man watching me through the window. He's not there anymore."

"I've sent someone down to check it out."

"Thank you. I hate to be paranoid, but after Mr. Deems . . ."

"It's better we check these things out," he answered. "Stay on the line with me until the security officer gets there."

"Okay," I awkwardly sat in silence listening to the dispatcher breathe. "It's taking some time. I'm sure the man is long gone."

"Remain on the phone, Miss."

"Okay." I bit my bottom lip and studied the window. I felt stupid. If only I had called on my cell phone, I could have gone outside and seen if I could confront the peeping man.

The sound of footsteps in the hall outside filled the air and the door opened. "Chef Cole?"

"I'm right here." I waved my hand from the spot behind the door where the phone was attached to the wall. "I'm going to hang up now."

"Okay, Chef," Hawthorne said. "You're in good hands."

"Thank you." I hung up the phone.

Ian Gordon, the Head of Security for Kensington Palace and a man I considered a friend, walked into the kitchen. "What's the matter?" He asked in his Scottish drawl.

"I saw a man peering in the window there, watching me." I pointed to the curtained window over the sink. The window was just about counter height and usually allowed me a nice view of the parking areas inside Kensington Palace. "I called security right away. I think he must have seen me get up and dial because he's gone now."

"Stay here." Ian gestured with his hand toward the small table. "I'll be right back."

I went to the table and sat down. My cell phone rested on the top of the table and I lifted it up and snapped a couple of pictures of the window. It was light in the kitchen and dark outside, making it hard to see anything outside. The man must have had his face right up against the glass for me to see him. A shiver ran down my back.

The door opened again, shaking me out of my thoughts. "There's no one outside right now," Ian said, studying me with an intense gaze. Ian was tall with wide shoulders and handsome as the day is long. He had gorgeous deep blue eyes with long black lashes and thick black hair cut in a military style. His nose was straight and his jaw square with a dimple in his chin. It was enough to make a girl's heart beat just a little quicker.

Not that mine needed to move any quicker

"Someone was out there," I said. "I saw him watching me, plain as day."

"Did you get a picture of him?" He asked, lifting one of his dark eyebrows questioningly as he looked at the phone in my hand.

"No," I said, shaking my head. I held out my phone's camera. "I didn't think to take pictures until you were out there."

We studied the picture I had taken. There was no sign of Ian in the window.

"Did you see any footprints or anything?"

"It's all pavement out there," he said. "Can you describe the guy?"

"Yes, I think so." I knew that eye witness accounts were usually very unreliable, but I would do my best to describe what I saw. "I could see his face rising just above the window-sill, so he wasn't very tall."

"And you're sure it was a man?"

"Yes, he had short hair and large ears that stuck out. I think his nose was thin and his face was sort of oval shaped."

"Could you see the color of his eyes or hair?"

"No, they just looked black through the window. But his skin was pale."

"It could be any number of employees on the grounds," he said, mostly to himself. "The palace is pretty locked up and secure. I doubt that it was a random stranger in the employee parking area."

"Okay," I took a deep breath to try to calm my beating heart. "So what are you thinking? Was it someone who works here peeking in?"

"Well, your light is on and it's late. It could have been a security guard looking to ensure there wasn't anything odd going on."

"Right," I shivered, glancing back to the window. "Then when he saw me go for the phone he could have identified himself."

"I agree," Ian said. "I'll check into the outside guardsmen and see where they were at that time."

"And if it wasn't a security officer?"

"There are cameras on the corners of the building. We will see what they show."

I slumped in relief. "Okay."

"What keeps you in the kitchen until eleven PM?" He asked, leaning against the wall.

"I was making a cake and going over the desserts to be served at this Saturday's event."

"You put in some very long hours for a personal chef," he stated matter-of-factly.

"I want to do a good job."

"Even Butterbottom doesn't put in the kind of hours you do," Ian said, crossing his arms over his chest.

"How do you know?" I asked. "Have you been peering in my windows, too?"

"I pay attention," he said. "No need to peer in your windows."

"That's what security cameras are for," I teased.

He frowned. "There are no cameras in your kitchen. I see your light on all the time."

"I'm kidding. Wait, if you see my light on that means you are working longer hours than I am."

"I'm dedicated to my job."

I laughed. "I guess that means neither of us has a life. You know, there's such a thing as work-life balance. No one is indispensable. I do have my day off."

"I do too," he shrugged. "I'd just rather be on my watch."

"Then if you don't mind will you walk me to my room? I'm still a little spooked by the face in my window."

"Sure thing." He held the door open for me as I turned off the light and locked up the kitchen behind me. The staff-only hallways were simple wood floors and beige walls. The kitchen was down a couple of flights from the servants' apartments, where my tiny suite was next to Penny's and a few other people who needed to have direct access to the duke and duchess. Like the children's head nanny and the nanny's assistant.

Did I mention that Penny was the duchess's personal assistant? They met in school and Penny had the dream job of taking care of her now-famous friend.

"I hear you are getting a new assistant tomorrow," Ian said as we walked down the hall to my room.

"Yes," I said. "Agnes Moore. She comes highly recommended."

"You go through assistants quickly."

I stopped at my door and gave him a look. "Chef Butterbottom likes to impress upon them my unworthiness. My first two left because of the murder. My last two because of the difficult working conditions when the kitchen garden was being redone. Let's hope this new girl has staying power."

I thought I saw his mouth twitch into what might have been a smile. "Good luck with that."

I laughed and shook my head. "Fingers crossed. I mean how often does a murder happen around here anyway?"

Chapter 2

The next morning, I went down to the kitchen at five-thirty. It felt a little spooky to turn on the kitchen lights after last night. I glanced at the window and noted that it was pitch black. No face stared at me. I shook off the feeling and put on a kettle of water.

I liked French press coffee in the morning. My assistants had all preferred tea, which meant that having a boiling kettle of water always on hand was helpful. The kitchen was small but mighty. There was room for a chef, a sous-chef, and one assistant. Attached to the side of the kitchen was a small greenhouse. The greenhouse had been knocked down and rebuilt since I've been here.

That meant the plants weren't as mature as I had hoped. At least the various leaf lettuces and kale and chard all grew fast.

Jasper Fedman, the kitchen's head gardener, had planted new raised beds of vegetables that the duchess had requested and had even allowed me to dictate a few plantings as well.

I poured the heated water over the coffee in my French press, stirred the water mixed with fresh-ground beans, and then covered it, putting it in a cozy to steep. A sudden sound in the glass-walled garden had me whipping around, my hand going to my heart.

"Whoa," Jasper said as he stepped into the kitchen. "Didn't mean to frighten you."

"I didn't know you were in the garden," I said as I clutched the counter trying to calm myself down.

"I'm planting carrots and onions today," he said. "I saw you turn the light on and wanted to pop in and see how you are."

Jasper was a good-looking guy who was working his way into my heart. He was tall and athletic, with blonde hair and a reddish beard. He looked kind of like the movie-version of Thor, and his blue eyes tended to twinkle around me. Today he wore jeans and a dark T-shirt that showed off his biceps.

"I think you startled a year off my life," I said.

He grinned at me and my heart melted. "Sorry, love, I'll knock before I enter next time."

I turned away and pulled down two mugs. "I'm making coffee, if you want some. Or I have hot water for tea."

"Coffee is fine by me." He turned one of the kitchen chairs around and sat down so that he could rest his arms on the back. "I hear you are getting a new assistant today."

"Yes, Agnes Moore," I said, glancing at the kitchen clock. "I expect her in the next half an hour or so."

"I hope she stays longer than the last ones."

"Me, too," I shook my head. "That is if the Peeping Tom doesn't scare her away."

"Peeping Tom—what are you talking about?"

I handed him a mug of coffee and placed a small tray with a creamer and sugar bowl in front of him. I sat down next to the table. "Someone was watching me through the window last night. I called security but they didn't find anyone. The ground outside the window is paved so there were no tracks."

"That's weird."

"Creepy," I said and sipped my coffee. I like the acidic taste of French roast mixed with the smooth taste of cream.

"He had to be someone who works at the palace," Jasper said. "No one else can get back into the employee parking area. What'd he look like?"

I gave Jasper the same description that I had given Ian. "Do you know anyone like that?"

"No one I work with." He sipped his coffee. "No wonder you hit the ceiling like a scared cat when I stepped into the kitchen."

"Hopefully it was an anomaly and won't happen again."

"What does Gordon say about it?" Jasper asked.

"He's going to have his men look through the security footage from last night."

"Maybe it's a ghost," Jasper said with a twinkle in his eye.

"If it's a ghost, he can't come in," I said.

The kitchen door flew open and a middle-aged woman stepped in. She wore a trench coat with a white button-down shirt and black slacks under it and sturdy black kitchen shoes. She was plump and about five feet tall. Her steel-gray hair was pulled back into a no-nonsense bun. "Good day, everyone," she said with a faint Irish accent. "I'm Agnes." She extended her hand to Jasper.

"Jasper Fedman," he stood, leaving his coffee cup on the table. "I'm the head kitchen gardener."

"He supplies the fresh organic herbs and veggies for the kitchen," I explained.

"I brought a bucket of fresh new potatoes," he said, pointing to where he left the bucket by the door. "I thought you could use them for the family's meals."

"Wonderful, thank you," I said, waving as Jasper left. He was gorgeous and had kissed me once. It was my first week in London, and he'd taken me out for drinks. We spent the evening talking. I had a boyfriend at the time, but we had been separated. At the end of the night, Jasper walked me to my door and, in that moment, kissed me. A lot happened between then and now. I broke up with my boyfriend and settled into my life at the palace. I wondered if Jasper was ever going to kiss me again.

"Nice to meet you, Chef," Agnes said and shook my hand as well. She unbuttoned her trench coat and hung it on the coat hooks by the door. "What are we cooking for breakfast today?"

I handed her a white apron and grabbed my chef coat. "Start by boiling some new potatoes," I said. "We can incorporate them into an egg casserole. I'm cooking breakfast sausages and bacon, as well as buns and cinnamon rolls."

"Sounds ambitious," she said and tied the apron around her thick waist.

"Not too bad," I said. I started the rolls last night and they are in the proofer for the final proof right now. "Would you like a cup of coffee or tea? I've got the kettle on."

"Tea for me," she said. "But I can fix it myself."

Perfect. It seemed like Agnes was going to fit right into the kitchen. Maybe this time I found someone who would stick.

*　*　*

It was late afternoon and I had finished the family's tea service when Penny came dragging into the kitchen. "You look beat,"

I said and began to make a pot of Earl Grey tea without her even asking. "How late were you out last night?"

Penny looked sheepish. "I got in about four this morning."

"That's about the time I was getting up to work," I said. "I'm glad I didn't go. Did you at least have a good time?"

"Oh, yes," Penny said. "Evie Green is over the moon about some guy. But it turns out he's married. She thinks that he might leave his wife for her."

"Oh, that's no good," Agnes said from the side of the kitchen where she prepped the salad for that night's dinner. "Married men who cheat are all snakes. If they cheat on their wife, believe you me, they will cheat on their mistress."

"Evie says this guy wouldn't do that to her."

"Did she tell you who it was?"

"No," Penny said. "She said it was still very new and all hush-hush."

"What about you and Rachel?" I asked. "Did you pick up anyone new and exciting?"

"Rachel says she has her eye on one of the guys at the palace, but she won't tell me who because it's still in the flirting stages. Really, next time I need to go out with you," Penny said, shaking her head. Her blonde hair danced in perfect waves. "I know you're not seeing anyone and you would be a great wingman, er, woman."

"Well, thanks, I think."

"Nothing good ever comes out of partying on a week night," Agnes said with a shake of her head. "You girls are better off staying home and catching up on your sleep. Trust me, you won't regret it in your fifties."

Penny sent me a side eye. "I might be dead when I'm fifty and then what good will my staying home be?"

"Don't even kid that," I said. "Did I tell you I saw some guy peeking in the kitchen window late last night?"

"What?! No, that's disturbing."

"Who would do such a thing?" Agnes asked, her hands on her wide hips.

"I don't know," I said, "But it was creepy. I called security. Ian came out and didn't find anything. He's looking over the video cameras now."

"Wow, after Mr. Deem's murder, I'd be spooked by that," Penny said.

"A man was murdered here?" Agnes asked.

"It was no big deal," I downplayed what had happened.

"Mr. Deems was one of Carrie Ann's previous assistants. He went toes up inside the greenhouse."

I gave Penny a serious shush look. "It was totally solved and the evil-doers went to prison."

"I thought you said your last assistants left because they didn't like the close quarters here."

"That's true," I said. "They renovated the kitchen green-house after the murder and we were stuck in Chef Butterbot-tom's test kitchen. It was a bit of a hardship, but that shouldn't happen again."

"Okay," Agnes said and went back to preparing vegetables. "So long as I know what's going on around here, I'll stay."

"Even knowing some guy was peering in the window?" Penny asked.

I sent her another look.

"What?" She mouthed and shrugged her pale-blue-sweater-clad shoulders. Penny was always well-dressed. Today she coordinated her sweater and a blue and white tweed pencil skirt and kitten-heeled pumps.

She made my white-shirt-and-black-pants outfit feel frumpy. But then again, I wasn't working with the duchess, and my outfits were generally covered by my white chef's coat.

While her hair was cut in a pretty, perfectly wavy lob, my mass of unruly hair was pulled back tightly into a ponytail.

"I trust security can handle a Peeping Tom," Agnes said.

"Yes," I agreed quickly and put my arm through Penny's, dragging her out in the hall. "I'm positive Ian will have things well in hand."

"Oops," Penny said as the kitchen door closed behind us. "Sorry."

"The last thing I need is to lose another assistant."

"You brought up the creepy Peeping Tom," she rightly pointed out.

I sighed. "Ian thinks it's someone who works at the palace. How else would they have access to the employee parking area?"

"Makes sense to me."

"Hey, how are the plans for the bridal shower?"

"Oh, yes, that's what I was going to tell you," she said. "The duchess has a conflict of interest and can't make the shower."

"But she's putting on the shower . . ."

"Yes, she knows, but some sort of state affair came up and, well, you know family business comes before hosting a party for her employee's sister."

"Her friend's sister who is also her friend," I reminded Penny.

"Oh, don't get me wrong. The duchess is beside herself that she has to cancel her appearance. She has gone ahead and reserved the Orangery for us."

"The Orangery? Isn't that bigger than her apartments?"

"Not too much," Penny said. "And really it makes sense to hold it in such a lovely place if her apartments aren't available."

"Except for one thing, I don't work in the kitchen at the Orangery. That's a public kitchen and it belongs to Chef Wright."

"But that's the good news," Penny said. "Since we simply have to change venues, the duchess worked it out so that you can still cater the affair. Chef Wright has graciously bowed out."

"Oh, I don't believe that for a moment," I said. "No chef graciously lets another chef into their space to serve food that is not on their menu."

"Well, Chef Wright is going to do just that." Penny patted my shoulder. "All you have to do is take your food to the Orangery and serve us there instead of at the duchess's apartments."

"I think I'd better meet with Chef Wright first," I said. The change of venue wouldn't be that bad except now I have to deal with another chef and his ego.

"I don't think you will have a problem with Chef Wright," Penny said. "He's not like Butterbottom. Chef Wright has a reputation as a lover of the ladies." Penny wiggled her eyebrows. "But he's married so don't let him get too close."

I shook my head at her. "I'm not the kind to hang around married men," I said.

"Right now, you don't seem to be the kind to hang around any man."

"What does that mean?"

"That means you need to get out and have a life," Penny teased me. "You can't rely on a Peeping Tom to fill your life with excitement."

"You make me sound like an old spinster." I pouted.

"I'm simply pointing out that you are young and gorgeous, and yet you're spending all your time tucked away in a tiny kitchen. The boys at the bar have been asking about you."

"Which bar?" I asked, as I had only been to two. One had been Jasper's family's bar, the other a local bar where they held Mr. Deems's wake.

"Jasper's bar, of course," Penny said and smiled at me. "You can't hide in your kitchen and expect men to come to you. That's all I'm saying."

"Fine," I said with a sigh and a bit of a smile for my new friend. "How about we plan to go out Monday? It's my day off and the shower will be over and done with."

"Perfect," she said. "I'll get the girls together to pick you up at nine PM."

"Fine."

"Good," she said and stepped down the hall. "Don't forget to get tarted up a bit—it will be good for you." She waved and hurried up the stairs to the family's living quarters and the office where she worked.

I had no idea what I would wear. My closet was filled with sturdy black pants and white button-down shirts. It seemed I would have to make a trip to a store to get some kind of going-out outfit. Whatever that might entail, I knew it wouldn't be as colorful as Penny's.

Next on my list was to make an appointment to see Chef Wright and ensure he really was okay with my catering a party in his domain.

Chapter 3

The Orangery is a brick enclosed pavilion inside the gardens at Kensington Palace and away from the Palace itself. It was open to the public for lunch and high tea from ten AM until four PM. The bridal shower was set for six PM on Saturday.

I made an appointment to meet with Chef Wright at the end of his day on Friday. That way the family had tea and it gave me plenty of time to cook supper after the meeting.

It was a lovely spring day, warm enough that I didn't need a jacket as I crossed the gardens to the Orangery. The wind blew stray hairs out of my ponytail, but I smiled as the sun hit my face. It seemed to be rainy or foggy at some point every day; I was lucky to be between clouds.

The gardens were decked out in their spring flowers. Tulips, purple status, pink phlox, hedges, and flowering trees filled the air with fragrant scents and the smell of warmed damp earth and green grass.

I saw that they had opened the doors to the pavilion to let in some of the light spring air. Inside, a few tables still filled with late tea and tourists.

"May I help you?" A young man in a white shirt, black slacks, and white apron asked when I entered.

"Yes, I have an appointment to see Chef Wright."

"Sure," he said. "I'll check with him."

I waited while the young man went to the back. It was my first time in the Orangery with its elegant columns, lovely view, and long, narrow seating area. As I was glancing around, I froze. I thought I saw a shorter waiter with big ears going around to the back. Was that the Peeping Tom in my window? I took a few steps toward where he was, but the young man interrupted me.

"Miss—"

"It's Chef," I said. "Chef Cole."

"Excuse me, Chef, Chef will see you now. If you'll follow me, please."

I followed behind the young man, who I assumed was a maître d'. "Excuse me, but I thought I saw someone I know working here," I said as we walked toward the kitchen. "He is shorter than you and has kind of big ears . . ."

"I'm sorry, I don't know who you are talking about," he said with an apologetic smile. "This is my second day here." He walked me through the kitchen to the small back office. "Chef Wright? Chef Cole to see you."

"Thanks, Mel," the man inside the office said. "Come on in, Chef."

I stepped inside the small, cramped office. Like most chefs' offices, it was filled with recipe books, menus, and the paperwork that comes with ordering food and controlling inventory and personnel.

The man himself was tall and lanky with a quick smile and a warm brown gaze. He held out his hand and looked me straight in the eyes as if I was the most important person in the world to him at that very moment. I must say, it was flattering.

"Hi," I said, shaking his hand. "I'm Carrie Ann Cole. I work for the duke and duchess—"

"Of Cambridge, of course, I've heard good things about the American they've employed. But I didn't hear how beautiful she was."

I felt the blush rush right up my cheeks. He gently enclosed my hand in both of his, and it was oddly intimate. I pulled my hand from his.

"Thank you," I said. My mother had taught me to acknowledge a compliment no matter how odd. "I'm here to talk about Saturday's bridal shower. I understand the duchess rescheduled the venue to be here in the Orangery instead of her apartments. I wanted to ensure that you were all right with my catering the affair. I understand this is your kitchen and I—"

"Of course, of course," he said and pointed to the chair across from his desk. "Please sit. Can I get you anything to drink? Tea? A cocktail perhaps?"

I sat down more out of reflex, and he walked over to his chair. "No, thank you, I'm fine. Are you okay with me catering on Saturday?"

"Oh, yes, of course," he said as he sat down. He poured us each a glass of sherry and pushed one toward me. "Cheers."

I lifted the glass to his and then took a sip. It was very good. "What a relief," I said. "Sincerely, I didn't want any trouble."

"Who would have trouble with a beautiful woman such as yourself?"

"Chef Butterbottom, for one," I said as I placed the sherry glass down on his desk. "My ex-boyfriend, for two. He would have a terrible time with someone else catering in his space."

Chef Wright tipped his head to the side. "You said ex-boyfriend?"

"Yes. We broke up over my decision to stay in London and work for the duke and duchess."

"He sounds like a terrible man. Who would throw away the love a gorgeous woman?"

I felt the blush creep up my neck. "I'm sorry, I didn't come here to talk about personal matters." I stood. "I simply wanted to make sure you were okay with my catering the party."

"Yes, of course, whatever you need," he said sincerely. He stood with me.

"Good, okay, well, thank you."

"Let me show you the kitchen," he said, coming around the desk. He opened the door and put his hand on my back to guide me out.

"I really don't think that's necessary," I said, stepping out of his reach. "I'm cooking and baking everything in my kitchen. We'll bring it over and unpack and serve it here."

I thought I heard a clicking sound and turned to look over my shoulder, but there was no one there.

"I really need to get back to my kitchen. There's dinner to finish and such." I stuck out my hand. "It was a pleasure to meet you and I'll be sure to return your kitchen to you clean and ready for Sunday lunch."

"Thank you," he said and walked beside me to the now deserted dining area.

"Wait," I said, stopping in front of the door. "I thought I saw a waiter here. He was about this tall." I put my hand to the bottom of my eyes. "He has short hair and his ears kind of stick out."

"It sounds like you are talking about Wentworth Uleman," he said. "Did you need him for something?"

"No," I said, shaking my head. "I just thought I saw him looking into my kitchen window the other day, then today I saw him here. I wondered who he was and what he wanted."

"That sounds like Wentworth. Don't mind him. He is a staple around here. Good guy, actually. He shows up to work every day and works anywhere he's needed in the palace area. His grandmum worked for Princess Anne, so they have a long family history here. He probably just wanted to get a look at the lovely American." Chef Wright winked at me. "Can't say that I blame him."

"He could stop and say hello like a normal human," I said. "If you see him, please tell him to stop peering in my window. It's disconcerting."

"Of course, of course," Chef Wright said. "I will see you tomorrow."

"Yes." I stepped off onto the path. "Have a good day."

Wentworth Uleman was the name of the man who peered in my window. The same man who I saw at the Orangery. I pulled up my cell phone and called Ian Gordon.

"Gordon," he said into the phone.

"Hi Ian, it's Carrie Ann. I think I know who was peering in my window the other day."

"Wentworth Uleman," he said.

"Yes! How did you know?"

"I was getting ready to call you. We identified him on the video. He was definitely lurking outside your window at the time of your call. I called him in to the office. He seems harmless. He said he saw your light on and wanted to make sure everything was okay."

"By staring at me like a creeper?"

"I've put a warning in his personnel record. He understands if he is caught doing anything like this again he will be let go."

"Okay," I said. "Good. I'm glad."

"I told you I would take care of things," Ian said.

"I know, thanks."

"Any time." "Let me know if he bothers you again."

"Oh, I will," I said as I walked through the garden. "I owe you a dessert of your choice. Do you like pie?"

"I'm partial to coconut," he said.

"I'll make one just for you."

"Goodbye, Chef."

"Bye, Chief." I hung up my phone. Chef Wright seemed a little too slick, but it was nice to have a calm man like Ian Gordon watching your back.

The garden was still lovely even as the afternoon turned to dusk. I hurried along because I had dinner to make. Agnes would have everything prepped by now, and I didn't want to be late.

There was a crunch of footsteps behind me when I stepped out onto the parking lot that separated the back of the kitchen from the gardens. I turned and threw a quick glance over my shoulder. There was no one there.

I must still be on edge about the Peeping Tom, or perhaps it was lingering doubts about Chef Wright. I shrugged it off and hurried to the kitchen.

Dinner was a Friday night favorite of fish and chips. The fish was fresh from a local fishmonger and filleted into tender pieces. We coated it with a gluten-free beer batter and egg and deep-fried it in olive oil. Next, we cut golden potatoes into fries and baked them until they were crispy brown. Mushy peas and a fresh green salad finished off dinner. Everything was packed up and taken to the family's dining room where it was served with milk, tea, and a dessert of the chocolate cake I had made the night before.

I enjoyed making English fish and chips. Yes, I even liked mushy peas. The peas were fresh from the indoor garden that Jasper had rocking and rolling.

The children ate at eight PM. The duke and duchess had a date night out with friends. Penny told me that even after their date night, the duchess would be up very early to prepare for the last-minute event she had to attend.

Agnes left shortly after taking dinner up to the family. I stayed in the kitchen and worked on piecrusts for the shower. I liked a coconut crust with chocolate caramel pie. Of course, coconut cream pies all needed coconut crusts as well. There was an almond flour crust for the lemon meringue pie. And good old American flaky crusts for the apple and cherry pies.

The kitchen smelled of flaky pastry and warm spiced fruit. I was washing dishes when I noticed a face peering in my window again. This time I didn't even stop to call security. I dropped the pan into the sudsy water, wiped my hands on the towel I had hanging from my apron strings, and hurried out of the kitchen down the hall and outside.

"Hey!" I called.

The young man froze with what appeared to be a camera in his hand. It was difficult to tell because it was dark out, and the parking lot lamp light was low emission.

"What do you think you're doing?" I asked as I approached him. "Are you Wentworth?"

The young man unfroze the moment I took a step in his direction and took off running. I suppose I could have run after him, but why?

Instead I shouted at his retrieving back. "I know it's you, Wentworth Uleman. Stop spying on me or else!"

I frowned as he disappeared into the darkness. What did he want? Why did he think he could just peer into my window and why did he have a camera?

I walked over to the spot where he stood and looked inside. With the light on, it looked as if the kitchen was a stage. Why would anyone want to watch me make pies?

Shrugging, I turned back to go inside. Once inside I sent Ian a simple text.

"Saw Wentworth peering in my window again. I confronted him, and he ran away. I think he may have had a camera. Anyway, all is quiet now."

I got an immediate phone call. "Hello?"

"What do you think you're doing?" Ian sounded put out and his accent got thicker when he was upset.

"We know who the guy is," I said. "So I wanted to find out what he wants."

"You don't confront a stalker," he said. "That's madness."

"It's not madness when you know who he is. What I want to know is why he's doing it. Besides, he ran off."

"I'm on my way. Stay in your kitchen."

"Yes, sir," I muttered after he hung up. I looked around the kitchen. Did Wentworth think I had secret recipes? A quick glance in the mirror by the door showed me that I didn't look untoward. In fact, the mirror by the door was to ensure I didn't go out of the kitchen with anything on my face or in my hair—like flour or butter or frosting. I didn't want to show up in the duchess's audience looking like I was making a mess out of her kitchen. Even if I did from time to time when I was working out a new recipe.

The kitchen door opened beside me and Ian strode in. His eyes flashed and his jaw ticked in the corner. It was a look that meant business. I crossed my arms in front of me in self-defense. "I did not do anything stupid," I said before he could get a word out.

"The palace has security for a reason," he said. "You don't have to go out and confront people who aren't acting right."

"But you and Chef Wright know who this guy is. I mean, he's shorter than I am. I doubt he would hurt me."

He stepped closer and I leaned back against the mirror and hooks where I kept a clean chef jacket for those times I needed to be seen by the family. "How about you not confront him and not find out if he can hurt you."

"I wanted to know what he was doing. It looked like he was filming something, but there's nothing to film but me baking."

My explanation didn't seem to affect the emotion in his gaze. It made my heart beat faster.

"I've got my men out scouting the grounds for him right now. When we find him, I'll find out what he was doing."

"I'm dying to know."

"Don't say it that way," he said and shook his head at me.

"It was probably nothing." I tried to shrug off the reaction I was having to his nearness.

"It doesn't matter if it was something or not, I can't have him peering into palace windows." He went to the window and looked out. I took the moment to admire his backside. "I'll have a security screen installed. You can roll it down at night. It will allow you to see out, but no one else to see in. The family has them on all their private windows."

"Thanks," I said, giving myself a mental shake. Stop staring at the man for goodness sakes.

"It smells good in here."

"I'm making pies for the bridal shower tomorrow." I moved to the sink, hoping motion would break the spell. "The venue has changed."

"Yes, I know," he said as he studied me. "Please tell me you did not go out there without at least a knife or a rolling pin or a heavy sauce pan to defend yourself."

I looked around and bit my bottom lip. I didn't even think I might need to protect myself.

"Just, don't do anything like that again. Okay?"

"Why?" I asked. I guess I was fishing for something from him that might relate to the emotion he stirred in me.

"I don't need any more violence on the Palace grounds," he said. He walked up and stood toe to toe with me. "I especially don't want to see any of my friends get hurt."

"We're friends?" I half whispered. The man could get my pulse jumping. But everyone knew he had one rule about his job. He never mixed work and personal relationships. Lots of women on the grounds tried to get his attention. Ian Gordon had deftly let them all down. It was suspected he had a wife tucked away somewhere—or maybe a husband. But I didn't believe that. I could tell by the way he looked at me that Ian was not gay.

He lifted my chin so that I looked him in those gorgeous blue eyes. "We're friends."

Every nerve ending in my body was on fire. He smelled so good.

The moment came and went without any hint from him that it meant anything more than what he said. He took a step back, breaking the tension. "Try not to run out after Peeping Toms anymore. Okay?"

"Okay." I stood frozen to the spot as he left the kitchen.

Huh, I thought. He said we were friends. He was worried about me. Maybe Ian Gordon wasn't as immune to the women he worked with as he let on. That was an idea that carried me through a long night of pie-making.

Chapter 4

Saturday morning dawned clear and bright. The family had breakfast at eight AM. The duchess took the children to the park to play for an hour or so before she had to come back and get ready for the state affair.

All morning, Agnes helped me load pies and tarts into coolers and warming carts and take them over to the Orangery kitchen where Chef Wright had freed up space for us to set up for the bridal shower.

I was surprised how long it took to complete the catering for the shower. Penny's sister was not only a friend of the duchess but of many other women from higher British society. There were twenty-five attendees, and all of them were well-connected. Most of the women attending were part of the duchess's sorority or the duke's social group.

It seems when I made friends, I made them in high places.

"Oh, pish," Penny had said when I made a comment about the duchess giving the bridal shower for her sister. "My father knows her father through business. It's not like I'm in the royal set or anything."

Still, it was hard for an American girl like me to understand how everyone fit in the social structure. But I wasn't blind to the fact that some of the women attending had titles that I would never see on an American name card.

On my last trip to the Orangery, ladened with a tray full of warm meat pies, I pushed open the door to the kitchen and ran into someone. "Oh, I'm so sorry," I said as I worked quickly to resettle the pies before they all ended up on the floor.

"No worries," a young man said.

I looked over to see that I had run into a young man with big ears. He seemed as startled by my presence as I was by his. "Wentworth?"

"I'm sorry, ma'am, er Chef, but I have to get out to the floor."

"Stop!" I said, following him through the door. I grabbed his arm and juggled my tray of pies while he fumbled with his tray with a fresh tea service on it. "I want to know what you think you're doing peering into my kitchen late at night."

"I'm sorry, but you must have the wrong person," he said.

"No." I felt my mouth grow tight. "I don't have the wrong person. I clearly saw you—twice now—standing outside my kitchen. Last night it looked as if you were filming me. What were you filming?"

"Excuse me, is there a problem here?" the maître d' came up to us. It was then that I noticed that everyone was staring. I guess I had unknowingly made a scene and done exactly what Ian had asked me not to do. I had confronted my Peeping Tom, face to face.

"No problem," I said.

"She has me mixed up with someone else," Wentworth said. "I'm trying to do my job here."

"So am I," I said, straightening up so I towered over him. I leaned in toward him. "I don't want to see you outside my window again. Do I make myself perfectly clear?"

"Yes, ma'am," he said. "I mean, Chef . . ."

"Good," I said. Then I glanced at the maître d'. "Then there is no trouble here." I walked back into the kitchen, my heart pounding. I put the pies in the warmer and leaned against the counter in relief.

"Are you okay?" Chef Wright came out of his office and over to check on me. "You look quite pale."

"I'm fine," I said. "No, no, I'm not fine. I saw your waiter Wentworth Uleman looking in my kitchen window again last night. It looked like he was filming me."

"Oh, that's terrible," Chef Wright said. "I'll speak to him."

"I already have," I said. "I ran into him out in the pavilion just now."

"Oh, no, what happened? Did he harm you or threaten you?"

"No," I said. "He claimed I had the wrong man, but there is no mistaking those ears. I saw him very clearly last night."

"Then I will have him fired."

"I spoke to Security Chief Gordon," I said. "He told me that he had already spoken to the man once before. They were looking for him last night. I have to assume they didn't find him since he is here at work today."

"You are clearly distressed," Chef Wright said and took a hold of my hand. "Come sit down. Let me get you some water."

"Thank you." I put my forehead in my hands. "I had no idea that I would be so upset when I came face to face with him."

I took the glass of water from the chef and sipped.

"I can't have a man working for me who does these kinds of things," the chef said, patting my hand. "I will go now and see that he leaves here immediately."

A twinge of guilt struck me. What if he was right? It was dark outside. What if it wasn't Wentworth at all who was looking in my window. Could I have him fired?

I took a deep breath. "No, please," I said and squeezed Chef Wright's hand. "Let the man finish his shift today. I'll have Ian Gordon check the video from outside my window and confirm it was Wentworth. I think it's only fair that a full investigation be had before you let him go."

"If you are certain . . ."

"I'm not certain," I said with a wry smile. "But I do want to be fair."

"You are not only beautiful, but you are kind. It is my pleasure to know you."

I felt the heat of a blush rush into my cheeks. "I've got to put this behind me and continue on with work. Thank you for your hospitality."

"It is my pleasure," he said, picking up my hand and kissing my fingertips.

Okay, that action crossed a line in my mind. Especially since he wore a wedding ring. I pulled my hand away and got up. "I won't keep you. I'm sure you have a family to get back to . . ." I glanced pointedly at his ring finger.

He smiled broadly. "Of course. It was my pleasure to help."

Thankfully the rest of the night went smoothly. I didn't see Wentworth again. I assumed Chef Wright escorted him from the building quietly while I was setting up for the bridal shower.

The shower itself was elegant, and Penny and her sister and friends had a wonderful time. There was laughter and teasing and gifts and games. Two hours later the ladies all exited to several limos that were waiting to pick them up and whisk them off to a few London hot spots, while the older women headed home.

I packed up the kitchen and left a lemon pie with a note of thanks to Chef Wright and his staff for allowing me to use their space.

Ian met me at the door of the pavilion as I pushed the final cart out toward my kitchen. "How was the shower?"

"It seems like it was a success even without the duchess," I said. "The women all had a good time."

"Good."

"I saw Wentworth," I said as we crossed the garden and stepped into the parking lot.

"I heard," he said and held the door open for me to the palace. We all had employee key cards and he swiped his to gain access to the hall entry of the kitchen. "I looked over the video from last night."

"And?" I asked as I pushed the cart down the short hall and opened the door to my kitchen.

"It was definitely Wentworth Uleman," he said. "I had Chef Wright escort Wentworth to the security offices when he got off his shift."

"And?" I asked again as I started to put the washed platters away. "Did he tell you what he was doing?"

"He claims that he saw you wave at him. That's why he peered into the kitchen window."

"Well, that's just ridiculous," I said. "I was inside baking pies. I only saw him because I felt as if someone was watching me and looked up to see him peering back at me again."

"I told him that this was his second offense. There won't be a third."

"You fired him?"

"I can't, but Chef can and I have written up a report asking Chef Wright to do just that."

"So he could come back tonight and look into my window again?"

"No." Ian pulled out a kitchen chair and sat down. "I escorted him from the Palace grounds."

"But he could come back." I bit my bottom lip.

Ian tilted his head. "I thought you might say that, so I'm going to stay with you until you retire for the night."

I laughed. "That sounds like a big waste of the government's money."

"No waste," he said. "I'm off the clock. So why don't you put a kettle on for tea and offer me a piece of pie?"

"Oh, I see, that's your true reason for being here."

"What?" He drew his eyebrows together as if caught off guard.

"For the pie . . ."

He laughed. "You caught me."

"Well, then, what kind of pie do you want?" I opened the last covered platter with four kinds of pie left over from the shower.

"I don't know," he said as he looked them all over. "Why don't you set the platter down on the table and hand me a fork. I'll tell you which type is more to my liking."

That made me laugh. I handed him a fork and a dessert plate. There was something about a man admiring my cooking that made me happy. Much happier than a man who tried to charm me with guile.

* * *

There was a banging on my apartment door. I stumbled out of bed and glanced at my clock. It was five AM. A half hour before my alarm normally went off. "Chef! Are you in there?" It sounded like Penny outside my door.

I grabbed my fluffy pink bathrobe, slipped my feet into mule slippers, and hurried to the door. I turned on the light and blinked against the brightness of the bulb.

My apartment consisted of a three-room suite. You entered into a great room that had a kitchenette near the door. Separated by a breakfast bar was a small, furnished living area with an overstuffed couch and coffee table. Between the breakfast bar and the couch was the door to my bedroom. Inside the bedroom was the bath area, across from the kitchen. It was a neat setup and just enough for a young woman who spent most of her time in the family's kitchen.

"Carrie Ann?"

"I'm coming," I said. I unlocked my door and opened it to find Penny standing in the doorway. "What's the matter? Why are you up?"

"Something's going on at the Orangery," Penny said. She was still dressed in a pale blue shift dress and jacket. The same clothes she wore to the bridal shower.

"Are you just getting in?"

"Yes," she said and didn't even blush about it. "We pulled in to see security at the Orangery. I thought I saw Detective Chief Inspector Garrote."

"Oh, no!"

Garrote was the Criminal Investigative Department Detective Chief Inspector who worked on the murder case of Frank Deems. Something bad had to have happened for the CID to be involved.

"I know, I thought you might want to check it out with me."

"Are you going to the Orangery?" I asked.

"Of course," Penny said. "Quick, get dressed. Let's go down together and see what's going on."

"Come in," I said, waving her inside. "I'll be just a few minutes."

I hurried off to my bedroom and quickly dressed for work, pulling my wayward hair into a tight ponytail and grabbing a jacket. It was spring in London, and that meant it was still chilly outside in the early morning.

"Hurry," Penny said through the door. "They aren't going to let us close if we don't get there soon."

"I'll be right out," I said and shoved my arms into the jacket while Penny and I left my apartment. Penny lived in a small suite down the hall from me. Our hall was the servants' quarters. The walls were painted a soft beige and the wooden flooring was well-worn.

We hurried down the hall, down the stairs, and out through the door just beyond my private kitchen. I could see the flashing lights of the police cars in the distance. People came out of the palace to see what was going on. Most had not stopped to get dressed like I did. But I was glad not to have rushed out in a night gown, robe, and slippers.

We approached the crowd to get a good look. All of the lights were on at the Orangery. The building wasn't usually open to the public until ten AM. Security and police came and went. They all had looks of concern on their faces.

"What's going on?" Penny asked a bystander.

"Someone said there was a murder in the Orangery," the man in a robe and pajama pants said. His hair stood straight up on the left side of his head while the right side was smashed down.

"A murder?" Penny nudged me. "Who? How?"

"I don't know," he shrugged.

I caught a glimpse of Ian Gordon. I pushed through to the

edge of the crowd. There the security forces held back the growing crowd. "Ian? What's going on?"

"Chef Cole, what are you and Miss Nethercott doing out here?"

"We saw the lights," I said. "We heard there was a murder. Is it true?"

"Billings," Ian said to a tall, thin man in a security uniform beside him. "Disperse the crowd."

"Ian?"

"Go inside, Chef," his expression was grim. "Someone will let you know if your presence is needed."

"But—"

"You can't help, Carrie Ann," he said. "Go inside." Ian turned his back on me and spoke to another security officer. Together he and Officer Billings began to break up the crowd.

"All right, folks, go on back to your rooms," Officer Billings said.

"Was there a murder?" This time it was Mrs. Worth, the head of the duke and duchess's household, who asked the question. Mrs. Worth was a formidable woman. Thin and very proper, she looked completely ready for her day. She wore a gray sweater set, a black skirt that hit her midcalf and a black quilted coat. Her hair was a perfect gray shoulder-length bob.

I had known Mrs. Worth only a short time, but I had never seen a hair out of place on the woman. Even at five-fifteen AM, she was immaculately turned out. Unlike the rest of the crowd, it was as if she sprang out of bed fully dressed for the day.

"I'm sorry, ma'am, but Chief Gordon did not give me the liberty to discuss the details." Officer Billings ducked his head. "Please tell your staff to go back inside. We will share any information as soon as we can."

"Tell Chief Gordon that I expect to hear from him before I see anything on the telly."

"I will, ma'am." The officer held up his hands. "Now everyone, go inside."

"Well," Penny said to me as we walked back across the parking lot. "If it is murder, at least this time you are off the hook."

"Thank goodness for that," I said. "I had enough of that adventure last time."

If you decide to investigate this one, let me know," Penny winked at me. "I love all the insider details."

"Please," I said. "It's not going to happen. I have work to do that is more important. Which reminds me, I'd better dial Agnes. I don't think they are going to let anyone inside the Palace gates this morning."

"Let's hope if there was a murder that neither of us knows the suspect," Penny said rather morbidly.

"From your mouth to God's ears," I said. The last thing we needed was another disruption to the household.

Chapter 5

I was right. They didn't let anyone onto the Palace grounds. That meant I was on my own for the family's breakfast, lunch, and tea. I kind of liked working by myself. It was hectic, but I could move in my own rhythm.

All the bustle kept me glancing out the window to see what was going on over at the Orangery. Security swarmed the place. I watched as an ambulance came and went. That meant that someone had gotten hurt. I sent up a little prayer that it wasn't serious. Although from the fuss, I suspected the rumor of murder might be true.

Penny came into the kitchen after tea. She was showered and dressed in a soft knit top and navy blue capris with navy blue flats.

"You look well rested," I teased.

"Sunday is my day off," she said, snagging a ginger cookie off the cooling rack. "Do you have any tea made?"

"I'll put the kettle on," I said.

"Have you been working all day?"

"All day," I said.

"Shoot, I was hoping you might have gotten the scoop

about what was going on at the Orangery. I know you have a special relationship with Ian Gordon."

"What? No, no there's nothing going on between Ian and me. He doesn't have relationships with people who work at the palace. You said so yourself."

"Right." She got two teacups and saucers and put loose leaf tea in the teapot. Penny had become my closest friend since moving to London and taking this job. She was in my kitchen nearly every day and knew where everything was kept.

"You know more people here than I do. What have you heard about what happened? I saw an ambulance so I know someone was hurt."

Penny sat down at the table and I poured hot water into the teapot to steep. "Well, word has it that there was indeed a murder in the Orangery. I guess Chef Wright was in early to work on some paperwork and discovered a waiter named Wentworth Uleman face down in a lemon pie."

I swallowed hard. "Wentworth Uleman? Are you sure?"

"Yes, I'm sure, why?"

"Because he's the man who has been stalking me," I said.

"What?"

"I caught him peering in the window a second time and when I confronted him he ran away. So yesterday when I saw him waiting tables in the Orangery . . ."

"Oh, no, you confronted him again."

"Yes, and Ian Gordon told me that he could confirm it was Wentworth in the video of the man peering into my window."

"What was he doing?" Penny asked. She poured herself a cup of tea. "It's not like you sleep in here or anything."

"I have no idea, but when I saw him the second night it sure looked as if he had a camera on him."

"He was filming you?"

"I hope not," I said. "I'm not exactly documentary material."

"And now he's dead."

"Allegedly dead," I said as I poured milk in my cup and then added the tea. "Aren't there twenty waiters and waitresses working at the Orangery? It could be any one of them."

"Except Evie Green told me that Chef Wright told her he was certain it was Wentworth by the man's ears. Then when security got there, they lifted his head out of the pie and positively identified him."

"Yikes," I said, making a face. I took a sip of tea to calm my nerves. I had left a lemon pie on the counter for Chef Wright and his staff. Was it my pie that Wentworth was eating when he died?

"I thought Evie worked in Princess Anne's household. How does she know Chef Wright?"

"Well, now that's an interesting thing. Remember I said that Evie had a new man in her life?"

"No!"

"Yes, Chef Wright."

"I thought you said her new man was married," I said and tried not to shiver at the memory of him kissing my hand.

"Yes, Chef Wright's married."

"Oh, that's right, he wore a wedding ring. Funny, but he doesn't act married."

"And he has two kids, but that doesn't stop Evie from seeing him." Penny rolled her eyes. "The girl has no sense. She insists that he only has eyes for her."

"She's wrong," I said. "I swear he made a pass at me yesterday. What a smarmy guy."

"Don't tell Evie that or she'll say you were the one who went after her guy."

"He's married."

"She doesn't care."

"Wow, that's messed up."

"There's no telling Evie Green something she doesn't want to hear."

There was a knock on my kitchen door and Ian strode inside. "Chef Cole, do you have a moment?"

Penny shot me an I-told-you-so look. "I've got to go. Talk to you later." She patted Ian on the shoulder on the way out. "Be easy on her. She's clueless."

"What did she mean by that?" Ian asked as he stepped down into the kitchen.

"I have no idea," I fibbed. "What can I do for you, Chief? Do you want a ginger snap? Some tea? I understand you've had a busy day."

"No, thank you," he said. "I need to speak with you. Officially."

"Oh." I stood. "Do I need to go to your office?" The last time he had to speak to me officially I was being investigated for a murder. Then he hauled me off to the security office for a day.

"I'm sure things will be fine right here," he said.

"Okay," I wrapped my arms around my waist. "What do you need to know?"

"Did you leave a lemon pie in the Orangery kitchen?"

"Yes," I said. "I had an extra and left it in Chef Wright's kitchen for him and his staff as a thank you for allowing me to use his space for the bridal shower."

"And did it look like this pie?" He held out his phone and

there was a picture of a ruined pie. It looked half eaten, but as if someone had tried to eat it without any utensils—or even hands.

"It might have," I said. "It's hard to tell by the state of the pie, but it does look like my pie pan."

"It is your pie pan," he said. "The bottom was inscribed with the duke and duchess's initials."

All of my dishes had the insignia of the Duke and Duchess of Cambridge on them somewhere. It was how we kept track of the family's possessions.

"Okay," I said. "What happened to the pie?"

"Chef Wright found Wentworth Uleman facedown in the pie at 4:55 this morning. The man was dead."

I shuddered. "What? My pie? How awful! I'm sorry to hear that. What happened? To Wentworth, I mean."

"He was poisoned."

"Poisoned? By what? I know it wasn't my pie."

"It appears to be from your pie," he said. "We've sent samples to the laboratory. Detective Chief Inspector Garrote will want to speak to you about the pie."

"But I didn't put any poison in the pie. Why would I do that? Chef Wright and his staff have been nothing but kind to me."

"That's what I'm here to determine."

"Do you really think I might have done this?"

"No, I don't think you would do this," he said. "But something happened from the time you left the pie until the time Chef Wright found Wentworth. We have evidence that you confronted Wentworth twice."

"He was looking in my window," I said. "You know that I reported him."

"I spoke to him a second time about that. I told Wentworth we caught him on tape and notified his boss of his bizarre behavior. Chef Wright assured me he escorted the man off the palace grounds that night."

"See, there was no need for me to poison the man," I pointed out. "I trusted you and Chef Wright to do your job."

"But, as of now, you are the only person with motive to kill the man."

I stood. "I'm sorry? Did I hear you correctly?"

"You heard me," he said. "We have complaints from you about Wentworth. Two times you have been caught confronting the man, once on camera and once in front of witnesses."

"I wanted him to stop peering in my window," I said. "I didn't know him well enough to want him dead."

"Well, now that's where things get a bit . . . strange." He ran a hand through his hair. "Wentworth had a camera on him when we found him. He had pictures of you."

"Doing what? Cooking?"

"Getting close to Chef Wright."

"Excuse me?"

"There are pictures of Chef Wright kissing your hand and standing what can be perceived as intimately close. There is some idea that perhaps Wentworth tried to blackmail you or Chef Wright."

"Why? I barely knew the man."

"We have pictures of you and him that appear to be intimate. Chef Wright is married. That means there are grounds to blackmail you."

"The man seemed to like to getting in my personal space," I said. "But trust me, we weren't having any kind of relationship."

"That's what I need you to tell the inspector," Ian said.

"I will, because it's the truth. What else did Wentworth have photos of? Chef Wright seems pretty loose with women. How do you know that Chef Wright didn't kill Wentworth?"

"We don't," Ian admitted. "But I can't and I won't discuss the investigation with you. For now, we need to relieve you of your duties to the family until we can rule you out as the killer."

"What?"

"We can't have a person who could have poisoned a man to his death serving food to the duke and duchess and their children."

"But—"

"I'm going to have to ask you to leave the kitchen," he said. "I'll walk you to your quarters."

"But the family has to eat dinner."

"Mrs. Worth has been informed of the problem."

"Who is going to cook for them?"

"Chef Butterbottom has been assigned to the family until further notice."

"Great." I flung my hands in the air. Chef Butterbottom was the head Chef for Kensington Palace and cooked for all the public functions. He was also my archenemy. He was sure I was ruining the children's palate with my American recipes.

"I need you to come with me," Ian said gently.

"But I have food in the oven and need to put away the other ingredients I have out."

"Chef Butterbottom will handle dinner."

"What happens to the meal that is in the oven and my chopped vegetables?"

"The Crime Scene guys will be going over everything with

a fine-tooth comb to ensure there isn't any poison in your kitchen."

"This is ridiculous," I said as I walked toward the door. "Why is it that whenever anything happens the first suspect is the American?"

"It's not personal," Ian said, holding the kitchen door open. A woman and a man stood in the hallway wearing jumpsuits and holding black equipment bags. They had CID badges on their collars. Ian escorted me out and the pair into my kitchen.

I sighed long and hard.

"Come on," he said and took a hold of my elbow. "Let's get you back to your room. Think of it as a tiny vacation."

"For how long?"

"Only until we gather more evidence," he said.

"You said it wasn't personal," I said. "Why does it feel personal? You know Butterbottom will be so happy to see me out."

"You aren't out," he said firmly as he escorted me up the stairs and down the hall to my room. "You're just on pause. We have to be careful."

"I am careful," I said as I unlocked my apartment door.

"Where were you last night between midnight and four A.M.?"

"Okay, see, that's personal," I said. "But for your information, I finished up in the Orangery around ten PM. I was back in my kitchen and sitting with you until eleven."

"When did you leave your kitchen?"

"I think around midnight," I said. The hall cameras should confirm that I went straight to my room and, believe it or not, went to bed."

"We'll review the tapes and the key card records," he said. "With any luck, you'll be back to work by Tuesday."

"Lucky for you tomorrow is my day off," I muttered.

He leaned against my doorjamb, filling my doorframe. "I am taking this seriously. I think you should too."

"Wait," I said and clung to my door. "If Wentworth had pictures of me, who else did he have pictures of?"

"CID is combing his apartment now to answer that question," he said. "Please, Carrie Ann, take this time to put your feet up. Go out and enjoy London in the spring. Leave the investigating to the professionals. Okay?"

"Good evening, Ian," I said. "Please get me my kitchen back by Tuesday, okay?"

"I'll do my best."

I closed the door and turned to my quiet apartment. Great, kicked out of my kitchen yet again. I had gambled my entire life on this move to London. So far it was off to a rocky start.

Chapter 6

"So here's what I was able to find out." Penny sat on the couch in my living area and leaned toward me. "You weren't the only one Wentworth was filming."

"I certainly hope not," I said with a sigh. We munched on hamburgers and French fries that we had delivered from one of the local pubs. "I don't know why Wentworth turned his camera on me. It's not like I knew him or even worked with him."

"My theory is that he was looking for someone, anyone to film."

"Why?"

"There may be evidence that he was trying to sell pictures to the tabloids."

"That's crazy. What tabloid would be interested in a personal chef? It's not like I blog or do anything remotely like a celebrity. In fact, I think my lack of fame is part of the reason I got this job."

"The duke and duchess are so famous that everyone is looking for a new angle to sell newspapers and news feeds."

"This angle is dull." I dipped a fry in ketchup and popped it in my mouth.

"Well, you did find a dead body and solve a murder."

I made a face. "I don't want to be famous for solving a murder. I'd rather known for my cooking. Now if I do become famous, it will be for all the wrong reasons."

"Oh, don't say that," Penny said. "There is still a good chance that you will be known for your cooking."

"So who all was Wentworth taking pictures of?"

"Rumor has it that he was following Chef Wright around snapping pictures of the man and his various lovers."

"Various lovers? Poor Evie," I said.

"Evie is a big girl who knew what she was getting into when she started to see him."

"They think I was one of his lovers," I said. "It's why they have me out of the kitchen. But I swear it was just the guy being smarmy with me."

"Smarmy? You used that word before. I had to look up the meaning."

"It's a good word," I said in my defense. "He stood too close and had that look in his eye. You know the one where a guy looks as if he is picturing you naked?"

"Oh, yuck."

"See, exactly," I said. "It seems to me as if Chef Wright should be the lead suspect."

"But it wasn't his pie that poisoned Wentworth," Penny pointed out rather unhelpfully.

"Who else was Wentworth photographing?"

"I understand he took pictures of visiting dignitaries," Penny said.

"So maybe someone didn't want anyone to know what they were doing while they visited. I think we need to see all of Wentworth's pictures."

"The police won't let us near them," Penny said and sipped her cola. "But never fear, I'm certain some newshound has already gotten ahold of copies."

"How?"

"The bloggers and papers never rest," Penny said. "If there's money to be made, there's someone looking into it. Besides, Wentworth didn't live in the palace. That means his camera, phone, and computer are open to being hacked by anyone who needs a few bucks."

"Crazy."

"Oh, you know what else I heard?"

"What?" I loved that Penny was a font of knowledge when it came to the Kensington palace staff.

"Old Butterbottom is enjoying taking over the duke and duchess's dinner."

"That's not news," I said with a frown.

"He's not the only one," Penny said. "There are others on his staff who felt as if you shouldn't have catered the bridal shower."

"What? Why?"

"Because they are jealous of your brilliance," Penny said and patted my hand. "Don't worry. There is nothing they can do to hurt you."

I did worry. Especially because I was kicked out of my kitchen at the current moment.

"Let's talk about our night on the town tomorrow," Penny said, changing the subject abruptly.

"Oh, I didn't think we were going anymore," I said.

"What? Why not? You promised."

"Fine," I said. "But I don't have anything to wear club-hopping."

"No worries," Penny said, jumping up. "Come on, let's raid my closet."

I followed her out to her suite of rooms. Her rooms mirrored my own. Her kitchen was on the right of the door and was filled with cozy bric-a-brac and a small teapot collection. While I left my walls beige, Penny covered hers with art and fabric in a cozy mishmash of colors.

She pulled me into her bedroom where her bed was left unmade, a scramble of bright blankets and white sheets. Like me, she had a well-worn wardrobe for her clothes. But unlike me, she had clothes that spilled out to the floor and the chair. She also had a closet rack filled with clothes that squished up against the wall, covering the bedroom window.

"Okay, you need something like a little red dress." She went over to her clothes rack and started pushing through the thick sprawl of hangers and outfits. "Yes!" She pulled out a gown that was made of jersey material that would cling to all my curves. It had no sleeves and a skirt that was so short I wouldn't wear it without leggings underneath.

"I don't know," I said doubtfully.

"Oh, no, you're going to wear it. You promised to get tarted up with me. Come on, you need to have a good time. You're missing out on London staying in Kensington Palace all the time pouring over recipe books. There's a whole world out there." She waved her hand at the wall where the blocked window was. "You never know. You might land yourself a prince."

"Oh, I don't need a prince," I said.

"I know you prefer a gardener or a security chief."

"Stop," I said. "I promised myself I wouldn't date people I work with."

"You broke your own rule when you kissed them," she teased.

"I never kissed Ian Gordon," I protested.

"We can change that once we get you all dressed for our night out tomorrow. I have a pair of red stilettos."

"Wait, my feet—"

"No protests. It's only for one night. I want you to have fun while you're young. This is London, baby!" Penny reached into her wardrobe and pulled out a pair of killer high heels. "Now, let's talk about what we're going to do with your hair."

* * *

Mondays are my errand-running days. The one day off I have all week and I usually spend it doing chores and paying bills. The fact that I was under suspicion for yet another murder did not deter me from going outside the palace gates. I made a trip to a local grocery store near the tube station.

"What are you buying this week?" the store manager asked. He was a young guy with ruddy cheeks and long blonde hair that fell into his eyes in an endearing way.

"I thought I'd try some of the more obscure cheeses," I said. I lifted my handheld basket to show that I had a box of crackers already inside. I didn't keep much food in my tiny kitchenette. There was no reason to since I had access to a fully stocked kitchen. But there were times when I wanted a late-night snack or had Penny over for wine. It would be nice to have some things on hand.

"Try the raw cheddar," he suggested.

"Raw?" I wasn't sure.

"It's good, it has different enzymes at work. Oh, and how about some mangosteen fruit?"

"What?"

"Some people call it the Queen of Fruits because it is said that Queen Victoria offered a reward to anyone who could bring her a fresh one. They come from Asia." He picked up a small purple fruit. "Tastes citrusy."

"Okay," I said. "I'm game."

I added a few of the fruits to my basket and kept walking when another customer caught his attention. I picked up a few more things on my list and went to the checkout where I spotted the tabloids. There were pictures of the Orangery and the crowd that had gathered to see what was going on yesterday morning. The headlines read: Photographer Uncovers Spy, Ends Up Dead.

"What?"

I pulled the tabloid off the shelf. A glance at the long line behind me at the checkout told me I couldn't waste any time reading the pulpy paper. I bought it and a second one that read: Duke and Duchess Watch in Horror as Man Dies of Lemon Pie.

Okay, now I know they were lying. There was no way the duke and duchess were up and watching out their window at four AM.

"Find everything you were looking for?" The checkout lady asked. Her name was Sally and she checked me out every Saturday. "Not like you to pick up the tabloids. Terrible things going on at the palace these days."

"People do awful things," I said.

"If you ask me, anyone who takes pictures of the royals and sells them to the tabloids deserves what he gets." Sally was a small woman with short white hair that was tightly curled, a puffy round face, and pale blue eyes. She always wore some sort of sweater, dark slacks, and a green and white striped apron on top of it all.

"I almost have to agree," I said. "But I can't condone murder."

"Ah, well, if a bad man slips and accidently kills himself I'm not going to cry over it." She expertly rang me up and bagged my goods. "You take care now."

"See you next week."

Once outside, I walked the blocks to the park and sat in the sunshine and thumbed through the tabloids. The spy story caught my attention. Apparently, there was a report that Wentworth had caught a diplomat from another country in the wrong part of the palace taking something from a woman. The photograph was grainy and out of focus. But it looked like the man was exchanging paperwork for cash.

The man was identified as Lord Heavington. The woman was dressed like one of an army of assistants who helped run the households in the palace. What did the papers contain?

The tabloid speculated that Lord Heavington was spying for his home country. That he paid the unknown woman for copies of the itineraries of the royal family. There was speculation that there was a plot to kidnap the young prince.

"That stuff's all made up, you know," a man said from over my shoulder. I gasped and glanced over to see Jasper Fedman standing behind me. He looked gorgeous in a white T-shirt and jeans.

I quickly stuffed the papers back into my grocery sack. "They say there are bits of truth to be found in the tabloids."

"There are?" he asked, sitting down beside me.

"Yes, I saw it in the movie *Men in Black*."

"Ah, right," he said, crossing his arms. "I believe they were talking about aliens."

"Aliens, spies . . . it's sort of the same thing, isn't it?"

He laughed. The sound was hearty and made me smile. "How are you, Chef?"

"I'm not so good," I said with a shrug. "They've kicked me out of my kitchen again. This time they have Butterbottom cooking for the family instead of me."

"Wait, I thought Mondays were your day off."

"They are," I said. "The duchess likes to cook for her children on Monday. But they kicked me out last night and the main kitchen cooked for them."

"Maybe old Butterbottom is jealous of your talents," he said.

"He has no need to be," I said. "You would think he has enough to do running his own kitchen." I shrugged. "Enough of that, how are you? How are the gardens?"

"The gardens are growing well. We have leaf lettuce out now, and I've got tomatoes and peppers and zucchini started for you. I also have squash, pumpkin, four varieties of beans as well as onions and herbs."

"You are amazing," I said.

"I know," he teased.

We sat in silence for a moment with our faces raised to the blue sky. "I hear that a fellow died face first in one of your pies."

"That's what they tell me," I said. "But not one of the twenty-five or so women who attended the bridal shower I catered is in the least bit sick."

"Did they eat your pie?"

"Every one of them had at least one piece."

"So odds are twenty-five to one of dying from your food."

I shook my head at him. "I think he died of something else and just happened to fall face first into my pie. Ian Gordon tells me that they should know the laboratory results soon."

"When did he tell you this?"

"I saw him in the hall this morning on my way out of the palace."

"He's keeping an eye on you then."

I sat up straight. "I suppose he is. I hadn't thought of it that way."

"He can be sneaky like that." Jasper stood and shoved his hands in his pockets. "But a little bird told me you were going out on the town tonight."

"Have you been talking to Penny?"

"Maybe."

"She is making me wear her clothes," I said. "I'm supposed to meet in her room at seven PM for her to do something wicked with my hair. I'm afraid." I smiled.

"You should be," he said. "Take a picture, okay? I'd love to see what you look like going out on the town."

"I think we might be stopping at your family's pub," I said. "You can see for yourself."

"That's an invitation I can't pass up," he said and winked at me. I watched as he strode away.

What had I just done? Maybe ventured my toe in the London dating pool. Maybe broken my own new rule of not dating people I work with. I wondered if he would really show or even if Penny would let me go someplace as low-key as Jasper's family pub.

I grabbed my bags and hurried toward the palace and inside. I had to show my key card badge even though the security men knew me by sight.

My apartment was quiet and freshly cleaned. Yes, one of the benefits of living in the palace was having a chambermaid who cleaned the apartments once a week. It was nice to concentrate on work and not have to worry about cleaning my own space. It was also a luxury I had never had before and never thought I would have.

Mrs. Worth explained it was a way for the administration to keep close track of any maintenance issues that might pop up. I understood—the building was one of the oldest I had ever lived in.

I put the groceries away and pulled out the tabloids. I grabbed a tea, sat down on my couch, and tried to find the kernels of truth in the sensationalism. The pictures were accredited to Wentworth. So he was selling pictures to the tabloids. I wondered if Lord Heavington was behind the murder. Who was the man? Why would he want to purchase palace secrets?

I popped open my laptop and typed his name into a search engine. Lord Andre Heavington was an Ambassador from a small Eastern European country. He had been in London for the last ten years and was a favorite of the social set. What was he doing in the picture?

There was a knock on my door. I opened it to find Ian standing in the hallway. "Hello."

"Chef," he said with a nod of his head. "Your kitchen has been released."

"Can I cook for the duke and duchess tomorrow?"

"That's up to the duchess," he said.

"But I'm not a suspect, right?"

"I can't comment," he said. "But the cause of death was definitely poisoning."

"Poison."

"Yes."

"It wasn't my pie."

"Can't comment."

"Have you seen the tabloids?" I walked back into my apartment to pick up the papers. "Wentworth was selling pictures to the tabloids. Have you looked into this Lord Heavington picture?" I showed him the picture of the ambassador buying something from an assistant.

"A man doesn't usually poison a person," he said skeptically.

"Oh, pooh, what if Wentworth was blackmailing him? He might take advantage of what was available."

"And most probably bashed the man on the head."

"Well, what about the woman who is in the picture?" I pointed at the blurry shot. "Do you know who she is? Do you know what she sold him?"

His mouth went into a thin line. "I'll look into it."

"Fine," I spat out. Then softened. "Thank you."

"Have a good day, Chef Cole," he said and walked off down the hall. Well, if nothing else, I brought the possibility of other suspects to him.

I texted Penny. "I got my kitchen back."

"Cool."

"But I can't cook until the duchess agrees." I sent a frowning emoji.

"Mrs. Worth is meeting with her now," Penny texted back.

I sat down on my couch. Maybe, just maybe, I would have my job back by the end of the afternoon.

Chapter 7

"Good news," I said as I entered Penny's apartments. "Mrs. Worth has informed me that the duchess is letting me return to cooking tomorrow!"

"That is good news," Penny said. "But you can't use it as an excuse not to go out tonight."

"Not even if I have to get up at five-thirty AM to prepare breakfast?"

"Not even." She pulled me inside. "I see you are wearing the red dress."

"Yes," I subconsciously pulled at the short hem.

"Where are the shoes?" She peered down at my flip-flop–covered feet.

"I brought them," I said, lifting the shoes in the air. "I didn't want to fall and break something on the way to your room."

"Oh, pish, you aren't going to fall and break anything. They're only five inches tall plus they have raised toes."

"It's like walking on stilts."

"Don't be ridiculous. Come on, we're going to do your hair and makeup."

An hour later, I toddled out of the palace to the cheers of the security guys.

"Looking good, Chef!" One guy called.

"A tasty dish," another called.

"Ladies, ladies, ladies, come with me," Penny's friend and private chauffeur for one of the royals, Ethan Craig, put his arms through ours and escorted us to the sedan he had parked in front of the palace. He opened the door for us and I felt like a bit of a celebrity as I tucked myself into the vehicle.

Ethan got into the front seat and put on his chauffeur's cap. "Where to, Penny?"

She grinned. "Let's pick up Veronica and her friends."

"Veronica?" I asked.

"Yes, don't worry Veronica and her friends are great. Veronica knows the doormen at a couple of London's hottest clubs. I promised to show you London and we're going to see it tonight."

"And we're off," Ethan said as he entered the traffic. Twenty minutes later we had squeezed four girls into the car and headed toward the London night club scene.

One of the girls—Maegan, I think her name was—pulled out a bottle of vodka and took a swig then passed it around.

"Um, no thanks," I said, waving away the offered bottle.

"Nope, you've got to do it my way tonight," Penny said, pushing the bottle back into my hand.

"Fine," I said and took a sip. We hit a bump and the sip became a swig. I swallowed hard and it burned all the way down my throat and into my stomach, but it soothed the uncomfortable knot that had formed there.

Yes, I had lived in Chicago, but I was a food nerd. I spent my entire life practicing recipes and going to visit kitchens and restaurants. I wasn't exactly the clubbing type.

"First stop is The Ministry of Sound," Ethan hollered back over the top of the blaring music. I handed the bottle off to one of the other girls. We crossed the River Thames and pulled up next to a club where people stood in line.

"Come on," Penny said, taking my hand as we poured out of the vehicle. I could hear the pounding music on the street outside.

"There's a line," I pointed to the people who curved around the corner.

"No worries, Veronica has us in," Penny said as she pushed me toward the bouncer.

He looked us over. "Veronica, you have a bigger group tonight. Who's the new girl?"

"She's the duke—"

"An American," I interrupted. "Penny promised me a taste of London nightlife."

"Well, we can't keep you waiting now, can we?" He winked at me, leered at my legs a moment, and then waved us all in.

"I can't believe you didn't tell him who you were," Penny complained as we entered the pounding, crowded club. A man at the main entrance stamped the back of our hands and Penny pulled me inside. "You should use that bit of a celebrity we talked about, you know. That counts for something."

"I don't want to get fired for trading off the duke and duchess's name," I said.

"You won't get fired," she said, shaking her head. "Look there's Prince Harry. Come on, let's get a drink and see who else is here."

The club became a blur of bodies. It seemed the women were all dressed like me, so I didn't feel out of place at all. Even with my short, tight dress, sky-high heels, and wildly teased hair.

The men on the other hand almost universally were dressed in T-shirts and jeans. A few of the richer guys wore button down shirts, but jeans all the same. It was strange. Almost as if the women dressed up for each other.

From the Ministry of Sound, we went to Fabric and then to XOYO and when Penny and the girls headed toward yet another over-crowded, pounding music dance floor, I called a driver to come get me. Luckily, I had an app on my phone that allowed me to get a personal driver. The girls waited for my car to arrive then I kissed and hugged everyone and promised to go out with them again sometime, then Ethan opened the car door and I slipped inside.

Inside the car was quiet, and I closed my eyes and rested my head against the back seat. "So we're going to Kensington Palace," the driver said. "Do you live there?"

"Yes," I said. "But I'm not a royal or anyone you can brag about. I just work there."

"No worries," he said with a shrug. "My sister works there. I thought you might know her."

"I might, but it's a big place, and I'm new," I said. My head swirled from overstimulation of sight and sound and three martinis, not to mention that slug of vodka in the car.

"She works as an assistant to the foreign department. She helps guide visiting dignitaries from place to place. Makes sure they don't get lost, that kind of thing. She can speak seven different languages."

"Sounds like you are pretty proud of her," I said. "What's her name?"

"Beth Branch," he said. "I'm David Branch."

"Nice to meet you David," I said and leaned forward. "Thanks for driving me."

"You're welcome." He stopped at the security gate at the back. "Say hi to my sister if you see her."

"I will," I said and got out of the car as gracefully as I could.

I took off the painful shoes and walked barefoot through the security gates and up into the apartments. A quick glance at my cellphone told me it was three AM and I didn't have much time before I had to be back in my kitchen.

"You look like you had a good time," Ian said when I opened the door to the entrance hall.

"I did," I said. "What are you doing up? Are you spying on me?"

"No," he said. "There was call about a disturbance near the kitchen."

"My kitchen?"

"Yes."

"Then let's go."

"You can't go barefoot."

"Fine," I put on the red heels. "I'm ready."

He gave me a look that sent me blushing.

"They're just shoes." I pulled at my skirt. "You go first." I turned him around and pushed him forward.

Lucky for me, he complied. We got to the kitchen and it was all locked up. He waved me forward and I opened it with my key. Reaching in, I turned on the light. The kitchen was a mess. It looked as if someone had come in and thrown a tantrum. Pots and pans were everywhere, drawers opened and dishes strewn about.

"Oh no." I sat down hard at the kitchen table. The seat was filled with flour from a bag that someone had emptied as if looking for something hidden inside. The white powder fluffed up around me and covered me in a fine layer.

"What the heck?" Ian pulled out his flashlight. "Don't move."

"I won't." I waved flour away from in front of my face. As I looked around at the mess, I realized I was not going to get any sleep tonight. I had to have this cleaned up and ready for the family's breakfast.

"It looks like they came in through the window," he said, examining the broken glass and crushed screen. "Although I don't know how. It was locked and secured with an alarm. I know the team didn't leave it open, and it's pretty crudely broken. They didn't seem to care that we have a video camera on the corner of the building."

"It's clear that whoever did this was either a vandal or looking for something. I don't know what they thought they would find since the CID has already been through the kitchen with a fine-toothed comb."

"I suspect it was vandalism," he said, studying me. "Someone may blame you for Wentworth's murder and this could have been revenge."

"Like a mad teenager's revenge." I stood up. I had waited while Ian looked over every nook and cranny of the kitchen.

"It's clear," he said. "I don't see anything dangerous. Quite a bit of debris, though."

"I need to get to my room and change so I can clean this up before breakfast."

"I'll send a crew to come down and board up the window."

He studied me again for a moment. "Do you want me to walk you to your room?"

I studied him back. Maybe it was the exhaustion from being out at the clubs, or maybe it was the remains of the drinks, but I thought there was a moment where something brave and wonderful flashed between us. He took a step toward me.

"Sorry, boss," Officer Billings stuck his head in the kitchen, breaking the moment and possibly saving me from months of embarrassment. "Don't mean to interrupt, but there's another disturbance at the Orangery."

"Right," he said. "See that Chef Cole gets to her room safely." He strode out and I let out a slow breath.

"Chef?"

"I'm okay," I said with a short smile. "Good actually. Do they need you?"

"I'm here to see to your safety."

"I'll be fine to get to my room," I assured him. "Can you see that the kitchen stays secure?"

"Will do."

I left the kitchen, took my shoes off and hurried to my room. I closed the door and leaned against it. "This close to disaster," I muttered. "Ugh."

Thankfully I didn't have the time to think about things too closely. I dragged myself to the bathroom. Time to shower and get dressed in my work uniform.

Chapter 8

"How did you make breakfast in this mess?" Agnes asked me when she arrived at six AM.

I had managed to clean up the half of the kitchen with the stove, sink, and fridge. The back of the kitchen was still wrecked from the break-in. The lights were on because the window was boarded over.

"I only had time to clean up half," I said briskly. "Grab an apron and let's clean up the cupboards."

"I meant no disrespect. If the rest of the kitchen looks like this now, I can only imagine the amount of work you did."

"Thanks, Agnes," I said. "Welcome back."

"I'm glad to be back, Chef," she said as she hung up her jacket. "Who took care of the family while we were off?"

"Chef Butterbottom made their dinner," I said. "I heard his pastry chef, Geoff Theilman, made their desserts."

"Huh," she said with a slight snort. "I bet he was over the moon about that."

"What do you mean?"

"I heard that Geoff let the entire staff know that he thought he should have catered the bridal shower, not you."

"What? Why?"

"Because he's the main kitchen's pastry chef. He's been grousing to the entire staff that an American chef should not have catered something so personal as a bridal shower thrown by the duchess."

"Well, I had no idea he even existed, let alone was upset that I did my job."

"And a good job," Agnes said. "I heard the reviews were crazy."

"There were reviews?" I asked.

"Yes," Agnes laughed as she grabbed a J-cloth to get the flour off the table and chairs. "The social media for the shower was awesome."

"Social media?"

"Twitter, Facebook, Instagram," Agnes said. "The ladies took pictures and shared all the goodness."

I leaned back against the counter. "The ladies social media-ed the shower?"

"You bet," she said and got out her phone. "See?" She showed me a Twitter stream called #duchessthrowsshower.

There were pictures of the decorations, the Orangery, the ladies, and, yes, even pictures of the pies. The food pictures were all positive, and it made me smile.

"Wait, is that a picture of the lemon pie?" I asked as she scrolled by one shot of two ladies in front of the dessert bar. The deadly pie was on a tall pie plate behind them. It was covered with a crystal pie cover.

"Did you make two lemon pies?"

"Only one," I said with a shake of my head. "When the shower was over it was still untouched, so I left it for Chef Wright and his staff to show my appreciation."

"But I thought they ate lemon pie," Agnes scrolled through several pictures. "See? Here's a lovely piece with sky-high meringue."

"Wait, yes, that is my pie. There's two pieces missing out of it." I frowned. "How was there a whole lemon pie left? I thought it was in one of our pie plates. It looked like my pie. Well, I assumed it was mine since mine were the only pies in the kitchen when I arrived."

"Do you think someone slipped a poison pie in with yours?"

"Why?"

"Well, if people got sick they would certainly say that on their social media."

"And everyone would get the impression that I'm a terrible cook," I said. "If that's the case, we're lucky no one else ate that pie."

"Did you count all the pie plates when you got back?"

"No," I said. "Why would I? Mine were the only pies served. I didn't think I needed to check the inventory."

"You should count them," she said.

"I'll do it after lunch service. I have to assume one is missing because CID identified the pie as being in a pie pan from my kitchen."

Lunch for the family consisted of several courses, to teach the children about official dining. We kept it simple with stuffed mushroom appetizers, potato and chive soup, roasted chicken, and rice pilaf, then pudding for dessert. Well, in England dessert was pudding so they had pudding for pudding. The thought made me smile.

By the time Agnes got back from taking lunch up to the family, I had done a quick inventory of my pie pans. Two seemed to be missing. I hadn't done an inventory of my kitchen since I first started. The pie pans could have gone missing at any time. I didn't usually keep the kitchen locked while we were coming and going throughout the day. Did someone pinch one of my pans and make a poisonous pie in it?

The thought seemed crazy. Technically there should be only one pan missing. Presumably the one that the police still had in evidence. Darn.

The missing pie plate made me paranoid. Someone had destroyed my kitchen. What if the same someone had been taking a dish here or there to frame me for more poisonings?

I pondered the absurdity of that notion while I continued working.

"You look worried," Agnes said as she brought back the used lunch service.

"I've got two pie plates missing," I said. "One is most likely in police custody. That leaves one unaccounted for."

"That's not good," Agnes said.

"I agree." I surveyed my cupboards. "I'm going to have to inventory the entire kitchen to make sure nothing else is missing."

"That's a big job."

"We'll get it done. But first, we need to work on tea."

Teatime came and I placed scones and macaroons on plates along with tiny cucumber sandwiches and ham salad sandwiches. Agnes took up the tea and I wiped the last of the flour out of the corner of the pantry. The kitchen was officially back to spotless, and I was officially running on zero sleep. I would have to do an inventory of my kitchenware another time when I had a clearer mind.

"Did you have a good time last night?" Penny had popped

into the kitchen to chat. Agnes, who worked only through tea-time, had left for the day.

"Sure." I put on a kettle for my French press. I needed coffee if I was going to get a late supper up to the family. Luckily today's supper was spring salad, fresh poached fish, and new potatoes. All easy to handle in my exhausted state.

"That doesn't sound very convincing," Penny said as she snagged a macaroon from the cookie plate and settled into the kitchen table.

"Tea?" I asked.

"Sure, what else do you have with cookies?" She grinned at me.

"Coffee, I need coffee." I poured water into her cup with a tea bag and then used the rest to make my coffee.

"You came home before us," Penny said. "You should be more rested."

"What time did you get home?"

"I think it was four-thirty this morning."

"Ouch," I said. You couldn't tell from looking at Penny that she hadn't had a full eight hours of sleep. The woman either was a great makeup artist or nightlife looked good on her. She didn't have a hair out of place or even a dark shadow under her eyes. Unlike me, I wore my lack of sleep as puffy eyes and a strange buzzing in my head. "Yes, well, at that time I was already in the kitchen." I proceeded to tell her about what happened.

"I heard them brief the duchess on the break-in," Penny said. "Did they take anything?"

"I'm not sure." I frowned. "I haven't had time to do a full inventory. But I did check my pie pans and there are two missing. One is with the police, but I don't know where the other is."

"Did they take it last night?"

"I don't think so. The cabinet where I kept the bakeware was exactly as I left it. Meanwhile, everything else was a big mess. You should have seen it. It took hours to clean up." I glanced around. "Ian said he thought it was a case of vandalism."

"Most likely," Penny said. "I heard them brief the duchess that someone broke into the Orangery last night, too."

"I had heard there was some kind of incident there last night, but I don't know the details. Was anything taken?"

"Not that anyone can tell anyway. The kitchen was still off-limits except for CID."

"Weird," I said. "Do you think the break-ins have to do with Wentworth's murder?"

"Why would you ask that?" Penny dunked her tea bag in and out of her cup, then added sugar and milk.

"Both the Orangery and my kitchen were broken into last night and both places were sites where CID investigated."

"Ah," she said with a knowing nod.

"What?"

Penny sipped her tea. "Ah, I bet it was someone trying to get pictures for the tabloids."

"What?"

"It's on the news that CID was here and where they investigated. My guess is that the tabloids will pay a lot of money to anyone who can get pictures of the scene."

"Why break into my kitchen and trash it?" I paused as I realized what it meant. "If they have pictures showing my kitchen as unkempt . . ."

"It would go with a story about how you poisoned someone with your pie."

"I didn't poison anyone."

"Well, I know that and you know that," Penny said. "But tabloids will pay a lot of money for the juiciest story."

"Please tell me you have never sold anything to the tabloids."

"Oh, no," Penny said, her eyes widening. "I would be fired. I stay as far away from anyone having anything to do with the tabloids as I can. Are you kidding me?"

"But you said—"

"That I've heard the tabloids pay a lot," Penny said, sitting back. "I've never done it, but I heard about other people—you know people like Wentworth—doing it. They say there's money in it if you don't get caught. I'm just saying that I wouldn't be surprised if you're the cover story on the evening news."

"Darn it!" I reached for my smartphone and brought up my news feed to see what was trending. I didn't see anything and sat down with a sigh of relief. "No news is good news." I flipped my phone at Penny to show her.

"Wrong news," Penny said and turned her phone so that I could see a photo of my trashed kitchen on a gossip website. The article's title mentioned me and said that it was my pie that poisoned Wentworth.

"Darn."

"I'll call the public relations department and see if they can't get it taken down," Penny said.

"I'll tell Ian," I said and dialed Ian's number on the kitchen phone. When Ian picked up I told him about the picture in the tabloids.

"I'll let Detective Chief Inspector Garrote know. Maybe CID can gain some clues from both break-ins. Can you come up to the security department tomorrow before lunch? DCI Garrote wants to speak to you."

"Sure," I said and we set a time of ten AM. I hung up and turned to Penny. "What did the public relations department say?"

"They are going to get someone to figure out what it would take to get the picture taken down."

"Maybe if Detective Chief Inspector Garrote were to haul the editor down to the station . . ."

"You are so funny." She got up, grabbed a dessert plate, plated more macaroons, and set them down on the table in front of me. "You know the chef business is cutthroat," Penny pointed out.

"Old Butterbottom will agree with that," I said and picked up a cookie. "Speaking of which, I haven't seen the guy lately. Do you know if he's all right?"

"He's been out of town at a training conference," Penny said.

"Ah, so even though his kitchen fed the duke and duchess Sunday night, he wasn't there to take the credit. Funny I was told Chef Butterbottom made dinner."

"Nope, just Chef Geoff."

"No wonder Butterbottom hasn't been down here to harangue me about the poison pie."

"Oh, I see," Penny said with a wink.

"What?"

"You miss the old guy."

"What?"

"I think you like the competition."

"I do not," the protest sounded false even to my own ears.

"Okay, maybe a little. He pushes me and I think I'm getting better because of it."

"It's okay," Penny said and patted my hand. "Your secret is safe with me."

Chapter 9

The next morning, I went to the security offices. "Good morning, Kathi," I greeted the secretary.

"Hi, Chef," she said. "Chief Gordon said to escort you to the conference room."

"No need to get up," I said with a short wave of my hand. "I remember where it is."

The tiny conference room was at the end of the interior hall right next to Ian's office. There was a two-way mirror that was embedded in the wall between the office and the conference room. Inside was a small table and two chairs.

Ian's office door was closed so I walked into the conference room and took a seat facing the door.

"Ah, Chef Cole," DCI Garrote said as he came out of Ian's office. "Good morning, thank you for indulging me."

"No problem. I'm always happy to help," I said. "How have you been?"

"All is well with me." He took a seat. "Tell me about your relationship with Wentworth Uleman."

We talked for close to a half an hour about Wentworth peeping in my window and how I left the pie for Chef Wright.

"I know you won't tell me about the investigation, but I can't be your best suspect," I said. "What have you learned about Chef Wright?"

"First of all, we have no suspects at this time. I'm still questioning people. Secondly, I'm not going to tell you anything about my investigation into Chef Wright."

"Fine, what about Lord Heavington?"

"Who is Lord Heavington and why should I tell you anything about him?"

I pulled out the torn page from the tabloid that I had brought with me. "Lord Heavington was one of the people Wentworth photographed. See?" I placed the fuzzy picture on the table. "According to this report, Wentworth snapped this picture of Lord Heavington buying information off an employee. It seems to me that Wentworth was blackmailing Lord Heavington. That would give him motive. Lord Heavington is a frequent visitor to the palace. That would give him means."

"I've seen this. I'm not without resources." He shot me a heated look that seemed to say he was disappointed that I didn't think better of him. "To begin with, we have not yet confirmed that this photo was taken by Wentworth Uleman or that he sold it to the tabloid," he said. "Next, we already checked Lord Heavington's whereabouts. He was in Rome for a conference."

I blew out a long sigh. "I know I can't be the only one who had a problem with Wentworth. What about the woman in the photo?"

"We are looking into her identity," he said.

"Is there anyone else Wentworth might be blackmailing with his pictures?"

"You know I can't comment further about an ongoing

investigation. May I ask why you think he was blackmailing people? Did he attempt to blackmail you?"

"No," I said. "No, I just don't see what other reason he might have had for snapping candid shots of people in the confines of the palace."

"That is for my investigation to figure out, Chef," he said. "Now, one last thing. Chief Gordon tells me that you think yesterday's break-ins were related to the murder."

"Yes," I said, pulling out my cell phone. I punched in the tabloid's website. "This is what my kitchen looked like after the break-in." I showed him my phone. The picture was of my kitchen covered in flour and tossed bowls and pots and pans.

"Allow me to take down the name of that website," he, writing the link into his little notebook. "We will look into this as well."

"How is Wentworth's family dealing with this?" I asked.

"His parents are planning a memorial for him next week," DCI Garrote said. "For now, we still need the body to do some final tests for the postmortem investigation."

"Please pass on my condolences."

"Do you know them?" he asked.

"No," I said. "But that doesn't mean I can't feel for their loss."

"Yes, of course," he said briefly.

"Can I go now?" I asked and headed to the door to leave.

"One more thing, Chef." He turned to look at me. "What is your relationship with Chef Wright?"

"I'm sorry?"

"Your relationship with Chef Wright," he said. "How would you describe it?"

"I barely know the guy," I said. "We met when the duchess

moved the bridal shower to the Orangery. I went to ensure he was okay with my working out of his kitchen."

"And was he all right with it?"

"Yes," I said. "He was surprisingly all right with it."

"There are pictures that make it look like you two are quite close," he said.

"We only just met," I said. "He kissed my hand. That was all."

"Okay," he said. "Thank you for your cooperation."

"That's it?"

"Yes, unless you have something more to add."

"No." I walked out. As I made my way out of the security department offices, I heard a call come through dispatch. It seems there was some sort of incident out in the parking area near my kitchen.

Curious, I hurried down the hallways, passed a few security checkpoints, and walked out into the parking area to see that a crowd had formed. I could hear what sounded like, "fight, fight," coming from the crowd.

Tearing through the crowd, I arrived at the front in time to see Ian drag two women away from each other. He handed a blonde to two members of security and held onto a brunette.

I recognized Evie Green as the brunette.

"What's going on here?" Ian asked. "Have you two lost your minds?"

"Tell her to stay away from my boyfriend," Evie screeched, grabbing for the other woman.

"I didn't steal him," the blonde said. "He chose to go with me."

"Ladies," Ian said. "Let's stop this right now. You're causing a scene. Billings, disperse this crowd."

"All right, people," Billings said as he pushed toward

the crowd. "There's nothing to see here. Go on about your business."

I turned to see Penny standing in the doorway with her hand over her mouth.

"What was that about?" she asked me. Today she wore a pale blue sweater set and black pencil skirt.

"Apparently Evie is fighting the blonde over a man," I said.

"That's Rachel," Penny said.

"Wait, your friend Rachel? Evie's friend Rachel?"

"Yes," Penny said. She turned to me. "Remember I said that Rachel was flirting with a new beau but we didn't know who? Maybe Evie found out who."

"Wait," I made a face. "Are you saying they are fighting over Chef Wright?"

"I certainly hope not. I told Evie he was a lady's man." Penny shook her head. "It would be awful if Chef Wright came between two good friends."

"I don't know if it was about Chef Wright, but it looks like they are both going to be sanctioned for this," I pointed to where Ian and his guys were taking the two women away in handcuffs.

"They made a scene," she said as we stepped into the hallway next to my kitchen. "One thing we don't do is make scenes on palace property."

"I hate to see them lose their jobs over a fight about a notorious playboy," I said.

"Playboy?" Penny laughed at me. "Where did you come from the 1950s?"

"What else would you call him?"

"I'd call him a player, and I have called him that." Penny walked into my kitchen and put the kettle on the stove.

"What was that all about?" Agnes asked from where she worked prepping lunch. Today the duke and duchess were out, so the children would eat in the nursery. We made finger sandwiches cut into teddy bear and gingerbread men shapes. There were finger-size organic carrots, celery, radishes, and a yogurt lemon dip. Finally, I plated sugar cookies in the shape of hot air balloons. Agnes was putting everything on the serving cart to take up to the nursery.

"Two women were fighting in the parking lot," I said. "Security took care of it."

"As long as no one else is murdered, we'll all be fine," she said. "I'm taking this up to the nursery."

"Thank you, Agnes," I said.

Penny poured freshly boiled water into a mug with a bag of Earl Grey tea. She snagged a cookie off the counter and sat down at my table. "I can't believe they had a knockdown, drag-out fight in the parking lot. Was it crazy? Did they attack each other?"

"I don't know," I said. "The fight was over by the time I got there."

"I'm going to text Evie," Penny said. She got out her cellphone and tapped off a message.

"Do you think she'll answer?" I asked. "I mean, she's probably in the security offices for the rest of the afternoon. That is if they don't escort her off the property."

"She'll get back to me." Penny blew on her tea before sipping it. "Don't worry, I'll get to the bottom of all this."

"I know you will," I said. "Without your in-depth knowledge, I would be lost in terms of who's who on the staff. Hey, wait." I reached into my pocket and got out the picture from the tabloid. "Do you know who this might be?"

"Wow," Penny said and held the photo up closer to her face. "It's really blurry."

"It's a tabloid photo that was part of Wentworth Uleman's stash when he died."

Penny looked up at me. "He sold this to the tabloids?"

"It was supposedly hacked off his computer," I said. "See? They claim this is Lord Heavington buying secret information off a staff member. The tabloid was running this story on the theory that Lord Heavington had his goons murder Wentworth because he was being blackmailed by the snooper."

"That's a far-fetched story," Penny said as she studied the picture.

"Yes, I asked DCI Garrote about it this morning. He said they questioned Lord Heavington, but he has an alibi. He was in Rome all week at a convention. But that doesn't mean the staffer wasn't involved," I said. "As of right now, no one can identify her."

"I sort of recognize this spot," Penny said, studying the picture as she munched on her cookie. "I think this is Princess Anne's administration offices," Penny said. "See this window? It looks like they are standing right by a pillar that sits outside the door to the admin offices. See this mark on the pillar?"

I looked at what she pointed to. It was faint. "Is that a heart?"

"Yeah," Penny said. "One of the young royals carved his love's initials with a heart. It's been there for nearly one hundred years."

"So we can place him," I said. "Does that help you figure out who the girl is?"

"I'll work on it." Penny stood. "Can I have this?"

"Sure."

"Thanks for the cookie," she gave me a salute and left.

The workmen came in to replace the glass in the window.

"We're putting in a pane that has blinds between the double glass," the head workman said. His nametag said Carl. "That way you can close it up with a flip of a switch and there won't be any blinds to catch dust."

"Sounds perfect," I said. "Thank you."

Agnes came in with the finished tray from the nursery's lunch. "Roast lamb for dinner tonight?"

"Yes," I said. "I'm braising the lamb shanks with oven roasted tomatoes. We'll serve it as the main course with toasted Orzo."

"It's amazing that the family consumes mostly what is raised on their own land," Agnes said. "They are certain it's organic and know breeder origins."

"Why don't you take a break while they install the window?" I said to Agnes. "I'll stay and keep an eye on the proceedings."

"Yes, Chef," she said. "Thank you."

Agnes didn't take any time in stepping out.

"It's a sunny day, Chef," Carl said as he removed the boards from the window. "Why don't you step out into the garden? We have this."

"I don't know," I said.

"We're certified and bonded, Chef," Carl said with a half-smile. "I've been a maintenance supervisor here for twenty-five years. We'll keep your kitchen safe."

"Right," I said, slightly embarrassed that I had wanted to keep an eye on my kitchen during the window installation. I took off my apron and stepped outside to drink in the warm spring sun.

The parking lot was busy, and I realized that even if Carl

wanted to do something nefarious to my kitchen, he couldn't. There were too many people around. That and cameras on the exterior that would record anything he might do.

So I decided to step out into the gardens for a while and enjoy the flowers.

"Hey, what a nice thing to see a lovely lady enjoying my handiwork," Jasper Fedman said. I turned to see him walk up. He wore tight, well-worn blue jeans and a T-shirt in a dark color that was covered with bits of dirt and leaves. His blond hair hung over his blue eyes. Jasper had smiley eyes. The kind that twinkled.

"Hello, you," I said as he placed a hello kiss on my cheek. "Have you been busy?"

"I keep myself busy with ensuring you have fresh foods." He crossed his arms and studied me. "You went out on the town and didn't come see me or my family at the pub."

I ducked my head. "Can I say I was at Penny's mercy? She rented the car and driver."

"Fine," he said. "This once I'll allow that." He slipped his arm charmingly through mine and walked with me down the garden paths. "I'm not really in charge of these gardens," he admitted. "I just wanted something nice to say. Where did you go on your night out on the town?"

"I don't really remember the names, but some really crowded discos. Penny and her friend Veronica seem right at home there, but I'd rather sit and listen to jazz and talk."

"Well, you should have come to the pub. I hear you looked killer."

"I beg your pardon?"

He shrugged and ducked his head. "The guys at the security booth told me you were wearing some sort of red dress with high heels. Why don't you dress like that more often?" He raised his right eyebrow.

"Maybe because it wasn't my dress or shoes," I said. "Penny dressed me. Also, it could be that I'm not cut out to walk around on stilts."

"I bet you looked amazing," he said. "So tell me what brings you outside besides this beautiful weather?"

"Carl and his assistant are replacing the window in my kitchen."

"Oh, right, I heard you had a break-in. Funny that they didn't touch the greenhouse."

"It may be possible that the break-in was meant to get photos for the tabloids. They only went to the crime scene and my kitchen."

"Why your kitchen?"

"Wentworth was found face first in one of my lemon pies," I stopped and looked at him. "Don't you know what all is going on around here?"

He laughed. "I've been busy with the plants." Then he winked. "They are less likely to gossip."

"But your family owns a pub," I said. "I know employees go there for drinks. There is no way you don't know what's going on."

"Of course I know about Wentworth. But I'm not following the story much, and unfortunately, I haven't been to see my aunt and uncle for about a week. The last time I went to their pub, my brother and I waited until closing to see a certain woman in a red dress. But she didn't show up."

I felt the heat of a blush rush up my cheeks.

"You did tell me there was a chance you'd come by," he pointed out.

"When Penny said a night out on the town, I thought she meant the local pubs."

"No worries, I enjoyed beating my brother at darts."

"I need to get back to the kitchen," I said as we turned back toward the parking lot. "I need to clean up after Carl and check on my lamb shank roast."

"Fine, I guess I can only hint so much," Jasper said. He stopped me. "Would you like to get a quick drink with me sometime?"

"Oh," I said, looking up at his handsome face. "Um, yes," I smiled. "I'm sorry, I'm not very good at this. I haven't been on the dating market in nearly five years."

"Well, good then," he put his arm back through mine and walked me to the kitchen. "I can teach you how to reenter the scene. When is a good day to go out?"

"I have Mondays off," I said lamely.

"I was thinking something sooner, like tomorrow night."

"I have to be at work by five-thirty AM," I said. "The last time I went out I came back to a ruined kitchen and was up for thirty-six hours straight."

"Do I hear you saying that sleep and work are more important than a nice drink with a handsome fellow?"

That really made me blush. "You make me sound like an old woman. I'm not even thirty."

"No, I know old women who socialize more than you," he teased. "Don't be talking bad about older women."

"Fine," I said. "Tomorrow night."

"Great, I'll pick you up at ten. That way you'll be done with your job. The duke and duchess eat at eight, right?"

"Yes," I said.

"Good," he brushed a kiss by my ear. "See you then."

"Wait," I said as he turned away. "What am I supposed to wear?"

He winked at me. "Something I've never seen you in would be a good start."

"Right." I opened the kitchen door. "Time to figure out what someone wears on a date."

Chapter 10

"I think I know who this is," Penny said as she waved the tabloid page around. It was after ten PM. She found me finishing prepping the kitchen for breakfast in the morning.

"Who?" I put on a kettle to boil. There was never a time when Penny didn't want a cup of tea. I had made chocolate biscuits earlier.

"It's Elizabeth Branch." Penny sat down at the table. I placed a small plate of cookies in front of her. "She fits the photo anyway. She's our age with dark hair and pale skin. She works in Princess Anne's administration."

"Should we go ask her about this?" I asked.

"You mean not let security figure it out?"

"Security isn't interested in this angle on the story."

"Then yes, I think we should go ask her," Penny said. "How about tomorrow night?"

"Can't," I said and poured her a cup of tea. I made chamomile for me. My nerves were jumping at the thought of my date tomorrow, and the last thing I needed was to add caffeine to the mix. I would never get to sleep.

"Why not? I'm sure you have the menu for the rest of the week made out."

"I'm busy tomorrow evening."

"Fine, let's go see her before dinner," Penny suggested. "I think she lives off the palace grounds. That means we need to catch her before she leaves work for the day anyway."

"Or we could invite her out for a drink at a nearby pub," I suggested. "Just not tomorrow."

"Why not?"

"I'm busy." I sat down and stuffed a cookie into my mouth while Penny's expression perked up.

"What are you busy doing?" She grinned. "I think I want to know."

"I'll tell you after," I said. "Have a cookie."

She studied me for a moment. "Fine, I guess we all need to have our secrets."

"I tell you what, I can pop over to the admin building tomorrow after breakfast and see if Beth is in."

"Wait, you know Beth?" She seemed surprised that I might know someone.

"My driver from the other night told me his sister was Beth Branch. I assume that Beth is short for Elizabeth."

"I think that's a safe assumption," Penny said. "Your driver from the other night?"

"Yes, the one who picked me up the night we went out and brought me back to the palace. He told me his sister was Beth Branch and to say hi if I saw her."

"So what are you going to do? Go see her and say, hi, you don't know me but I met your brother. Did you kill Wentworth Uleman?"

I laughed. "That does sound rather awkward. What excuse can we use to ask her questions?"

"There's a big staff meeting at the administration building once a week."

"I don't go because . . ."

"You're not part of the palace administration. But Mrs. Worth is, and she has been delegating the meeting to me."

"And are we safe to assume that Beth Branch's boss is also delegating her to go to the meeting?"

"Yes," Penny said. "It's tomorrow at two PM. Do you want to come?"

"How are you going to sneak me in?"

"These things are usually a lecture hall filled with staff standing in the aisles taking notes for their bosses. No one pays attention to who goes and who doesn't."

"Fine, I'm there," I said. I sipped my tea and debated asking her if I could go through her closet to see if she had any appropriate date wear. Then I remembered her closet and decided I'd just have to figure out what to wear on my own.

"What?"

"Thanks for dressing me up the other night," I said. "It was crazy."

"And fun." She popped a cookie in her mouth. "You have to admit it was fun."

"Yes, it was fun," I admitted. "I would have never done it without you."

"Good, so here's a list of five guys who asked me for your number." She held out a piece of note paper.

"What? What guys?"

"Five guys from the other night. They tried to give you their numbers but you didn't take them so they gave them to me."

"Oh, I don't remember anyone trying to give me his number."

"So it'll be a surprise when you see them again." Penny put the new numbers into my phone. "That will be fun. Let's see if we can't get you on some first dates. Men here love Americans. They think you all are fearless."

"I don't think I need any numbers," I protested, trying to get my phone back.

Penny kept my phone out of my reach until she finished inputting the numbers and texting the guys.

I grabbed my phone. "I can't believe you texted them."

"Talk to them if they text back," Penny urged. "You need to get out more."

I bit my tongue. I was not going to tell her about drinks with Jasper-not yet. Not when I wasn't sure of where it would go. I tried changing the subject. "Have you heard from Evie?"

"I texted her, but she hasn't gotten back to me. I heard both women were suspended from work for a week."

"Ouch," I said. "I would hate to lose a week of work."

"I agree," Penny said. "All the more reason not to date someone from work."

I tried not to cringe at the thought that I was making a huge mistake by having drinks with Jasper. I had to ask myself: If I really liked Ian, why did I say yes to going out for a drink with Jasper? Was it because I feared Ian rejecting me? I mean, Penny was the one who told me Ian didn't date women from work. Since she is so plugged into the local gossip, I had to believe her. "Aren't you curious how Evie found out about Rachel and Chef Wright?"

"Yes," Penny said. "I'm hoping to see Evie tonight. I'll get the entire scoop and share it with you."

"I knew you would."

* * *

Ten o'clock the next morning, Butterbottom was back. I watched him pull into the parking lot and get out of his car. Chef Butterbottom was a very big man with a bald head and beady eyes. He wore white chef pants and shirt and pulled a briefcase out of the vehicle.

A couple of his sous-chefs came running out of the backdoor of the palace to help him carry whatever equipment he had in the car. The whole thing was quite a scene as the Chef bellowed at and berated his workers.

I shook my head. How could I have not noticed old Butterbottom wasn't around this last week? I wondered what he would say when he found out my kitchen was once again under suspicion.

At least I didn't have to worry that I would get fired. Butterbottom hadn't hired me, and right now I was very glad of that fact. Who was I kidding? The very British chef would have never let me get out of Chicago let alone come to work for the family. He'd told me so himself once.

Agnes chopped veggies for the lunch salads. I grilled chicken with boiled potatoes and peas. Fresh rolls were in the oven baking.

There was a pounding at my kitchen door. I glanced at Agnes and she went to open the door—which was not ever locked when we were in the kitchen cooking. There was no need to knock.

"Chef Cole," the deep voice of Butterbottom rang through my kitchen.

"Come in," I said, checking my meal one last time before stepping away. "Hello, Chef. What brings you to my kitchen?"

"There is a charity bake-off in three days," he said standing in my doorway. "One of the other chefs had to cancel. There is now an open spot. This is one of the duke and duchess's charities."

"Are you asking me to participate?" I raised my eyebrows.

"I'm letting you know there is an opening," he said. "I'm sure you won't want to compete as you aren't as well-versed in English traditions."

"What's the competition?"

"It's a classic British pie competition," he said. "Something you likely won't touch because you will most likely fail, but I am obliged to let you know of the opening."

"Pie?"

"Three savory and two sweet," he said. "Here is the information." He handed me a flyer for the event. "That's all. I've done what was asked of me." He let the door slam closed behind him.

"Clearly he doesn't know you are very good at pie-making," Agnes said with a sniff. She came over and looked at the flyer. "The event will take place in Hyde Park and will be filmed for later broadcast on the BBC. Oh, now you have to do this. Once you win the competition people will understand why you are the duke and duchess's private chef."

"I'm not sure I want to trade off their names to create my own celebrity," I muttered. I went over to my tiny desk and brought up the website.

"Didn't you hear Butterbottom?" Agnes asked. "It benefits the duke and duchess's charity."

"I'll send a note to Mrs. Worth to see if she will okay my entering." I typed up a quick email and sent it. My thoughts were immediately on what type of pies to make. Clearly crust was a key. It would have to be flaky and light, but also substantial enough to hold a meat filling.

There was a one-thousand-pound entry fee that I would have to deal with. I studied the entry fee for a while until I got a ding that I had an email. I clicked over and saw that Mrs. Worth had procured the duchess's approval that I be a part of the competition. Even better, the household would pay my entry fee.

"Yes!" I said. "I'm signing up."

"Good for you," Agnes said. "Now, would you consider making my Grammy Duricott's secret pie recipe?"

"I'm not sure—"

"Oh, it's good," Agnes said with a nod. "People used to beg her for the recipe, but she made us all swear to keep it in the family."

"And you would let me make it on television?"

Agnes winked. "Only if you mention Grammy."

"It would be my pleasure to make your grandmother's famous pie."

"Good, it's settled," Agnes said. "You're going to practice your pies, right?"

"Of course," I said. "I'll serve them to the duke and duchess for lunch."

"Or you can make one and I'll take it home. If my family approves, then you're good to go."

I laughed. "Sounds like a plan."

Maybe if I won a pie contest on national television, it would wipe away the idea that my lemon pie might have killed someone. Of course, it could backfire. But I wasn't going to think that way.

Chapter 11

I was late for the meeting. Hurrying to the administration offices, I checked my phone. Penny had texted. "Where are you?"

"Here," I texted back as I arrived at the door. The small room looked like a lecture hall. It sloped down to the center dais and was packed with people sitting and standing. There was no room to go further inside. An older man droned on and on about things as the power point presentation flashed behind him.

"As you all should know, there was a murder on the premises a few days ago. Please remind your staff members that it is a terminable offense to talk to the tabloids. Anyone caught leaking information or selling pictures will be dealt with summarily."

I spotted Penny sitting next to a neat brunette. She saw me at the same time. I waved at her. She patted an empty seat next to her. Great, I would have to elbow my way over there. Nice way to go unnoticed.

The older man continued on about the number of visitors in the gardens and on the tours and basic safety to keep the royal family's privacy.

I shook my head at Penny. She frowned and waved harder causing several heads to turn. I did what any self-respecting woman would do. I ducked out into the hallway.

"Hello, Carrie Ann."

I turned to see Ian walk up the hallway behind me. "Hi."

"How are you? Any more troubles in the kitchen?"

I gave him a weak smile. "Things have been quieter."

"Good. I'm glad." His expression softened. "What brings you to this part of the building?"

"I'm meeting Penny to talk to someone."

"Mind telling me why?"

"I think we identified the woman in the tabloid photo with Lord Heavington."

"And you didn't tell me?"

"I wanted to make sure we were right before bothering you."

"Let me guess, you think it's Beth Branch."

"Yes," I straightened. "How did you know?"

"There is video of her meeting with Heavington at other times. CID is questioning Heavington. I'm here to pick up Beth and take her in for her side of the story."

"Do you think Beth was selling secrets?"

"I certainly hope not. We take these things seriously here." He paused. "How are you doing? I mean with everything going on?"

His gaze warmed me. "I'm fine," I said with a short nod. "Just fine."

The meeting must have ended because people started leaving the room. Ian and I waited outside the doors, watching the crowd. Penny and Beth didn't come out. When the crowd thinned enough that you could go into the room, we went inside.

Penny was talking to Beth. She looked up. "Carrie Ann," Penny called my name and waved me over. "Chef Cole this is Beth Branch. Beth, Chef Cole."

"Hi, nice to meet you," I said and shook her hand.

"Nice to meet you as well," Beth said. "You are pretty famous, you know."

"How so?"

"For taking on Chef Butterbottom, of course," she said with a small laugh. "That man scares everyone else at the palace."

"I know," I said. "I lost two assistants because of it."

"Beth Branch," Ian stepped in to the conversation. "I need you to come with me."

"Okay," she said quizzically. "Why?"

"It has to do with Lord Heavington," I said, pulling out the tabloid picture. "Is this you?"

"Oh," she said and her shoulders slumped.

"So it is you?" Penny asked.

"Yes," she said. "But I didn't kill anyone. It was a lark really."

"A lark?"

"Heavington told me he'd give me a thousand dollars for every one of Butterbottom's recipes I could sneak out of the kitchen."

"You were selling recipes?"

"Yes," she said, looking from one of us to the other. "Of course. Heavington was writing a Royal Palace recipe book. I thought everyone knew that. He got a million-dollar advance to write a recipe book based on the tables of the various royals he has dined with. The problem was that Heavington didn't actually have any recipes."

"So this is a picture of you passing a recipe on to Lord Heavington," Ian said.

"Yes," she said. "What did you think I was selling?"

"Something important enough to kill over," Ian said. "Why don't you come with me and we'll sort it all out."

"Right," Beth said.

Beth and Ian walked out of the lecture hall. I turned to Penny. "We might have solved the murder. I mean she might not have murdered Wentworth over the picture, but if Heavington's publisher had caught wind that he actually didn't have any recipes . . ."

"A million dollars is a bit of a motive for murder."

"Exactly," I said. "The problem is that Heavington wasn't in London at the time, and he can prove it."

"Unless he paid for a hit man to do it," Penny suggested. "After all, he was paying Beth to get him the recipes from Butterbottom. I bet he paid a lot of people to sneak him official recipes from all over."

"Yes," I agreed. "But how do we prove it?"

"By contacting Heavington's admin, of course," Penny said.

"Why?"

"Administrators know about everything," she said with confidence.

"But he wouldn't tell them he was hiring a hitman," I said.

"No, but they would note any big budget item on his accounts."

"Seriously?"

"Yes, they have accountants who keep track of everything," Penny said. "I bet he expensed the money he gave to Beth for the recipes. It wouldn't surprise me to find that he had a reason for making a large withdrawal last week."

"But isn't poisoning someone with pie kind of unprofessional? I mean when you hire a hit man, don't they usually use a gun or something swift and exacting? How would they have controlled who ate the pie? Do you think they forced him to eat the pie?"

"Ugh, those are all good points," Penny said as we walked back to the duke and duchess's apartments. "I suppose CID would have already thought of all that."

"If not, then Ian will see that they do," I said. "He seems to be on top of things like that."

"The question is whether Heavington is a better suspect than you."

"And what professional would he hire who can get inside the palace grounds and set me up as a killer?"

She opened the door to my kitchen. "It does seem all a little implausible."

"Yes," I said. "Thanks for introducing me to Beth. At least now we know she wasn't selling state secrets."

"Don't tell Butterbottom that," Penny said with a laugh. "I'm sure he thinks his recipes should be state secrets."

"Speaking of Butterbottom," I said, "guess who stopped by to ask me to participate in a charity cooking event this weekend?"

"No!"

"Yes," I said with a grin. "I think the duchess put him up to it."

"It certainly had to be someone higher up. He would have never come down himself."

"And he came down himself, stood right in the doorway," Agnes said, waving at the door we had just stepped through.

"Didn't so much as ask her to come as to tell her there was an opening, but she probably wouldn't want to take it."

"And did you take it?" Penny asked.

"Oh, I took it," I said.

"What kind of competition?"

"It's in Hyde Park this Saturday and it's sponsored by one of the duke and duchess's charities," I said. "I got the approval to be a part of the competition and the budget to pay the entry fee. I'm going to be making pies!"

"Oh, no . . . not after you are under suspicion for poisoning a man with pie."

"What? No," I said. "This is perfect. I can prove that my pies are delicious and that I'm a good chef."

"I don't like it," Penny said.

"Why not?"

"What if something happens to someone who eats your pie on national television? You will never work again."

"Oh, please," I said. "Nothing will happen. Trust me. None of the ingredients will leave my custody and I'll taste the final pies before anyone else."

"I don't know," She said with a shake of her head. "I don't like it. It's too coincidental that Butterbottom brought this competition to your attention."

"I don't think he had a choice," I said.

"I still don't like it."

"Pish," Agnes said. "I'll be with her. It will be fine. She's going to make my family's secret pie."

"Trust us, Penny," I said. "I know you do. You eat my food all the time."

"It's good food," she said with a sigh. "Listen, I have to go back to work and report on the meeting. I didn't mean to put down what you're doing."

"I understand, you have concerns," I said. "But it's fine. Don't forget to contact Heavington's admin about his spending habits."

"I won't." She snatched a cookie off the platter and ducked out of the kitchen.

"Don't worry, Chef," Agnes said as she patted me on the back. "You're going to win that pie competition. We have my secret recipe."

Chapter 12

I was not going to be late for my drink date. I stared at all the clothes in my closet. Ninety percent were white chef shirts and black pants. Unlike Penny, I didn't have a closet full of party clothes. Not that I wanted to wear party clothes. I highly doubted a little red dress was appropriate for drinks after work.

So what was appropriate? It had been so long since I had a date, I wasn't sure. I could ask Penny, but I didn't want her sticking her nose into something this new. It might go nowhere.

I thought of Jasper and his winning smile. It also might go somewhere fast. I sighed and pushed the clothes in my closet around. It wasn't producing anything more than what I'd seen before. Which meant I had to pick something I had and let that be that.

What did I have? I had a blue-and-white patterned midi fit-and-flare dress that buttoned up the front. It had short sleeves and a rounded neckline. Not exactly a little red dress, but not black pants, either.

I slipped on the dress and did a neat twirl. It was great if I was a nanny taking the kids to a park. It wasn't the best for a date. I sighed. It would have to do. I wasn't going to show up for drinks in my work outfits.

I twisted my hair up into a quick top knot, applied lipstick and slipped on blue flats and that was that. I didn't have a moment to spare when someone knocked on my door.

"I'll be right there," I said and hurried to open it.

"Well, you look different," Ian said as he studied me. "Are you going somewhere?"

"Hello, Ian," I said, ignoring his question. "What brings you here?"

"I wanted to let you know that we finished our investigation into Beth Branch. She also has an alibi for the night of the murder."

"So that's a dead end?"

"Yes," he said.

"What if Lord Heavington paid someone to kill Wentworth?" I leaned against the doorframe with my arms crossed. "He did like to pay people to get him what he wanted."

"We can look into that," he said. "But it's highly unlikely that a hit man would use poison."

"Unless they want to frame someone."

"You feel as if you are being framed?" He raised an eyebrow.

"Yes."

"Why?"

"What? Someone used my pie plate and maybe my pie—"

"It was your pie."

"To kill someone," I finished. "They used me to cover up their crime. I won't stand for it."

"I see," he said.

"Hello, darling," Jasper said as he stepped down my hall.

"Ian," he nodded as men do to acknowledge each other. Jasper brushed a kiss on my cheek.

I felt a flush of heat rush up my cheeks. There was so much maleness in the hall that it threatened to take my breath away.

"Are you ready?" Jasper asked me.

"Yes," I said. "Let me get my sweater." I stepped into my apartment and grabbed my blue sweater and my purse.

"You two have a date?" Ian asked. I noticed that his eyebrows drew together slightly and his mouth firmed into a tight line. Was he upset by the news? He stepped to the other side of the hall out of the way and crossed his arms over his chest. If I didn't know better, I'd say he was jealous.

"Just drinks," I clarified.

"Yes," Jasper said at the same time. He looked at me. "Drinks," he corrected himself with a smug smile and stepped into the space between Ian and me.

"Have fun," Ian said and walked off.

"We will," Jasper replied a little too brightly. I locked my door and we stepped out of the palace. "It's a nice night. Do you care to walk?"

"Sounds great," I said. I was glad to be wearing my flats and not Penny's sky-high shoes.

"I know this little hole in the wall. It doesn't look like much from the outside, but it's cozy inside, and the bartender makes a fantastic Pimm's cup."

"A Pimm's cup?"

"Oh, no, you haven't ever had a Pimm's?"

"No," I said. "Is it a beer?"

"It's a cocktail," he said grinning ear to ear. "Oh, we need to educate you on good British cocktails." He put his arm through mine. "My friends are going to love you."

I felt the heat of a blush rush up my cheeks. "They are going to love making fun of a sadly undereducated American?"

"No, no, they are going to love you. We are going to have a blast tasting all the different cocktails."

I put my hand up in a stop motion. "I have to work in the morning."

"I'll get you home safe," he said with a wink. "Gordon will be watching me, I think."

"No, it's me he's watching," I said. "He thinks I'm involved in Wentworth Uleman's murder."

"I think there's a bit more to it than that," Jasper said as he steered me toward a door in the middle of an alley. The name above the door said Uncle Joe's.

"Is this another relative of yours?" I asked. The last time I'd gone for drinks with Jasper I learned he'd taken me to his uncle's pub.

"No relatives this time." He flashed me a smile. "Just friends."

The inside of the place was dark but very soothing. I heard cocktail jazz in the air. The interior was like something right out of *Mad Men*, without the cigarettes. Waitresses had bee-hive hairdos and boxy tops with body-hugging pencil skirts.

There were small tables and cool lines of chairs. The colors were orange and turquoise. The pictures were abstract cityscapes.

"Wow," I said as he steered me to a small table in the left corner.

"Stay right here a minute and make yourself comfortable," he said. "I'll get Stephanie to come over and bring you a Pimm's."

I settled into the chair, certain that I wasn't dressed nearly as stylishly as the rest of the people who sat in the tiny bar. Lucky for me Jasper was wearing jeans and a button-front shirt. I fit with him, if not with everyone else.

"Say, aren't you that chef who made the pie?" It was a young guy in a plaid shirt, blue suit coat with thin lapels, and slim-legged blue slacks.

"I'm sorry?"

"The pie they found that guy face down in, you know. The dead guy," a second man said. The second guy was dressed similarly to the first. It looked like they might be work buddies.

"Hey, bugger off," Jasper said, pushing his way around the second young man.

"No, this is the chef, right? You're the chef?"

"Come on guys, let these two be," a waitress pushed the young guys back to the front.

"I guess my reputation stretches back to the 1960s," I said.

"They think they're being cool," he said. "Dressing like they are in some sort of movie. I asked Stephanie to see we're not disturbed."

"Hey kids," the waitress came over. Her shirt was buttoned in the front, but curve hugging. Her blonde beehive was nearly eight inches tall. "I've brought the requested Pimm's." She put the glasses down in front of us. "Pimm's cups are traditionally made with lemonade, lemon soda, and ginger beer. We add Créole Shrubb."

"Créole Shrubb?" I asked.

"It's an orange liqueur from Martinique," she said.

"Stephanie scours the internet for all the coolest drinks," Jasper said. "Pimm's is the drink to order at Polo matches. Have you ever been to a Polo match?"

"No," I said.

"Oh, Jasper," Stephanie said. "You have to take her." She leaned toward me. "I go just to people watch."

"Sounds like fun?" I looked from her to Jasper.

"Taste the drink," he said. "I ordered five more."

"You ordered six drinks?" I was astounded. "I should have had more to eat."

"Taste it," he said.

I did what he asked. It was quite good.

"See? You should trust me."

"I do trust you," I said. His gaze warmed and he touched my hand.

"Good, because I only mean you the best kind of courtesy."

We laughed and talked until the next drink came out. This one was a sidecar.

"I've heard of a sidecar," I said and tasted it. "It's pretty good. What's in it?"

"Cognac, orange liqueur, and lemon juice," Jasper said.

"I don't think I've ever had cognac." I drew my brows together. "Is it brandy?"

"Yes," he said. "A French brandy. Do you like it?"

My eyes widened. "It's very warm."

His smiled widened. "I like how your eyes light up when you're surprised."

Maybe it was the drinks, but I truly enjoyed the complements of this handsome man. Next was a classic Daisy. Then a Mr. Stair which was a pear drink. About the time we hit the next few drinks I was smiling at Jasper and feeling warm. The flavors all blended together with the jazz music and the stress of my new job and the investigation slipped away.

Luckily the young men who wanted to know if I was the

murder chef had left us alone. Jasper finally ordered tapas and we ate trying to calm down the effects of the alcohol. No, I didn't drink all those drinks. I just tasted them, but six tastes could still knock me for a loop. I was used to working all the time not having evening drinks.

"I know a secret," Jasper said as he leaned in toward me.

"What secret do you know?"

"Our Security Chief is pretty jealous of me right now."

"What? Why?"

He took my hand and kissed the back of it. "Because I'm spending time with a beautiful chef and he's not."

"Don't be silly, Ian doesn't date anyone who works for the palace."

"Wait, are you saying that you are only with me because you don't think he wants to be with you?"

'No," I said. "No, that's horrible. I'm not that horrible."

He studied me for a moment. "No, you are not that horrible. But I had to check."

"I think it's time to go home." I stood. Or, rather, wobbled up a bit. "We have to work in the morning and I have pies to practice for Saturday's competition."

He stood with me and paid the bill while I stepped outside. It was misting and cool. The streets were quiet after the music from the club. The weather damped everything, even sound.

"Hey, you are that chef, aren't you?" It was the young man from inside. He came over to me.

"Do I know you?" I asked and peered at him. I used my best Chicago attitude. It's the kind that you had to have when you lived in a big city. A sort of "stay back" vibe.

"Naw, Chef, you don't," he said. "I'm Nigel Bloom. I'm a reporter for an underground paper called *Fake News.*

"I don't have anything to say to the press."

"Not even *Fake News*?" He raised a well-manicured eyebrow.

"Especially not for *Fake News*," I said.

"What if I tell you that I don't think you did it?"

"Did what?" I hedged.

"You didn't make that pie." He crossed his arms over his chest.

I tilted my head and kept my thoughts to myself.

"Someone else made the pie," he said. "Someone with more to lose. Someone who needed Wentworth Uleman dead."

"And who would that be?" I had to ask.

"That's what I'm trying to find out," he said. "Maybe you can help me with that?"

"Help you with what?" Jasper asked as he stepped out of the bar.

"Find out who really killed Wentworth Uleman," he said.

"Who are you?"

"Nigel."

"He's a reporter from *Fake News*," I said as Jasper put his hand on my waist and pulled me protectively toward him.

"I think you need to leave us alone," Jasper said.

"Fine, but I'm on your side, chef." He pulled out a business card. "Here's my card. Call me if you need anything."

I took the card. "How do I know you won't make me look bad?" I asked.

"He's the press," Jasper said. "He'll make you look however it takes to sell papers."

Nigel shrugged and walked off. "You never know when you might need a friend in the papers."

I looked at Jasper.

"Don't mind him," Jasper said. "He works for *Fake News*. How important is that?"

I grimaced. "I'm learning how important tabloids are."

"You're going to get a lot of that just because you work at the palace. Don't let them in. It's the way to madness."

I glanced behind at Nigel's retreating back. "He said he wanted to prove my innocence."

"Trust me," Jasper guided me toward the palace, "people will say anything to earn your trust. The guy is looking to make a buck."

In my heart I knew that Jasper was right, but I was curious to know who Nigel thought killed Wentworth and why. Maybe when I got home, I'd search for the *Fake News* site on the internet and see what kind of journalism Nigel practiced.

Chapter 13

All the next day I couldn't help but think over the exchange with Jasper. The one where he accused me of liking Ian more than him, but settling on the man I could get. I didn't like the implication and worse, I hated that there was a ring of truth to it.

"I'm heading home," Agnes said. It was after teatime and she was done for the day. "We're all set for tomorrow's competition. Everything is boxed and bagged and ready to go. You have the recipes ready, right?"

"Yes," I said. "I'll practice a couple more times tonight. That said, I'm ready to go right now."

"You'll do great, Chef," she said. "I'll be here bright and early in the morning."

"Yes, we need to be at the site and set up by eight AM."

"You can count on me." She lifted the pie I had made for her family. "They're going to love this."

"I hope so," I said with a smile. After she left, I went over all the details of the coming competition one last time. I saw there was a line about notifying the security chief of your intention to compete. It seemed they needed to know to ensure there was plenty of security for each chef attending. I glanced at the clock. It was seven PM. Supper was done, and I was able to run out for a bit. I figured I'd check and see if Ian was in his office.

The secretary was out for the day. I could hear the dispatches in the next room. It was strange to be in the office after hours. I saw that Ian had his light on so I popped into the doorway and knocked.

"Ian, I need to—" I suddenly noticed that there were two people in the room. Ian had been kissing a lovely young woman. She was my height and tucked up against his heart. "Oh, I'm sorry—" I held up my hand and took a step back into the hall.

"It's all right," Ian said. "Come in, Chef."

The woman looked at me curiously. She had an oval face with big China-blue eyes and long blonde hair that flowed around her shoulders in soft waves. She wore a sapphire-blue shift dress and sparkly flats. "Is this Chef Cole?"

"Yes," Ian said. "Chef Cole, Carrie Ann, this is Lana McMann. Lana, Chef Cole."

"Nice to meet you," I said and gave her a wry smile. Why was my heart beating so hard? It was clear Lana was Ian's girlfriend. I swallowed hard and concentrated on Ian. "I'm so sorry to interrupt. Also I forgot to let you know that Agnes and I will be at a pie-baking competition in Hyde Park tomorrow."

"That's the one Chef Butterbottom is attending." Ian didn't seem to be embarrassed that his hand hadn't moved from Lana's waist.

"Yes," I said. "I just read that I was to notify security about my attendance. I'm sorry I didn't notify you sooner."

"It's not a problem," he said. "Mrs. Worth informed me the moment they paid your registration."

"Oh, um, okay. Good." I stood there rooted to my spot.

"Is that all Chef?"

"Yes," I said. "Have a good night." I took two steps back into the hall. "Nice to meet you." I turned to walk carefully down the short hall and out of the security department offices.

"Stupid, stupid, stupid," I muttered to myself. When the elevator didn't open immediately, I took the stairs. How could I have thought that Ian saw me as anything other than a coworker? That woman looked like a magazine model.

How could I have thought for a second that what Jasper said about Ian last night might be true? I could feel the heat of a blush rush up my cheeks.

I got back to my kitchen and moved mechanically through the steps to finish supper and get it up to the duke and duchess. After that, I did the dishes and closed the kitchen. Tomorrow I had to get up early to be ready for the competition. Right now all I wanted to do was to retreat to my room and try not to think about Ian kissing that gorgeous blonde.

* * *

Saturday morning Agnes and I packed ingredients for making the five pies for the competition. We vowed to keep the ingredients in our own custody for the entire day. It turned out to be harder than I thought.

We arrived at the pavilion set up in the park. I carried a cooler, and Agnes carried two baskets worth of ingredients.

I went to the registration table to introduce myself and ask where we were to set up.

"I'm Chef Cole," I said to the two women at the table. They looked up my name and pulled a name tag out.

"Okay, here is your name tag." The woman at the table plopped various registration items on top of the cooler I carried.

"Wear it on the right side of your chef coat at all times. This is your passport in and around the event. Also included in your packet is the schedule of events and the timetable for interviews and producer meetings.

"I'm sorry?"

"The producers will be interviewing each chef at various points in the competition. The schedule is set. You're in position four in the tent. Here's a map. Alex here is the producer's assistant assigned to you today. Follow him." She waved me off to the right.

"Chef Cole," A young guy who looked all of eighteen held out his hand. He was thin and about five feet seven inches tall.

"I'm sorry, my hands are full." I lifted the cooler, careful not to lose the paperwork she had placed on top.

"Right," he said. "Let me take that for you."

"No, thanks," I said. "We'll do it."

"But I'm here to help get you settled in and set up."

"Fine, you can take the paperwork, but the ingredients aren't leaving my hands or Agnes's."

"Who is Agnes?"

"She's my assistant for today," I nodded over my shoulder to where Agnes walked carefully balancing the two baskets.

"Right," Alex said. "We have guys who will take care of all that. Right now, I need you to go to makeup and get ready for your first on-camera interview."

"No," I said. "Nothing is leaving our sight. So if you want me some place faster, then you need to take me to my baking area first."

He frowned at me, but Agnes and I simply stared him down. "Fine," he said with a huff. "Follow me."

I thought I heard him mutter something about a diva, but

I didn't care. If anyone died because of pies that I cooked on national television, I would never work again. Yes, I'd rather go on television with no makeup than chance the loss of my career.

He led us to a tent that was set up with six baking areas. "You are in position four, near the front."

"The front?"

"The cameras draw the eye to the back where the more popular and well-known chefs will be working." He pointed to the last two spaces and I saw four of Butterbottom's sous-chefs setting up his space. One was busy cleaning an already spotless area.

"Himself is there, huh," Agnes blustered. Her face had grown red from the walk and carrying the heavy baskets. I put the cooler down on my space.

"Where are the other chefs?" I asked.

"All in makeup where you should have been five minutes ago."

The other spots were all filled with assistant chefs and production people prepping the ingredients for the first pie—an appetizer pie.

"I've got this, Chef," Agnes said. "I won't let it out of my sight."

I frowned. I would have to trust that no one would mess with my stuff when I wasn't here. I pulled out my pocket camera and small video stand.

"What's that?" Alex asked.

"It's a video camera," I said. I'm going to record my space."

"What, why?"

"We need to ensure no one tampers with her things," Agnes said. "Trust me, Chef, I'll keep an eye on it."

I set the camera on the tripod and checked that it recorded

the countertop. "I trust you, Agnes," I said. "It's everyone else that I don't trust." Once it was up and running I looked at Alex. "All right, show me the way to makeup."

We hurried out of the tent to a smaller tent nearby where I was tucked into a chair and my hair was pulled back into a low ponytail and poofed on top. There was so much hairspray in it I was pretty sure it wouldn't have budge in a stiff wind for at least two weeks.

Next was a makeup artist named Hannah. "Good thing you have great skin," she said as she tapped my face with foundation.

"Why?" I asked trying to keep my expression neutral so that she could apply everything correctly.

"You have to be on set in ten minutes," she explained. "Skin like yours doesn't take as much work."

"Good?"

"Yes," she laughed. "Very good."

I could hear Chef Butterbottom yelling at his makeup team in the far corner. Lucky for me I was a last-minute replacement and therefore far away from the more popular chefs.

"I said stop making me look so orange." Butterbottom got out of his chair. "I demand a new makeup artist." He tore off the white towel that was stuck under his chin to keep the makeup off of his white shirt. "Where is my tea?" Someone brought him a cup. "Not this! Where is *my* tea?"

Staff members with head gear went scurrying over to his part of the tent. They fawned over him until he calmed down and sat back in the chair. A new makeup artist was produced and all was quiet for a moment.

"Not all chefs are divas," I said as Hannah lined my eyes with a neutral brown pencil.

Hannah laughed. "Trust me you don't have to be a chef to be a diva. I've had people off the street turn into a nightmare in the prep room."

"Seriously?"

"Yes," she said with a short nod. "They think we're going to make them look bad."

"Nice to see you in the competition, Chef Cole," Chef Wright said as he passed my makeup chair with his handler on the way out of the makeup tent.

"Are you one of the competitors?" I asked.

"Certainly," Chef Wright said with a laugh. "Along with Chef Butterbottom and Chef Elsie."

"Who?"

"Chef Elsie, she cooks for the Duke of York and his wife. I guess with you and the rest, they have the entire palace out of chefs for the day." He winked at me. "Let's show them what we've got."

"He likes you," Hannah said as she watched Chef Wright walk off.

"He's married," I said.

"Everyone knows he has an eye for the ladies," she said as she brushed mascara on my lashes. "I hear he has at least two mistresses."

"All the more reason to stay away from him," I said.

Hannah laughed. "They told me you were smart."

I sent her a small smile. "Let's hope I'm smart enough to bake my way to the top today."

From the makeup tent I was whisked away to another tent where I was interviewed.

"So Chef Cole," the host, Sir Albert Nash said. "We understand that you are fresh off the plane from the USA."

"I've been here a few months," I said.

"And that you scored your enviable job as personal chef to the Duke and Duchess of Cambridge from the couple's trip to New York City."

"Yes," I said.

"So what is it like to be a native New Yorker?"

"I wouldn't know," I said. "I'm from Chicago."

"Ah, yes, the Windy City, the City of Big Shoulders, Second City."

"Something like that," I said.

"Where were you trained? Chef Butterbottom was trained with Britain's greatest chefs as well as at Le Cordon Blue in Paris. Chef Wright has a similar pedigree."

"I went to the Le Cordon Bleu College of Culinary Arts in Chicago," I said. "Then I studied in Paris and London as well as Madrid and Mumbai."

"You seem pretty young to have been studying so long," the Nash said with a crocodile smile.

"I'm older than I look," I said with my best soft smile.

"You were a last-minute replacement in this competition, weren't you? What made you decide to try your hand at British pie-making?"

"Actually, it was the fact that the proceeds go to the duke and duchess's children's charity. Chef Butterbottom told me about the opening and invited me to enter. I checked with my employer and they generously agreed to pay my entry fee."

"How wonderful of the duke and duchess," the Nash said. "I understand they will be attending the finale."

"Then I hope I'm one of the finalists so that they will be proud."

"Really? You know you are not even seen as a threat to the other chefs."

"I know," I said. "But everyone loves an underdog."

"And cut," the director said.

The Nash immediately turned from me and called for his assistant to bring him a cup of tea.

"Chef Cole." Alex touched my shoulder. "We need you to take your place in the competition kitchen for the opening shots."

"Okay." I followed Alex out of the interview spot. The sun was bright and people had begun to gather in the park. The baking kitchen was raised up off the ground for a better view for those who filled the chairs in the park.

The stage was a tented area with transparent sides so that the audience could fill the park on three sides of us.

"Oh man, I paid twenty pounds a ticket to be put in front of a nobody," I heard a man say as I took my spot alongside Agnes.

"Wait, isn't she the duke and duchess's American Chef?" the woman next to him said. "I hear she killed someone with her pie."

"You don't say," the man said. "If she makes it past the first round, I might be able to sell the tickets to someone for a profit."

The woman smacked him. "We can't be that lucky."

I shook my head and put on a clean chef's coat. "How are our ingredients?"

"I haven't left them," she said. Then she patted my camera. "This trusty little guy will show you."

"All right," the director said. "Let's start this shoot. Chefs, you will look at the hosts as they introduce the challenge. Then I want you to start baking. We will bring the crew by your station to set up individual shots of your recipe and plans for the pie."

Albert Nash then bounced into the tent fully on script. He introduced a Edwina Storm and a David Young. "Welcome, ladies and gentleman, to the second annual charity bake-off. This year we are highlighting good old English pies—both savory and sweet."

The director called cut. Makeup artists scurried in to do touch ups while the cameras were reset.

We spent the next hour standing by our stations looking happy and expectant before the judges finally gave us our assignments. "Chefs, you have one hour to create and bake an appetizer pie. On your marks, get set, bake!"

Finally, I could get start baking. I planned on making a fresh spinach quiche and bake it in individual finger-size cups. I went straight to work, careful to taste each ingredient in front of my camera.

The judges came over to film a segment asking me what I was making and how I felt about my stiff competition.

"I'm confident in my pies," I said. "But I'm looking forward to see how my work compares with all the other great chefs here."

"Good job on being humble," Alex whispered. "People like that."

I shrugged. "If I'm an underdog then I need to act like one."

I continued with the pies, rolling out flaky crust made with butter, flour, salt, and vinegar. The key to a good piecrust was not to handle it too much and to keep the dough very cold.

I prebaked the tiny crusts then added the egg, spinach, cream, and cheese filling.

"Twenty minutes on the clock," came the call from Nash. I glanced around to see that only one other chef still needed to put pies in the oven. Butterbottom glistened with sweat and grabbed a white tea towel to pat off the perspiration. Chef Wright looked confident as he bent down to check his oven.

"Time to prepare the plates," I said to Agnes, who pulled two small plates out of our basket and handed them to me. I garnished them with fresh tomato, basil, and mozzarella.

When the minipies were done, I let them sit as long as possible to cool and make the filling firm, not runny.

"Five minutes," came the call. "Five minutes."

I quickly plated my pies. Two garnished plates for the judges and one big plate to serve the people outside. I had done my best, and I had tasted each ingredient to ensure nothing was tampered with.

"Five, four, three, two, one, and hands up!" Said Nash. There was a lot of cheering from the chefs, their assistants, and the crowd.

We waited long moments for them to set up the cameras to film the judging. Finally, our dishes were brought up before the judges and placed side by side. Apparently, there had been a mishap with one of the front chefs. Chef MacLode had tried to make cheese pies but the edges of the pie had burnt while the filling wasn't quite jelled.

I felt bad for him and was glad mine at least had cooked well. Maybe I wouldn't be the first chef to go home.

Chapter 14

I made it through the appetizer round. Next up was the meat pie round. Agnes was nervous since it was the unveiling of her family's recipe. I patted her hand to let her know that I was going to do my best to make her family look good.

"Congrats on finishing your first and last round," Chef Butterbottom said to me as he passed by. "You will be undone by the English meat pie."

"Good luck to you, too, Chef," I said with a smile.

We all went to our stations and waited while the Nash and judges were filmed. "For your next round, you have two hours to make two classic English entrée pies. On your marks, get set, bake!"

I decided to set up my presentation as a picnic. We emptied one of Agnes's baskets and she prepped it with checkered linen.

Agnes's family pie contained steak and kidney with a savory gravy. I paired it with a classic beef and Guinness pie. I started with a puff pastry crust and ensured I tasted each ingredient on my table. My little camera still ran whenever I cooked in case I had to prove later that I tasted everything both before mixing and after.

Raw ingredients like meat I left untasted until they were braised and cooked. But it would be clear that I tasted the final product.

"That's a little paranoid, don't you think?" Chef Aster said. She was the chef directly beside me and was one of the Buckingham Palace chefs.

"What?"

"Tasting all your food, what are you afraid you'll poison someone?"

"I'm not afraid of poisoning anyone," I said. "A good chef cooks by taste."

"Right," she shrugged. "Maybe in America."

It was embarrassing that she figured out what I was doing. Maybe I was paranoid. Or maybe everyone watching was waiting for me to kill someone with my pie.

When it was time for the meat pies to come out of the oven, Chef Aster got very upset. It seemed that her oven never got hot enough. Her pies were still raw.

I looked at Agnes and she looked at me. How did that happen? I suspected that there was sabotage going on to up the suspense on who would win.

"Plate your pies, Chefs," Albert Nash said. "You have five minutes."

We hurried the pies into the picnic basket display and plated two judging plates for tasting.

"Down to the final seconds and in five, four, three, two, one, and times up. Step away from your pies."

I put my hands in the air and waited while they shot our reaction video. My plates looked good. The pies were crescent shaped, making them easy to take to picnics. The display looked good with a garnish of potato salad and a bottle of red wine.

"Cut," the director said as they set up for the next shot of the judges coming in. I took the opportunity to wave over my wrangler, Alex.

"What can I get you, Chef?"

"What happened to Chef Aster's oven?"

He glanced over at the weeping chef and the half-baked pies. "It appears it didn't keep its temperature."

I studied him. "Was that intentional?"

He looked me in the eye a long moment. "Everything is intentional, Chef. The show is storyboarded weeks in advance."

"I see," I said. "And what chef did I replace?"

"Chef Nice," he said. "He's the head Chef at The Drake downtown."

"All right," I said. "So my guess is he has never been suspected of poisoning anyone with his pie."

Alex laughed. "No, he never has. Why?"

"It's been made clear to me that I'm here because people are waiting to see if anyone dies from one of my pies."

"You mean like that Wentworth guy did?"

"Wentworth did not die from my pie. He was poisoned."

"But wouldn't it make for great telly?" He grinned at me.

I opened my mouth to speak but nothing came out. Then the director shouted for us to take our places. It was time to shoot the end of the round and see who was going home.

* * *

"Welcome to the dessert round," Nash said. "We started with six chefs and now four remain. This round will be a play-off round where two chefs will go head to head. The winning chefs of each bracket will face off for the final round and a chance to be named the winner of the title, Best British Pie Maker.

"For this round, we will pair Chef Cole with Chef Elsie and Chef Butterbottom, you will be directly competing with Chef Wright. Each of you will make the same pie—bilberry pie—and you will be judged on plating, taste, wow factor, and crust.

Your ingredients are in the box provided. Chefs, on your marks, get set, bake!"

I opened the box to find flour, butter, salt, vinegar, bilberries, sugar, tapioca, and an egg. I grabbed some apples from my own ingredients and started making my crust.

I instructed Agnes to continue with our picnic theme and create a beautiful basket presentation that included a dessert wine, sharp cheddar cheese, and a small bowl of cream.

I was the only one adding apples to my bilberry pie. I made the crust and carefully fluted little custard cups as my pie pans. The thought was that I would pop out the pies so that they could be eaten with your hands or on a plate with a picnic fork.

Quartering the apples, I placed them in a saucepan with sugar, then I added butter and let them cook down a bit. Next, I added the bilberries and cooked the mixture for two more minutes before letting it cool.

The cooled filling was spooned into the small pie pans and I added decorative lattice work on the tops, brushed them with egg white, and sprinkled on sugar for shine.

Then, fingers crossed, I checked the temperature of my oven and stuck the pies in to cook. The camera crew and two judges showed up at my space for an individual shoot. I added more apples to the pot, along with sugar and butter, and stirred them while the judges asked me questions.

"Are Americans familiar with bilberries?" Judge Storm asked.

"We are more likely to make blueberry pie," I said. "Occasionally we'll get a shipment of bilberries to make pie if there is a special request."

"What is the favorite pie of the duke and duchess?" Judge Young asked.

"The duke loves cottage pie and I think the duchess is partial to lemon."

"Like the lemon pie Wentworth Uleman was found face down in?"

"I hardly think anyone likes killer pie," I said.

"So it wasn't your pie?"

"I didn't make that pie," I said. "But I am making this one, and I've personally tasted all the ingredients." I pointed to my little camera. "I have the video to prove it."

"Well, judges, since she has become her own walking taster, I'd say you can enjoy tasting her pie without fear of death," Nash said with a chuckle.

"The only thing she has to fear is losing," Judge Storm said.

I smiled. "I'm not afraid to lose. It's been a pleasure just participating."

"That's the spirit," Albert Nash said with a nervous laugh. "Okay, let's move on to Chef Butterbottom."

I pulled my pie out with ten minutes to spare and allowed it to cool. I have to say that it was the best-looking pie I'd ever made. None of the ingredients ended up on the floor and my equipment worked just fine. It looked like this might be a non-sabotaged segment. Good. It would be nice to have my bilberry pie go up against Chef Elsie's.

"And we are counting down the final seconds of the semi-final bake-off. Five, four, three, two, one, hands up!" I raised my hands from my plated pie. I looked at Chef Elsie and she looked at me.

"May the best pie win," I said and shook her hand.

"As long as it's my pie," she said with a grin. We brought the plated pies forward for the judges to talk about and taste. It was difficult to stand and listen to the judges talk about the pies. Memories of cooking school came rushing back. I had busted my bum to please the chefs and they had made me look bad with practiced ease. This time was different, but the emotions brought up by the memory were disheartening.

In the end, it seemed they loved my filling, but my flakey crust might have been too thin. I bit my bottom lip and waited as they critiqued Chef Elsie's pie.

"Nice depth of the crust," Judge Young said. "But it appears a little doughy."

Judge Storm took a forkful. "The taste is quiet exquisite, but the fruit filling is a touch runny."

I glanced at Chef Elsie who looked a bit steamed at the judges.

"The winner of this pie challenge is . . ."

"Chef Cole! You will be moving on to the finals in this bake-off. Congratulations!"

I held my hands over my mouth in surprise and then turned and gave Agnes a big hug. I was in the finals. When it came down to it, my bilberry pie was judged better than Chef Elsie's.

This was so awesome. I went over and shook Chef Elsie's hand and thanked her for a good competition. "I'll get you next time," she said, a grumble in her voice.

Then we stepped off the stage to watch the judging between Chef Wright and Chef Butterbottom. I held my breath. Both men were stiff competition. But if I had my choice, I would have Chef Wright win. It would be easier competing with him than competing with snobbish Butterbottom.

"Well, gentlemen, you both made superb pies," Judge Storm said. "But we must pick a winner."

"And that winner is . . ." the Judge Young waited until the director gave him the signal to announce. "Chef Butterbottom. Congratulations, Chef, you have made the finals in today's bake-off."

Darn.

Butterbottom shook Chef Wright's hand and turned to me. "All right, Chef Cole, I'm coming for you."

I swallowed hard. Butterbottom had made it his mission since I arrived to show everyone that he was a better chef than I was. He liked to say that I was the worst chef in London, but I now had proof that I was, at least in this competition, better than three other chefs.

"And cut—" the director said. Alex came over as the makeup artists worked furiously to touch up our makeup. All the heat and steam from baking put a real shine on our skin.

"I'm so glad I have you," Hannah said. "Butterbottom won't stop sweating. What a nightmare."

"All right," Alex said. "Congratulations, Chef. The director wants you to move your set up to the front right. Chef Butterbottom will be moved to the front left. That way we can get the lights on you and keep you in the camera shot the entire time.

Agnes and I carefully moved all the remaining ingredients, our dishes, and our other things to the vacated front kitchen. Butterbottom's assistants went straight to work, cleaning, shining, and placing all his things right where he wanted them.

I could hear the audience outside. People were betting on the winner, and I was not the favorite. I didn't mind. I was simply happy to be in second place. I noticed the director talking to Butterbottom. I thought I heard him say that Butterbottom had the win in his hands.

That wasn't upsetting at all. It was kind a relief to know what the outcome would be. I was still surprised that they didn't have Chef Wright or Chef Elsie as one of the finalists.

"Congratulations," Chef Wright said from behind me. I turned and he stuck out his hand.

"Thank you," I said as he shook my hand and then he leaned in to give me an unwelcome hug and a peck on the cheek.

"Best of luck."

"Right." I took a step back to put space between us. "How is Evie?" I asked him. "Or is it Rachel now?"

He smiled at me, his eyes crinkling. "What's wrong with both?" He winked. "Best of luck."

"All right, people, let's get the final shoot in before we lose daylight," the director called. Chef Wright left the tent/staging area to watch from the chairs with the other losing chefs.

I stepped over to Chef Butterbottom and stuck out my hand. "May the best pie win."

He sneered at my hand. "Everyone already knows who makes the best pie."

I pulled my hand back. "That would be me." I winked at him.

The cameras were rolling and I wanted to give them a good show. It was all for a good cause—children's charity. I rolled

129

my shoulders and tilted my neck like a fighter getting ready for a fight. Nash loved it. The cameras moved off me to the judges.

"Chefs, for your final bake you must make a Yorkshire curd tart. We are looking for a classic crème base and a warm, homey taste. Don't forget your crust must hold up to being lifted from the pie pan yet be flaky and delicious. The ingredients are in the box in front of you. On your marks, get set, bake!"

Chapter 15

I started out with a sweet shortbread pastry. I was sure to taste every ingredient. These ingredients were supplied and I wasn't taking any chances. I formed the ingredients into a ball and put it in the refrigerator to chill for thirty minutes while Agnes stood guard.

A Yorkshire curd tart was made with cheese curds, flour, sugar, butter, raisins, egg, lemon zest, and nutmeg.

The piecrust rolled out to perfection and I placed it in tart pans. Then I added beans to hold down the crust as I prebaked it for fifteen minutes, ensuring that my oven didn't go out or my crust get too brown.

Once I pulled the piecrust out, I filled the it with lemon curd and then the cheese curd mixture. Then I put it in the oven to bake. A quick glance at Chef Butterbottom showed me that he was about five minutes ahead of me in making his tarts. I had used smaller tart pans so that they would cook more quickly. Cheese tarts were best served cool, and that would take at least twenty minutes. A glance at the clock told me I had thirty minutes left. I was cutting it close.

Butterbottom had already begun to create his presentation.

I stuck to my picnic theme. I prepared white ceramic plates that mimicked popular paper plate shapes, then created a warm ginger sauce to decorate the plate.

A quick check on the tarts showed that they were done. I pulled them out and put them in the chilling box to cool. Agnes stayed beside the box.

I worked quickly and efficiently. I wasn't worried. I knew it wasn't in the script for me to win. That said, I wanted to do my best possible work to show everyone that the duchess was not wrong to hire me.

The judges came over to interview me one last time.

"How did you learn to cook Yorkshire curd tart?" Judge Storm asked. "I highly doubt cheese curds are sold in American groceries."

"You would be surprised," I said. "People in Wisconsin love their cheese curds. Living in Chicago, I had access to all kinds of cultures and flavors. It was a pleasure to learn all about British pie-making."

"So they do have cheese curds in America?" Judge Young asked.

"Yes," I said. "We are much more than fast food."

"And who is your assistant today?" Judge Storm asked.

"This is Agnes." I tugged the older woman forward. "She is my assistant at the palace."

"Hello, Agnes," Albert Nash said. "How does it feel working with a chef whose first assistant was murdered?"

"Well, we certainly don't dwell on murder." Agnes puffed up. "It's a pleasure working with talent like Chef Cole. I enjoy feeding the duke and duchess and their lovely children."

"We've noticed that you and Chef Cole are tasting

everything and keeping tight security on your bake today. Can you tell us why?" Albert Nash asked.

"There was some speculation that Chef's pies might not be safe," Agnes said. "We know Chef doesn't deserve that reputation. In fact, I believe Chef is being framed. We want to ensure everyone's safety."

"Are you sure you're not trying to prove Chef Cole's innocence?"

"There's nothing to prove," I said. "We're simply acting with an abundance of caution."

"Sounds like you have nothing but the best intentions," Judge Storm said.

"Exactly," I said.

The crew then moved over to interview Chef Butterbottom, who was supremely confident that his pie would win. And why not? They told him he won before we even started the round.

I wiped sweat off my brow and started plating my tarts.

The camera crew, host, and judges took their places at the front of the tent.

"We are on the countdown to naming a champion in the British Best Pie competition," Nash said. "Chef's you have ten seconds . . . five, four, three, two, one. Time's up."

I put my hands in the air and turned and hugged Agnes. We had made it through the competition with some of the best pies of my life and no one sabotaged me. I turned and went over to Chef Butterbottom to shake hands. "Good competition."

He gave me a back handed compliment: "Not bad . . . for an American." I took it. At least in all this Butterbottom was beginning to understand that I was good at my job, and that I was here to stay.

They filmed the judging segment next, and Agnes and I cleaned up our area, carefully packing all the remaining ingredients in the cooler. We washed and dried the dishes and placed them in the baskets.

Hannah came over to touch up my makeup for the last time. "Best of luck," she said as she finished dabbing at my face. "You deserve to win."

"You are too nice," I said. "I know Butterbottom is slated to win. But it was fun to film this and to compete with so many great chefs."

"You never know," she suggested. "The producers might go for a twist in the finals."

I shook my head at her. The director called us all to our places for the finale shoot.

I stood beside Butterbottom in a fresh chef coat and listened to them critique my pie as having a smooth buttery flavor, and the crust was thankfully done to perfection.

Next, they talked about Butterbottom's pie. It, too, was perfection.

"To prevent a dead-even tie," Nash said. "We will now go back over all of your pies for the day and the winner will be the Chef who proved without a doubt that they are Britain's Best Pie Maker."

"And cut—" the director called. "Chefs, please stay on your marks. We're going to shoot a short bit where the judges go over all of your work."

I let my mind wander and studied the crowd that had gathered outside the tent. The ticket holders were seated on both rolled-up sides of the tent. Gawkers and those who stood surrounded the tent. There were a lot of people there.

I felt nervous for the first time. I'd been so focused on

baking that I hadn't thought about what the crowd would think or how they would react. The couple who had commented on being seated in front of a nobody were fastened to their chairs even though I had moved.

I saw the other chefs standing at the front of the tent. Chef Wright winked at me, and I sent him a smile. The man was a flirt. I scanned the crowd for familiar faces. Not that I would see that many.

Then I made eye contact with Penny. She was with Evie. They waved, and I waved back.

"We are going to taste your pies one more time," Nash said. The assistants brought out the pies. My pies held up well for a day under filming lights. I looked over at Chef Butterbottom's pies. They looked spectacular. In comparison, mine looked like a home cook made them.

My shoulders bowed a little. Still, I could proudly say I entered the competition and got farther than anyone thought I would. I certainly hoped it was due to my efforts as a baker and not the talking points of murder or the duke and duchess.

"Chefs, we have finished our final judging. You were both strong competitors and the good news is you are both competing for good charities. Chef Cole, you are competing for the Children's Charity and Chef Butterbottom's efforts go to the Women and Children's Clinic. As a bonus, all of the pies made today will be auctioned off, and any funds raised will benefit the winning charity.

Without further ado, it's time to name the winner." Nash took a card out of the inside pocket of his suitcoat. "And the winner of Britain's Best Pie Maker is . . ."

I held my breath.

"Chef . . ."

I bit my bottom lip.

"Butterbottom."

Chef pumped his fist in the air. "Yes!" The crowd went wild to see one of its favorite chefs acknowledged. Agnes patted me on the shoulder. "Good job, Chef."

"Thank you." I patted her back. "Good job to you, too." Then I stepped over to Butterbottom's camp and shook everyone's hands. The cameras continued to roll, but my part in the competition was done. I stood straight. At least no one died from eating my pies.

Suddenly there was a scream and someone shouted to call an ambulance. I turned to see that Chef Butterbottom hunched over in pain. Then his assistants began to double over one by one. Each held his stomach and moaned.

Oh, boy.

"What's going on?" I asked. "Are you okay?"

"Ugh, food poisoning." Butterbottom raced for the trash outside the tent. Shockingly, he and his entire crew turned an odd shade of green and acted as if they were dying. Maybe they were.

The emergency techs were on the scene taking care of everyone. Agnes and I stayed out of the way. The judges looked queasy, but so far only Butterbottom's crew was hurt.

So much for auctioning off the winning pies. The production crew would be lucky to be able to give the pies away. CID showed up nearly as fast as the EMT's. DCI Garrote walked into the tent and glanced from me to the pies and back. "Tag those pies for evidence," he barked at the patrolmen who followed him.

"This is going to get complicated," I said to Agnes. "We

should get out of the way." We picked up the cooler and baskets and headed out the side entrance of the tent.

"Stop right there, Chef," DCI Garrote said. "I need everyone to stay right where they are until we determine what has happened here."

"Okay." I sat down on the steps that separated the tented stage from the ground. I noticed that the crowd had been cleared back from the chairs, but people continued to watch with fascination. I suppose this was a bit of a train wreck.

"What do you think happened?" Agnes said to me from the stair below mine.

"Maybe they got some bad ingredients," I shrugged. "The judges seem to be okay. Strange."

"I don't think Chef Butterbottom and his crew pretested their pies like we did."

"It wouldn't matter," I said. "The judges didn't get sick. I wonder if Chef Butterbottom drank anything that the judges and we didn't."

"I think he had tea brought in," Agnes said. "Probably had bad milk or something."

"Huh," I said.

We waited there while they hauled Chef Butterbottom off in the ambulance along with the four members of his staff. Everyone else was checked out, but no one else was sick. CID was taking samples from every cup plate and saucer in Butterbottom's kitchen.

"Are you ladies all right?" a tall, thin ambulance technician asked. His nametag said Hyde.

"Yes." I stood. "I feel fine. Agnes?"

"I'm fine as well," she said, standing beside me.

"Good," he said with a shy smile. His blond hair fell into his blue eyes. "I've brought you some water. You could be here a while until Detective Chief Inspector Garrote gets to you."

"Thanks for checking on us," I said.

"And thanks for the water," Agnes said. She opened her bottle and went to take a swig when it was slapped out of her hand by a policewoman. "What are you doing?"

"Do you know that man?" The policewoman asked.

"No, but we don't know you, either," I pointed out.

"Until this thing is resolved, you should think twice before eating or drinking anything around here. Okay? We don't know the source of the sickness yet."

"I think we've narrowed it down," DCI Garrote said as he approached us.

"What is it?" I asked.

"Is it in the water?" Agnes asked.

"It appears someone poisoned Chef Butterbottom and his staff."

Chapter 16

"Poison?" I asked. "Are they going to be okay?"

"For the most part," the inspector said. "They will be out for at least twenty-four hours. The doctors tell me that the poisoning, while severe, was not life-threatening."

"Oh, thank goodness," I said sincerely.

"The poison, however, is one we may have seen before." The Inspector looked at me.

"Where have you seen it?" I asked.

"The ambulance techs fear it is the same poison that killed Wentworth Uleman."

"No!" I put my hand over my mouth.

"Yes," he said, his mouth a thin line. "I have to ask you Chef, did you poison your competition?"

"What? No!" I protested. "No, he already won. Why would I poison him?"

"Because he won," DCI Garrote said. "It is pretty fishy that Butterbottom and his crew are all sick and you are not."

"That's ridiculous," I said. "I didn't have access to any of his ingredients." I turned to Agnes. "We were both too busy prepping our own stuff to even go over to his things. Plus, there were four assistants at his station. It seems like one of them might have seen something."

"And we will interview them all," he said. "Once they are stable enough to comment."

"We were very careful with our ingredients," Agnes said. "We tasted every one and tested each pie before anyone else was able to eat them. That might be why we aren't sick."

"It's true," I said. "The last two rounds used ingredients provided by the producers. Besides, you can ask my show wrangler, Alex. He was with us every minute we weren't on camera."

"I'll be sure to question him," DCI Garrote said. "But I have to ask you, do you have access to household chemicals? Gardening chemicals?"

"No," I said. "Of course not."

"Aren't you dating a gardener?" He looked at me intently.

"What?" Agnes also peered at me.

"I went out for drinks with him," I said. "That's all."

"I see," the inspector said. "And couldn't this gardener who you went out to drinks with have access to gardening chemicals?"

"I don't know," I said. "I suppose he could. He is a gardener. It didn't come up in our date-night conversation."

"I see," he said and made a note. "I will need to see all of your things. We will be testing the baskets and containers for any trace evidence that might be on them."

"Wow, testing everything is a big job. It's going to take a while, isn't it? What happens to evidence like my pie pan?"

He gave me a look. "Once the investigation is complete and the poisoner brought to justice, the articles that can be returned will be returned. In this case, the pie pan is the murder weapon, therefore it will never be returned. I would suggest you requisition a new one."

"Right," I said with a sigh. The CID techs took our things away to process them.

At the end of the day, the duchess had cooked for her family for the entire day. I came in second in the competition, and the winner, my supposed rival, was still in the hospital recovering from having his stomach pumped.

Not exactly my best day.

I let Agnes go home since we didn't have anything to bring back to the kitchen. The pie auction was cancelled. I hated to see the food wasted, but they couldn't take the risk of more people getting sick.

What poison was used?

Detective Chief Inspector Garrote wouldn't or couldn't tell me anything more than it may have been the same thing that killed Wentworth. I assumed it was some sort of household or gardening chemical since that is what he asked me about. But what could kill one person immediately and only make five other people sick?

I guess it depends on Wentworth's autopsy. Maybe he had something else in his system like alcohol or drugs. Or maybe he had a much larger dose. Or maybe it wasn't the poison that killed him at all. Maybe the poison was something the killer used to distract the police from how Wentworth was really killed.

My mind wondered in circles while I made tea in my kitchen. I hadn't seen Jasper since our "quick drinks" date. I hadn't seen Ian either. Heat rushed up my cheeks at the memory of seeing him kiss Lana. How could I think he might like me? What a mess.

"Here you are," Penny said as she sailed into the kitchen. "I'm hearing all kinds of rumors about what happened after the show. You need to dish, now!"

"I saw you at the show." I got up and took out a teacup for her. Luckily, I had a pot of tea ready. "You were with Evie. So have you chosen Evie over Rachel?"

"Oh gosh no," she said with a laugh and sat down at the table. I put the cup of tea in front of her and a small plate of cookies.

"No cookies for me, thanks," she said.

"What are you afraid I might have poisoned them?"

"Is that what happened to Butterbottom?" Penny poured two teaspoons full of sugar into her cup of tea.

"That is what Detective Chief Inspector Garrote seems to think," I said. "Something about finding traces of the same poison that took out Wentworth."

"Egad!" Penny exclaimed. "They didn't find any on you, did they?"

"No, Agnes and I watched our things like hawks. The funny part is the poison made Chef sick after the competition. It's almost as if it were an afterthought."

"Huh, did they find the poison in the pies chef made?"

"They must not have," I said. "The judges didn't get sick."

"Maybe it was in the tea chef drank after."

"It was warm outside under all those lights. I wonder if he drank enough water."

"An Englishman drinks tea first and foremost," Penny said. "They could have spiked his tea. Do you know what the poison was?"

"I have no idea," I said. "And I'm glad I don't, because that would only make DCI Garrote more suspicious of me."

"Why would he be suspicious of you?"

"Because Butterbottom and I were in the finals."

"But Chef didn't get poisoned until it was all over."

"That's what I said. He didn't pose any threat or risk to me afterwards. Why would I or anyone poison him?"

"Maybe you want to take over his kitchen for a few days," Penny said, wiggling her eyebrows at me.

"Oh stop, that was never on my mind."

"But he was able to take over your kitchen for a meal after Wentworth was murdered."

"That might be true," I said, "But Chef was out of the country then, so it wasn't even a plus for him. I mean, today the duchess cooked for her family. How would poisoning Butterbottom help me?"

"You do make a good point," Penny said. "I wish I knew what the poison was. Then we could try to figure out who the killer is. Who did you see at the competition today?"

"There were so many people coming and going," I said. "I was focused on ensuring none of my food was poisoned. I didn't want that to get on the evening news. I would be fired for sure. In fact, that's a good reason not to poison Chef—it only points a suspicious finger back at me. Someone is trying to frame me."

"But who? And why? Are you sure you didn't see anyone you know?"

"I saw you and Evie," I said. "But I hardly think either one of you could have gotten close enough to poison chef." I looked at Penny. "You don't particularly seem like a killer to me."

Penny put her hands up. "I'm on your side. I've been helping you investigate. Why would I try to frame you?"

"Exactly," I said. "And I don't know Evie well enough for her to frame me. Where does she work again?"

"Evie is Princess Anne's administrator."

"Is she still having an affair with Chef Wright?" I had to ask. "I mean, even knowing that Rachel also slept with him?"

"Evie is crazy in love with the man," Penny said. "I wish I could say all of this changed her mind."

"But it didn't."

"No," she said. "If nothing else it spurred her to want to be even closer to him. She told me that he promised to leave his wife for her."

"Classic," I said.

"Right?" Penny sipped her tea. She eyed the plate of cookies. "Okay, I'll have a biscuit."

I glanced at the clock. It was midnight. "It's late and I have to get up early." I stood, then stopped. "Wait, it's Saturday night, er, Sunday now I guess. Why aren't you out at a club having fun?"

Penny shrugged. "I need a break from Veronica and all that."

I narrowed my eyes and put my hand on her forehead. "Are you getting sick?"

Penny laughed and pushed my hand away. "No."

"Then what is it?" I studied her for a moment. "Wait, you started dating someone, didn't you? Someone who works on Saturday, maybe?"

A blush ran up Penny's cheeks.

"Who is it?"

"No one you know," she said with a sigh. "I can't tell. It's still too early."

I sat down. "Oh no you don't. Dish."

"You didn't dish about your date with Jasper."

"How did you know about that?"

"There are no secrets in the palace," Penny said.

"Except yours. Please at least give me a hint. Is he royal or one of the employees?"

"Oh, gosh, no, not royal," Penny said. "I'm too far outside of their set. But he is pretty important."

"Of course he is. Or he wouldn't have caught your eye. Now who is he?"

"I'm going to keep this one to myself for a while, if you don't mind."

I frowned. "Fine. You spent the day with Evie. Have she and Rachel reconciled yet?"

"Oh, gosh, no, that isn't going to happen," Penny said. "Evie really is possessive of Chef Wright."

"What about Rachel? Don't tell me she is still with Chef Wright, too."

"Oh, no, no," Penny said. "Rachel said that it's very clear that Chef Wright is not going to leave his wife. She's looking for someone who is going to concentrate only on her."

"So why not tell Evie that?"

"Because she is upset and wants to keep Evie angry as payback."

"Some friendship," I said. "Just so you know, I didn't want to talk about my quick drinks date with Jasper because I didn't know how it was going to work out."

"And how did it work out?" She asked as we placed the dishes in the dishwasher and left the kitchen.

"Not so good," I said as we climbed the stairs. "He asked if I'm only dating him because Ian won't date me."

"Ouch."

"I know, right? I think we recovered from it, but I'm not sure. Sometimes I overthink things."

"Unless it's true," Penny gave me the side eye. "Do you have feelings for Ian?"

"I don't know the man well enough to have feelings," I said as we entered our hall. "Besides, I went to see him last night to inform him of my entry in the competition."

"And?" She asked. "Did he do something?

"He didn't do a thing," I said. "Except kiss a beautiful woman named Lana in his office. It's clear they are in love. He couldn't keep his hands off her."

"That's right," she said and stopped at her door. "I hear he has a girl in Brighton."

"Well, there you have it. Dating Ian is out of the question."

"Are you sure there isn't a question?" Penny asked and raised her eyebrow.

"The only question I have is why I'm being framed as a poisoner."

Chapter 17

Sunday started off well with Sunday brunch for the family. Agnes had the day off and I took the trays up to the family's dining room.

"Oh, Chef," the duchess stepped in as I handed off the plates. "Do come in for a moment."

I stepped into the room. Staff had already set the table up. The dishes would be served on the sideboard. The family was small but we kept with tradition. The dining room smelled of coffee and sausages and my famous cinnamon rolls.

"What can I do for you, ma'am?" I asked.

She smiled at me. She wore close-fitting jeans and a striped three-quarter length T-shirt. Her bouncy hair was down around her shoulders. It struck me how thin she was. No wonder designers loved to dress her.

"First off, I wanted to say congratulations for coming in second yesterday at the bake-off."

I felt the heat of a blush rush up my cheeks. "Thank you. Thank you for sponsoring my entry."

"Of course," she said. "Children's charities are one of our biggest concerns." She paused. "I also wanted to thank you for the wonderful job you did at the bridal shower. I know I can count on you to go above and beyond your duties."

"You're welcome."

"I understand there have been some bumps in the road since you have been here. I certainly hope you won't let anything drive you away." She sent me a soft smile. "William loves your pastries."

"Thank you, ma'am," I said. "I won't."

"Good," she said. The sounds of children running down the hall echoed throughout the elegant surrounds. "Have a good day."

"You, too," I hurried out the side door of the dining room. The butler had returned my empty cart to the hallway. The servants' halls snaked in and around most of the main living areas. They were there to keep us out of sight so that the family could live their lives discretely.

I glanced up as I stopped at the elevator door. There were cameras in the halls. That was to keep us and the royals safe. Somewhere on the other side of the camera, Ian and his men ensured as little as possible disturbed the occupants.

It had to be difficult living a life where you were always in the public eye, even when you were in your own home.

* * *

"Garrote was wrong," Penny said gleefully as she sailed into my kitchen.

It was just after I had served dinner and I was busy doing dishes. "How was he wrong?"

Penny grabbed a mug from the cupboard, tossed a tea bag into it, poured hot water in her cup, and sat down by the table.

"The poison that made Butterbottom sick was not the same thing that killed Wentworth Uleman."

"How do you know that?" I asked as I rinsed dishes.

"The news reporters said that Wentworth died of cyanide poisoning."

"Okay?"

"And Butterbottom and his crew were poisoned with isopropyl alcohol."

"Wait—so it wasn't the same killer?" I finished rinsing the last dish before grabbing my own cup of tea and sitting next to her.

"No, they think it could still be the same killer or it could be a copycat." Penny sipped her tea with an animated her expression. "Most likely whoever poisoned Chef couldn't get their hands on any more cyanide and turned to something more readily available."

"Ugh," I groaned. "So we have two potential killers running around trying to frame me?"

"If there is a copycat, I don't think they were trying to frame you or they would have made sure CID found traces of the poison in your possession."

"So why poison Butterbottom?"

"That certainly is a good question," she sipped her tea.

"Except no one knew what poisoned Wentworth until today's newscast, right?"

"They might have guessed wrong," Penny shrugged.

"Or the killer only had a little cyanide and had to change poisons." I tapped my finger on my chin. "So why did DCI Garrote ask me if I've been around garden or kitchen chemicals?"

"Maybe he hadn't gotten the report yet," Penny mused.

"Here's my big question. How do you get cyanide to poison someone? I mean isn't it illegal?"

"Let's find out." Penny grabbed her smartphone and did a search. I picked up my smartphone and started searching as well. "Oh, they can make it from peach pits and cherry pits and such."

"Except those fruits are all out of season," I said. "Not only would they have to get ahold of a bunch of out-of-season fruits, but they would have to grind the pits. That's a lot of work."

"It could be why they switched to isopropyl." Penny tapped on her phone.

I studied the information on cyanide. "Wow, that's nasty stuff." I looked up poisons. "Did you know that rhubarb leaves could poison someone? It is rhubarb season. It would be much easier to grind that up and put it in a pie."

"But not as immediate." Penny scrolled through the text on her phone. "It's pretty clear they wanted Wentworth to be found with his face in your pie."

"Huh?" I studied Penny. "I know there wasn't any poison in my pie. That means someone used my pie pan without me knowing or someone slipped it into my pie before Wentworth ate it. Do you think the intended murder victim might have been someone else?"

"I hadn't really thought about that," Penny said. "But you're right. Anyone could have slipped poison into your pie. You left it on the counter for the staff."

"Maybe it was intended for Chef Wright," I said.

"And yesterday's poisoning was meant for Chef Butterbottom. Maybe someone is taking out the palace chefs. Which means you could be next."

"I certainly hope not." I put down my tea. The flavor suddenly tasted sour to my tongue.

"I can be your taster," Penny said with a grin. "You haven't had any of those petit fours yet have you?" She pointed to the glass-covered platter filled with the tiny tea cakes.

"Too late," I said. "I've not only tasted them, but the family had them for tea."

"Oh," she sounded so disappointed.

"But you can have some if you want," I said.

"Super." Penny jumped up and got a small plate and put three icing covered cakes on her plate. She bit into one the moment she sat back down. "Seriously, I'm here if you need a taster."

I shook my head. "How do you stay so trim when you eat like that?"

She shrugged. "Good genes?"

"You know women around the world hate you," I teased.

She shrugged and bit into her cake.

"So tell me about this mysterious romance you have that keeps you from going clubbing on Saturday night."

She sighed and put her elbows on the table. "He's a vicar."

"What? No—you mean like a preacher?"

"Yes," she said. "His name is Dale Ruthart and he is the cutest thing I've ever seen in my life."

"How did you two meet?"

"My mother's best friend got married in a little church and Dale presided over the ceremony. Lucky for me, my mother insisted I dress like a lady—which I did."

I tilted my head. "Does your vicar know you go out clubbing?"

"No." She sipped her tea. "All he knows is that I work here, and that I work a lot."

"So you're lying to him."

"Not lying," she said. "I no longer go clubbing."

"So you've known him less than a week," I teased.

"Long enough to know he has the most gorgeous eyes I've ever seen on a man. That's saying a lot. Oh, and he works with poor children at an afterschool program. Isn't that something?"

"It's something." I sipped my tea. I could tell from her expression that she truly thought this vicar might be the man for her. "Do you see yourself as a vicar's wife?"

"Well, why not? I have experience running a large household."

"That you do." I stood. "Do you have a picture?"

"He won't take a selfie with me," she pouted. "He says it's a bit too narcissistic for him."

"Surely he has a picture," I said. "What is his parish? They must have a website, right? Wouldn't he have a professional picture?"

"Oh, gosh, you're right," Penny's eyes lit up. She tapped into the search bar of her cell phone. "Here, St. Anthony. Ah, there's my guy. Isn't he cute?" She pushed her phone toward me. There, in full choir dress, was an earnest-looking young man with a round face, round, bright blue eyes, and blond hair pushed away from his eyes.

"Oh, he is quite good looking," I said with a smile and handed the phone back to her. "I see what you see in him."

"You should see him without a shirt."

"You saw him without a shirt already?"

She blushed. "I might have peeked when he was changing

out of basketball clothes. You see, he invited me to come see what he does with the kids' afterschool program."

"But you hate kids," I pointed out and took her tea mug and empty plate to the sink.

"I don't hate kids." She raised her chin. "I happen to like the little prince and princess."

"You hate kids," I said. "You tell me that all the time when we go into the park to eat lunch."

"Well, that's unruly park-going children." She stood. "I have never been around afterschool-program kids. I didn't know, I might have liked them. I know for sure that I like to see Dale all sweaty after playing a game of ball."

We walked out of the kitchen, and I turned out the lights and locked the door. "Well, that's a start I suppose."

"It is, isn't it?" Penny said with a secret smile. We walked through the hallway, up the stairs and down our hall. The floors were all wood and creaked with our steps. The beige walls were very clean and the baseboards dust free. Mrs. Worth ran a very clean household. I never saw the maids who cleaned the halls, but it was clear they did. I bet you could practically eat off the walls.

I stopped outside Penny's door. "Do you think you'll ever have children?"

"I don't know," she said. "I hadn't thought about it much. The thought of going through a pregnancy like the duchess did, not once but twice. I don't know."

"Well, you just met your vicar. It will be a while before you need to think about it."

"Do you think he'll want children?" She whispered with concern.

"He's a vicar who helps with an afterschool program," I said. "Sounds like he wants children. Good night, Penny." I walked off to my room feeling a bit sorry for her.

"Good night," she said, disappearing into her rooms. I opened my door, turned on my light and sighed at the cozy peace of my little suite. Maybe it will work out for Penny and the vicar, I thought. Weirder things have happened. I put my keys in the small basket on my breakfast bar and headed to my bedroom, turning on lights as I went.

Thinking about children made my mind go to thoughts of dating again. Jasper was really handsome. He wanted to go out with me but thought I had a thing for Ian—which, if I was being honest with myself, I did.

I frowned. Why did everything have to be so difficult?

Chapter 18

"Hey, how are you?" I asked when I ran into Jasper in my kitchen garden. Even though it was my day off, I had come out to pick salad greens for my lunch. The radishes and green onions were also ready. But I had to admit, all that was just an excuse to run into Jasper.

"Good, good," he said, hefting a bag of soil up onto his broad shoulder.

"Listen, I'm so sorry we left things in such a weird place," I said, confronting the subject. I had been thinking about it ever since Penny had told me about her vicar. It was time to be brave and reach out.

"Hey, I started it."

I put my hand on his left bicep. "I want you to know that I don't consider you second choice. Only a crazy person would consider you seconds. I'm not crazy."

"No, you're not." He said dumped the soil into a newly made wooden box that would become a raised bed.

"I don't want things to be awkward between us." I stepped back while he worked. "I happen to like your fresh veggies."

He sent me a smoldering look and a wicked grin. "There's more to me than my fresh veggies."

Yikes.

A blush rushed up my cheeks and I found myself taking a step back before I held my ground. I'm a grown woman. It wasn't my fault I've never been seriously seduced. Was it?

I laughed and it sounded fake to my own ears. What does a woman do with such a man? Sigh, I guess. "I bet there is," I managed to squeak out.

"So, quick drinks again sometime? Or shall we move on to dinner?"

"Quick drinks." I raised my hand when he started to look disappointed. "You know I'm fresh out of a long-term relationship. Let me enjoy all the stages. Okay?"

"Okay," he said. "So tomorrow?"

I laughed again. "Wednesday."

"Cool." He winked at me and moved toward the greenhouse door.

"I do have a quick question."

"What?"

"Do you use garden chemicals?"

"No, the greenhouse is strictly organic. Why do you want to know?"

"Just wondering," I said. "See you Wednesday?"

"Take care, Chef. And enjoy your day-off salad."

"Right." I really did blush to my roots. There was no denying I'd gone out to the garden to find him and he'd caught me. At least I learned that any chemicals that might have been used for poison weren't his.

"Oh, that boy likes you," Agnes said when I stepped back into the kitchen. Monday was my day off but not Agnes's.

156

Agnes had Saturday and Sunday off. Then she was in the kitchen Monday in case the duchess needed extra help. Like today, the duchess had an important meeting and Agnes was called upon to make lunch.

"You saw that?"

"It's a glass wall," Agnes pointed out. "I'm not blind."

"Right, okay, well, I have fresh veggies for the lunch salad. Why don't you make that while I poach the fish?"

"Now, chef, no need for you to work on your day off," she said with a smile. "I can handle the children's lunch. I know you just came down to search out your young man."

I tried to hide my blush by making tea. "What? I spent the morning running errands. I thought I'd stop into the kitchen and see if you needed anything is all."

"Right," she laughed. "Nice to see you blush. Means you're human."

I let it go. I liked Agnes. She must feel the same, or she wouldn't be so quick to tease me.

I watched as Agnes put together a simple lunch of poached white fish on quinoa, spring greens salad, and a quick trifle dessert made of berries and whipped cream. I'm sure even Chef Butterbottom couldn't find fault with it. Not a single deep-fried fish stick in sight.

I was always amazed at how well the children ate. But then my mother told me that children only eat junk food if you teach them to eat junk food. The duchess was ensuring they grew to love fresh, simple meals. Having ensured that Agnes truly didn't need me, I left the kitchen and headed to the park to catch some sunshine.

"Chef Cole! Carrie Ann!" I heard Chef Wright call my name in the hall and I turned.

"Chef Wright, what brings you into my part of the palace?"

"I heard about Chef Butterbottom's poisoning and I wanted to see if you were affected as well."

"I wasn't," I said. "How are you? How's your team? Was anyone else poisoned?" I don't know why I didn't think about the other teams earlier. Right now, Chef Wright was making me feel a little too self-involved.

"No, only Butterbottom and his crew," Chef Wright said. "I understand they found a toxin in the teacups they drank out of."

"I heard that," I said. "Scary. I don't understand who could have done such a thing. I thought the security was quite good for the event."

"Yes, well, there were a lot of ticketed people wandering around," Chef Wright said. "It could have been anyone."

"I heard a rumor that you might have been the target. Do you think that's true?"

"Who me?" He pointed at himself and laughed. "Not hardly. I heard the same about you."

"Not hardly," I said with a half-smile. "It does seem that someone is trying to take us out one by one."

"Well, it will take more than a few sips of isopropyl to take down Butterbottom. The man has an iron stomach."

"It's because he's an iron chef." I laughed at my own joke.

"Is he?" Chef Wright looked confused.

"No," I said. "I mean, I don't know. I just said it because it was a funny pun."

"Right."

"I heard that isopropyl wasn't the poison used to kill Wentworth. So it might not even be the same poisoner. Do you think they meant to kill Wentworth or just make him sick like they did Chef Butterbottom and his crew?"

"I have no idea," Chef Wright said. "I understand that poison is a strange thing. No one really understands dosage or even how to control it."

I looked at him sideways. "Are you saying that the killer misjudged how much it took to kill Butterbottom?"

"I don't think anyone knows what it would take to kill ol' Butterbottom." He winked at me.

"But you think they were trying to kill Butterbottom, not just make him sick?"

"Maybe," he said with a shrug. "Or maybe they were trying to make my team sick and Wentworth was accidently overdosed."

"Huh." I thought about that. "Maybe Wentworth was an accident. It would explain why the poisoner switched to isopropyl. But why try to make you and your team ill? Why make Butterbottom sick?"

"That's the question, isn't it?" He said.

"I do have another question."

"What, dear?"

"I-"

Penny and Rachel came around the corner interrupting me. Rachel had a moment of pause when she saw Chef Wright with me.

"Carrie Ann," Penny said with surprise. "You're out of your kitchen."

I laughed. "I do get out every now and then. It's my day off. You should know that. You're the one who got me out on the town."

"She did?" Chef Wright asked.

I could feel Rachel tense up at his words. "Yes, she gave me my tourist night on the town last week."

"I even dressed her up," Penny said with pride. "She looked amazing."

"I bet she did," Chef Wright said.

"Excuse me, I've got to get back to work." Rachel walked off. Her back was straight and her head held high.

Chef Wright seemed to shrug her off. If I didn't know that the two of them had been having an affair, I would wonder why she snubbed us. As for Chef Wright, he didn't seem at all moved by her discomfort. That made me wonder what kind of man he was.

"What brings you to the palace halls?" Penny asked Chef Wright. "I thought you had your hands full hiring a new waiter to replace Wentworth."

"Ah, that's why I'm here," he said. "I was on my way to the administration offices to interview some new candidates."

"This hallway isn't exactly on the way to admin," I pointed out. We were in the hall adjacent to my hall. Granted, it was a shortcut from the apartment to my kitchen, but the admin was in the opposite direction.

"I'll be honest," Chef Wright said. "I was hoping to run into you."

"Really, why?"

"Yes, why?" Penny crossed her arms over her chest. Today she wore a smart skirt suit in a pale blue tweed. Chef Wright was dressed in a green button down and khaki pants.

They looked like a hardworking couple. Meanwhile, I looked more relaxed in my day-off cotton fit-and-flare dress. I'd dressed hoping to look nice for Jasper and not look like my usual professional chef self.

"I haven't seen her since the competition," Chef Wright said. "I wanted to congratulate her on winning second place."

"You could have sent an email," Penny pointed out.

Chef Wright shrugged. "What can I say? I prefer to say congratulations in person."

"How is the staff at the Orangery doing since Wentworth's murder?" I asked to change the subject and lighten the mood. "Are they worried that there might be a killer among them?"

"I've had several staff members quit," he said. "A few left after Wentworth's demise, but more left when they heard of Butterbottom's illness. It's why I have to conduct interviews."

"I've heard that you aren't the only one with staffing issues over this," Penny said. "No one wants to work in a place where people are getting poisoned. Especially if they are working for minimum wages."

I looked at Chef Wright. "How is business at the Orangery? Has it fallen off since the murder?"

"No," he said with a shake of his head. "It's actually picked up which is why I need to hire and train people quickly."

"It's picked up? I thought for sure people would stay away, worried about food poisoning."

"Actually, the tourists seem to have a morbid fascination with death," he said. "We do have some people who want to tour the kitchens now to see where Wentworth died and perhaps solve the mystery of his murder."

"Who gains from the pickup in traffic?" I asked.

"The Orangery and other tourist sites here at the palace are run by a charity," Penny said. "The nonprofit would see gains from more foot traffic."

I frowned. "So no one would stage a poisoning to gain more profits."

"No," Penny said.

Chef Wright eyed me. "Are you still trying to solve this crime?"

"I'm still considered a viable suspect," I said with a small shrug. "So, yes, I would like to figure out who is doing this and why. That way I can get back to concentrating on my work."

"I hadn't considered you as a suspect," Chef Wright said.

"Tell Detective Chief Inspector Garrote that," I said. "When Butterbottom and his crew got ill, I was the first one he came to question."

"What reason would you have to hurt Wentworth or Butterbottom for that matter?"

"Remember that Wentworth was peering in my window taking photos. Looking for something to sell the tabloids, I assume," I said. "And it was my pie he ate."

"Pish, nothing of value came from the pictures that boy took," Chef Wright said.

"DCI Garrote said it isn't the picture he sold to the tabloids that got him into trouble," I said.

"They think Wentworth was blackmailing members of the staff to keep pictures out of the tabloids," Penny said.

"Like the picture of Lord Heavington buying stolen recipes," I said.

"Wait, what? What recipes?" Chef Wright asked.

"Lord Heavington has sold a recipe book concept based on all the royal kitchens he has visited," I said. "Apparently, he was purchasing recipes, without permission, to fill his book."

"He better not have taken any of my recipes . . . Wait! One of my staff was selling him recipes?"

"We don't know that," I said. "We only have him buying recipes from Beth Branch. She works for Princess Anne."

"I'm going to have a sit down with my staff," he said. "Selling recipes is stealing money from our employer. I can't have stealing in my ranks."

"Just poisoning?" Penny asked.

"No," he said. "No one on my staff did that. It was her pie after all."

"See," I said. "Everyone thinks I did it. Well, I didn't. I don't have time for this. It's my day off." I pushed through the hall toward the parking area and headed outside. Even Chef Wright pointed a finger at me. All because it was my pie pan.

My pie pan . . . a lot of people knew I was making pies for the bridal shower. I hadn't kept that a secret. In fact, I had ensured that everyone knew so that they wouldn't have any complaints over the menu. I suddenly wished that the police had kept the pie itself. I had proprietary ingredients. A simple test would tell if it was actually my pie.

Chapter 19

I fumed over the conversation the rest of the afternoon, trying to figure out ways someone could have stolen a pie pan and set me up.

"What are you frowning about?" Agnes asked when she returned from taking tea to the children. I was back in my kitchen. It was the only place I felt welcome right now.

"I'm trying to figure out how Wentworth's killer got the poison into the pie without anyone noticing." I poured hot water into my teacup. "I had the crazy thought that they simply put their pie in my pie pan, but that wouldn't work."

"Why not?"

"Because they would have had to know which pie I left for Chef Wright's staff, make the same pie, then switch it out. How would they have gotten ahold of my pie pan?"

"They could have taken a used pie pan you had stacked up and left to wash in the kitchen," Agnes suggested. "You did say you have two missing pie pans."

"But how would they know what pie I left?"

Agnes shrugged. "You've got me there. Maybe they injected the poison into the pie. That would be easy."

"How would they ensure that Wentworth would take a bite out of the part of the pie with the poison. I mean injecting doesn't go uniformly through the pie."

"So what do you think happened?"

"I wonder if they tested the fork he ate the pie with," I mused.

"You think the silverware was poisonous?"

"It's a thought," I sipped my tea. "But I think they tested the pie and said that the pie was poisoned. That sounds like something was baked evenly into the entire pie."

"That makes the most sense."

"So how did they do that? I mean how did they get ahold of my pie plate and how did they know I was going to leave a lemon pie?"

"Did the pie have meringue?" Agnes asked as she cleaned up the kitchen and prepared to go home for the day.

"Yes," I said. "I put a nice five-inch meringue on the top to seal in the lemon custard."

"Well, there you have it."

"Have what?"

"The simple answer," Agnes said. "It would be easy to take your pie, remove the meringue, whip new meringue with the poison, and re-cover the pie. It wouldn't take that long, especially if the pie was left to sit and the meringue shrunk."

"Crazy," I said. "Whoever might have done that would most likely have done it in Chef Wright's kitchen. Don't you think?"

"Yes," Agnes said.

"I should go see Chef Wright and ask him if anything was out of place after the murder. Well, I mean anything that wasn't disturbed by CID."

"What if he can't tell?" Agnes asked. "I understand the crime scene guys do a pretty good job of going through everything."

"I think it may be worth checking with him." I stood. "I'll be back before you finish cleaning up. If not, go ahead and do the prep for tomorrow's breakfast."

"Thank you for coming in on your day off. My grand-daughter has her school play this evening. I appreciate you covering for me. I might be gone when you get back."

"Don't worry, whatever you can't get to I'll do in the morning."

"Thanks, Chef."

I left and walked across the parking lot toward the Orangery. It was bustling with clients, just as Chef Wright had said. It made me frown to think that people were so morbid as to want to dine in a place not because of the history or beauty of it, but specifically because a man died there. I went around to the back entrance so as not to attract too much attention. The last thing I needed was for a crowd of people to start speculating that I was doing anything other than cooking for the duke and duchess.

"Hello?" I called inside the kitchen. There were people coming and going. Two staff members in aprons washed dishes. A third plated sandwiches and tea cakes. Waiters and waitresses came and went. Hey, hi," I said to the woman plating. "I'm looking for Chef Wright."

"Yes, well, aren't we all." She blew her bangs out of her eyes.

"He's not here?"

"He's been gone over an hour," she said. "It's closing time, and I need to know what to start for tomorrow's menu."

"Do you have any idea where he went?"

"No," she said. "I suppose you can ask one of his many

girlfriends. My guess is he's with one of them . . . you." She sent me a long, side-eyed look.

"I'm not one of his girlfriends. I'm the personal chef for——"

"I know who you are," she said. "Listen, Chef, let me give you a piece of advice. Don't go snooping around Chef Wright, okay? The man is not going to settle for one woman. He never has and he never will."

"I told you I'm not one of his girlfriends," I said. "I don't want to be. I have a question about the day of the murder."

"I can help you with that." She handed the plates to two waitresses. "I was here that day. In fact, I was with Chef Wright when he found Wentworth."

"I thought Chef Wright was alone when he found Wentworth."

"Yeah, he wants everyone to think that. You know, he wants everyone to perceive he's a good worker, always stays late, gives two hundred percent."

"He's not?" I drew my eyebrows together.

"No, he's not," she grumbled. "Talk to the real staff. We're always covering for him."

"So wait, you were with him when he found Wentworth's body facedown in the pie?"

"You can sort of say that," she said.

"Say what? That you were with Chef Wright or Wentworth was facedown in the pie?"

"Wentworth wasn't exactly facedown in the pie. Look, I told CID this. I came in early to make sure the kitchen was ready after your bridal shower."

"I left it spotless."

"Yes, you did a good job. I wasn't expecting anyone else to

be there. I turned on the lights in the kitchen and started looking over the stations to ensure they were clean. Then, surprise, Chef walks in. I asked him what brought him in so early. He said something about not being able to sleep that night. Seems his wife sent him to the couch where he should be."

"Ouch."

"Yes, well, Chef's conquests are legendary, and I don't like them. So sue me. Anyway, Chef asked me to make coffee. I was starting the brew when I heard Chef yell. I dropped what I was doing and found Chef in the breakroom. Wentworth was in a chair with his head back and his mouth open. There was some kind of foam dried up on his mouth."

"Was he dead?"

"As a doornail." She leaned in close. "I swear you could see the little crosses on his eyes like in the cartoons. Anyway, Chef is screaming like a little girl. So I went over and thought the least I should do is verify the guy is dead, right?"

"Sounds right," I said. I had some experience with finding a dead man. It's surreal. You have to check the body to make sure that what you think you're seeing is real.

"I went over and touched his shoulder, and he fell face first into the pie. I jumped back and might have let out a scream of my own. Meanwhile, Chef is running to the back door."

"Who called security?"

"I did," she said. "They called the cops. You know the rest."

"That means that he didn't suffocate in the pie."

"No," she said. "He was dead. But the pie was in front of him at the table and there was a slice cut out."

"Was there only one slice?"

"Yeah, I think so. Why?"

"Why was Wentworth sitting alone in the breakroom eating a slice of pie out of the pan?"

"Gosh, I hadn't thought to ask that question. I don't know. It's not like the guy was homeless. Maybe someone was with him." She frowned. "No, I didn't see a second plate. Weird."

"Really weird," I said. "Listen, was anything out of place in the kitchen?"

"What do you mean?"

"Well, did it look like I left anything undone? Like I made meringue and then didn't quite clean it all up?"

"No," she shook her head. "I assumed you baked all the pies in your kitchen."

"I did," I said with a sigh. "And I cleaned up any sign of the bridal shower before I left."

"You think someone snuck in and created a new pie in your pan?"

"That's reaching," I said. "But thanks. Can you tell me where Chef might be? I really want to talk to him."

"I have no clue. He just up and left."

"When was the last time you saw him?"

"He was heading for the walk-in freezer," she said. "Over here." She opened the freezer door and there on the floor was Chef Wright. The man was blue and stiff.

"Crud," she said.

"Oh, dear," I said at the same time. We both rushed to his side. I felt his wrist. She felt his neck. His skin was ice cold. His lips and fingers blue. "I can't feel a pulse." I looked at her.

"Maybe he's just frozen, you know? Maybe we should drag him out of the freezer."

I glanced out the freezer door and noted that the staff had

started to gather. "Someone call security," I shouted. Then I looked at the woman. "What's your name?"

"Sandy."

"Well, Sandy, I don't think we should move him. If he's as dead as I think he might be then we're contaminating a crime scene."

"And if he's not?"

"Then the warm air from the door being open should help to unthaw him a bit." I looked at the crowd. "Does anyone have a blanket or towel?"

Several people stepped in and handed me kitchen dish towels. I covered his expose skin. "Let's try not to touch him, okay?"

"Got it." Sandy stood. "Okay, people, there's nothing to see here. Go back to work until you're told otherwise." She glanced at her wrist. "At least it's after four. There won't be any more people coming in." She looked at the remaining waiters and waitresses staring at Chef Wright. "Come on then, let's get all the customers out of here safely, okay? All right." She glanced my way. "I'll try to clear the place as best I can."

"Do you think that's wise? What if he was killed? The murderer could still be here."

"Then let's make sure no one else dies today," Sandy said. She stuck her head out to the kitchen. "Don't touch anything. Don't drink or eat anything. Understood?"

"Yes, ma'am," came the reply.

"Good, let's see to our guests then. Henry, move everyone to the party room and keep them comfortable until security lets them go. But don't give them anything that isn't bottled or canned. Do you understand? I don't want any more trouble."

"Yes, ma'am."

I could hear sirens in the distance. Suddenly Ian stood outside the freezer door.

"Chef Cole."

"Hi, Chief," I said.

"I had hoped I wasn't going to see you for a while."

"Yes," I said. "Me, too."

Chapter 20

"I think he's dead."

Ian stepped into the freezer. "Did you cover him in towels?"

"Yes. In case he was alive and his heart beat just too weak for us to find."

"Right." Ian hunkered down and tried to find a pulse. "Nothing."

"Sandy suggested we move him out to warm him, but I thought we shouldn't move him."

"That's best." Ian stood and looked around. "Who all was in here?"

"Sandy opened the door and I stepped in with her. She left to try to get the staff and the guests in a safe place."

"Okay."

The ambulance techs showed up with a stretcher and medical cases. "What do we have here?" The male tech asked. His name tag said "Hermit."

"We opened the freezer and found him on the floor," I said. "We didn't want to move him, so we covered him in towels to keep him from freezing further."

The two techs squatted down to assess the situation and Ian took me by the elbow and drew me out of the freezer. "You're freezing."

After he mentioned it, I noticed that I was indeed cold. My fingers were blue and my nose had started running. A shiver went through me.

"Here, sit." He pulled out a chair. "Can I have a blanket here?"

The second ambulance tech stepped out of the freezer and handed Ian a blanket.

"Is he dead?" I asked.

"We believe so, yes," said the tech with "Finney" on his name tag. "CID is on the way."

"So you don't think he's hypothermic?"

"No," Finney said. "We've hooked up a heart rate monitor and it's flatlined. No sense in trying to revive him. Did you find him?"

"Sandy and I did." I pointed to the sous-chef who was keeping the staff safely away.

Ian wrapped the blanket around my shoulders. I was chilled to the bone. Not because of the time in the freezer but because another chef was dead.

"Please tell me it's not poison," I said.

"I can't comment," the tech said.

"Crap." I felt tears well up in my eyes.

"You okay?" Ian put his hand on my shoulder.

"Yes, sure. I was just talking to him this morning."

"Chef Wright?" Ian asked.

"Yes, I ran into him in the halls. He said he was on his way to the admin building to interview new staff." I looked at Ian. "Did he make it?"

"I'm sure he did," Ian said. "Then he must have come back here. What brings you here? Don't you have a dinner to make for the family?"

"It's my day off, and I wanted to talk to Chef Wright. I had an idea of how Wentworth might have been killed." I covered my mouth with trembling fingers. "I wanted to warn him."

"About what?" Ian asked softly.

"I don't know." I looked at him. "That someone might have used his things. That they might be trying to poison him. I left the pie for him."

"It's all right." Ian squeezed my shoulder. "CID is on the way. I'm sure they'll want to talk to you."

"Right." I glanced at the time. It was five-thirty PM. "Oh, no!" I jumped up and shivered, still fighting off the freezer cold.

"What?" Ian had turned to talk with another member of security. He turned back to me when I got up.

"Agnes has to leave. Her granddaughter has a school play. I have to get back to the kitchen."

"I'm sorry, Chef," he said and took my hand. "You have to stay and give a statement. DCI Garrote is on his way. He'll be here soon."

"But—"

"Text her. I'm sure she'll understand."

I pulled out my phone. "I need to go."

"Text her. I'll make sure you are the first one to be interviewed."

I noticed a member of the coroner's office had come in. I texted Agnes. What the heck do you say? Go ahead and go to your granddaughter's play. I'm running late because I found a dead body?

"Sorry, I got held up. Leave me a list of what needs to be done in the morning." There, I thought. That was a vague but might hold her over.

"He's been dead less than an hour," I heard the coroner say. "It's hard to tell for sure because the freezer slowed down the process."

I winced. Chef Wright was dead. I looked at Sandy who had gone pale and sat down hard. "Someone get her a blanket." I grabbed my blanket and put it around Sandy's shoulders. "It's okay."

"I can't breathe." She looked at me with a wide-eyed expression.

"Put your head between your knees," I suggested. "It will help if you feel faint."

"Excuse me, Chef Cole?" A young police officer addressed me. "Detective Chief Inspector Garrote would like to speak to you now."

"Yes, of course," I said. "Can you stay with Sandy?"

She nodded.

DCI Garrote looked tired and rumpled in his suit. I think I knew how he felt.

"I need to get back to my kitchen," I said.

"Yes, Chief Gordon told me," he said. "I do have a few questions."

"Of course," I said. We went over everything again from the time I left my kitchen until the time we found Chef Wright's body. As I finished my story, Evie Green came rushing in.

"No!" She screamed and threw herself on Chef Wright's body, which had been placed on a gurney and was being wheeled out. "No!"

She let out a heart wrenching sob. Two officers pulled her

---

away and let the coroner zip up the black body bag. Evie fell to her knees and covered her face with her hands. She was clearly distraught.

Rachel followed Evie through the door and stood with her arms around her waist looking horrified at the scene.

"How did these two women get in here?" DCI Garrote called to his staff. "Please keep people out of my crime scene."

"Can I go now?" I asked.

"Yes, but I expect you to be free for more questions at a later date."

"Yes, sir." I slipped away from the chaos. So both of Chef Wright's mistresses were saddened by his passing. I wondered briefly if his wife would be as well. The guy was a bit slimy, but that didn't mean he should have ended up dead.

I walked quickly through the crowd and back across the parking lot to my kitchen. A glance at the clock told me it was six-thirty. Agnes had done an excellent job of cleaning up and prepping for breakfast.

I fixed myself a cup of tea, hoping to ease the churning of my stomach. I could see the commotion going on at the Orangery. I wondered if Chef Wright was murdered or if his passing was just a bizarre accident. I was betting on murder.

I put on an apron, washed up, and started baking. It's what I did when I was upset, and Chef Wright's death truly upset me. He had died just next to a room full of people working. No one noticed.

I sighed and rubbed my forehead. I didn't want that to happen to me. I concentrated on making sweet Danish dough with all its layers of butter. After making the Danishes, I put then in the fridge to wait to be baked up in the morning. Next, I made a big batch of peanut butter chocolate chip cookies.

After that I made brownies. If only I kept baking, then none of this would have happened.

The door to my kitchen swung open, startling me out of my thoughts. "Oh, my goodness," Penny said as she rushed in. "I heard you found Chef Wright. He's dead, isn't he?"

"Yes." I started to make more cookies. I could freeze those to be served later. My grandmother always had a million different cookies in the freezer. She would take out a few of each kind and let them thaw, then serve them on giant platters with hot cocoa and coffee. I worked on autopilot, creaming butter and sugar.

"Oh, my goodness," she said again and sat down. "We were just talking to him."

"I know."

"Where did you find him? I heard he was with a woman. But I also heard he was found in a cupboard."

"We found him in the walk-in freezer," I said. "Where did you hear about the woman and the cupboard?"

"Oh gosh, rumors are rampant right now. That's why I thought I'd come down and get the scoop from the source."

My phone buzzed in my pocket. I pulled it out. It was a text from Nigel Bloom. How did he get my number? It read: "Heard you found Chef Wright dead. Can I have an exclusive?"

I sighed.

"Who is it?"

"It's that tabloid reporter looking for an exclusive. I have no idea how he got my number." I put my phone away. Best not to address it until the palace gave a statement to the press as a whole.

"Maybe he knows someone at the phone company? Or maybe he paid someone to find it. Either way, you can't tell him before you tell me. What was it like? Where did you find him? Why was it you who found him? Just how many cookies are you baking?"

I shook my head at her. "I bake when I'm upset. It comforts me."

"Where's Agnes?"

"She had a family thing tonight. I'm afraid this whole thing might have ruined her night."

"Why?" Penny held the door open for me. I pushed the cart through.

"They blocked everyone coming in and out of the palace area. I've been watching security slowly letting people leave. I hope she got out in time to attend her granddaughter's school program. I should have stayed in my kitchen and away from the Orangery," I said. "Now everyone is going to think I'm either a murderer or simply bad luck."

"Yikes." Penny leaned against the counter. "What happened? Did he get trapped inside? Did he freeze to death or was it poison again?"

"They don't know," I said. "I don't know. Listen, I have to finish making this before I ruin all this dough."

"I'll come back later," she said as she straightened. "I'll bring something stronger to drink than tea."

I raised a corner of my mouth in a half-smile. "I don't think they make anything strong enough for what I've seen today."

"Are you going to talk to the tabloid reporter?"

"What? No, I'm in enough trouble. I don't know how the duchess is going to take all of this."

"All the deaths?"

"All of the dead people I find," I said.

"Well, it's only been two, right?" she pointed out. "I mean you didn't find Wentworth and Butterbottom wasn't killed. That means you only found Mr. Deems and now Chef Wright. She can't hold that against you. Can she?"

"I don't know," I said. "Even if she doesn't, there are others who will worry about the future kings of England."

Chapter 21

The next morning, I was called into Ian's office. They put me in the conference room. I studied the small space with the two-way mirror and wondered when they were going to name it after me.

"Thanks for coming in," Ian said as he entered with a file folder.

"I didn't think I had a choice," I said, tilting my head. "Is the duchess going to fire me?"

"Why?" He seemed surprised by the question.

"There seems to be a lot of death around me. If I had small children, I would take them somewhere far away."

Ian sat down across from me.

"Especially future kings of England," I said and felt defeated.

"Did you sleep last night?" He asked.

"Is it the five-pound bags under my eyes that gave it away? Look, just rip the Band-Aid off. Tell me that I'm being let go and . . ."

"I'm not the one who lets people go," he said. "That would be Mrs. Worth's job. Has she called you in yet?"

"No," I said.

"Then don't make a problem where there isn't one."

"Comforting," I muttered.

"Chef Cole, Carrie Ann, I'm going to ask you some of the same questions DCI Garrote will ask. We both have different reasons for our investigations and a need to know."

I put my elbows on the small conference table and rested my chin in my hands. "Why are your investigations different?"

"I need to look into the security and safety of the palace grounds. DCI Garrote is looking for a killer."

"Do you think it's only one killer? Was Chef Wright poisoned? Do you think it's all related?"

"You are full of questions," he said, his gorgeous eyes emotionless. "I can't answer during an ongoing investigation."

"I see. Do you think DCI Garrote will answer my questions?"

"That's up to him."

"What do you need to know, Chief?"

Ian wasn't acting like my friend any more. I wondered if it was because of my walking in on him kissing Lana. Or was there something about the investigation that was bothering him?

"Chef Cole—"

"Please, you know you can call me Carrie Ann, even officially."

"Chef Cole, please tell me why you were at the Orangery after teatime last night."

"Like I told you yesterday, I went to look for Chef Wright. I had an idea of how the pie that killed Wentworth could have been poisoned—not by me."

"How?"

I explained about the meringue. "The poison could still be on any of his mixing bowls and things CID may not have thought to look at because everyone assumed I had made the pie in my kitchen. I thought I should warn him and his staff."

"Why not call me or DCI Garrote?"

I sent him a short smile. "You and the good inspector need more evidence and less supposition. You taught me that."

"I see. And why did you go into the freezer?"

"I asked Sandy where Chef Wright was. She thought he was with one of his mistresses, but he'd been gone awhile. I asked her where the last time she saw him was."

"The freezer." He took notes.

"Yes," I said. "We went over to the freezer, opened it up, and found him on the floor. The rest you know."

"Have you spoken to Sandy before?"

"No, not as far as I can remember. We just met yesterday. I don't think she was one of the assistants he had taken with him to the competition. I don't even know her last name."

"Sandy Earnest," he said. "She wasn't at the competition because she was charged with running the Orangery in Chef Wright's absence that day."

"Speaking of the competition, how is Chef Butterbottom?"

"He's fine. He starts back at work today."

"Oh, good," I said. "Do you think his poisoning was somehow connected?"

"That's for the Inspector to discover," he said. "It didn't happen on the palace grounds."

"But the Orangery is on palace grounds, and you are looking into that. It would seem that the answer is inside Chef Wright's kitchen. The only link I have to Chef Wright's death is that I found the body."

"Indeed." He sat back. "All the video corroborates your story. You were nowhere near the Orangery at the estimated time of death window."

I sat back with some relief. "Right."

"It's still curious that you insisted on seeing him. He might have gone missing for another few hours or even overnight had you not pushed Chef Earnest into looking for him."

"Did you know that Sandy was with Chef Wright when he found Wentworth? Did you know that Wentworth wasn't found face first in my pie, but that happened after Chef Wright shook him?"

"I'm aware of the details."

"Well, it would have been nice for you to share them with me."

"Some details are best not shared," he said. "Chef Cole, it's our job to investigate. It's best if you stay out of it. The fewer details you know the better for you."

"That's not true." I felt crushed. My voice trembled and my eyes welled. "I can't go on working thinking that you believe I killed Wentworth."

He covered my hand with his. "You're just one of many people we're looking into."

"Oh. Good." I wiped my eyes. "Do you think that Wentworth and Chef Wright were killed by the same person?"

"Right now, there is no proof that the same person is responsible for both murders," he said. "Chef Wright wasn't poisoned."

"Oh," I sniffed and sat back. "I guess that's good? Or is it bad? Are there two killers?" I felt a shiver run down my back.

"I can't share any details."

"You need to check the bowls and utensils in Chef Wright's

kitchen," I said. "If I'm correct and someone removed my meringue and recovered the pie with poison meringue, they could have left evidence in the kitchen."

"DCI Garrote and I will look into it," he said and for the first time his gaze looked sincere. "I need you to stay here. DCI Garrote is here to ask you some questions."

"Okay."

He stood, and when he reached the door, he turned to look at me. "I didn't think for one moment you did this, Carrie Ann." He left.

I felt some relief. It was nice to know that someone besides me was looking for Wentworth's killer.

My time with Detective Chief Inspector Garrote ran over lunch. I answered all his questions. Most of them were questions I'd already answered. I guess they needed me to answer again to see if my story remained the same. It did, because why lie?

On my way back to my kitchen I ran into Chef Earnest on her way up for questioning. "Are you doing okay?"

"I guess I'm fine," she said. She wore black slacks and a white top just like I did. Her thin blonde hair was pulled back, showing off her round face and baby blue eyes. "It's so strange, though. Everyone is looking to me to take up the slack now that Chef Wright is gone." She shrugged. "I've been doing it for years. It's just now everyone acknowledges it."

"I understand he wasn't poisoned," I said. "I'm glad that means no one else is in danger."

"That we know of," she frowned. "CID was just in the kitchen pulling bowls and utensils off the shelves. Do you know what they were looking for?"

"I think they're checking for traces of cyanide," I said. "I told them about the meringue theory."

"What meringue theory?"

"I think the killer could have scooped the meringue off my pie and replaced it with poison meringue."

"You think the killer used our utensils?"

"Don't worry, they'll only keep something if they find traces of poison on it."

"I'm not worried about getting it back. Not if they find cyanide on it."

"They are only looking for trace amounts." I put my hand on her arm to soothe her rising fear. "Trace is a good thing. It means they're closer to finding the killer."

"Who has cyanide anyway? Any idea how they got it? I mean, I don't think you can just buy it on the street. Can you?"

"I don't know," I said.

"Chef Earnest," Kathi called. "They are waiting for you in the conference room."

"Got to go," she said.

"Contact me if you need anything," I said.

"Same." She walked back to the conference room.

I was glad that someone had taken my theory of the meringue seriously. It was also nice to know that I wasn't considered the only suspect. Heading back to my kitchen I had to wonder: Who were the other suspects? Clearly they hadn't told me everything if they knew that Wentworth wasn't found with his face in my pie like the tabloids suggested.

Speaking of tabloids, I should get ahold of Nigel. He might know something that could help me. It didn't matter so much if the police cleared my name if the tabloids continued to make me look like a killer. I needed to do some PR.

I got back in time to find Agnes doing the lunch dishes. "Well, they certainly held you awhile," she said as she scrubbed a pot. "Are you all right?"

"I'm fine," I said. "I guess I'm less of a suspect than they let on."

"Well, that's certainly good news. What do they know about the dead man you discovered yesterday? I hear they have closed the Orangery for the day."

"They aren't telling me anything about Chef Wright. Except that he didn't die of poisoning" I put on an apron. I grabbed ingredients to make petit fours for the family's tea. I had at least six different cookies baked the night before and ready for tea, but I liked to offer something other than cookies.

"That changes things, then," Agnes said. "Not the same killer?"

"I don't know," I said. "I suppose it could be the same killer. They just found a different means to kill Chef Wright. They may not have been as successful as they wanted with poisoning. I mean, they may have wanted to kill Chef Wright all along and instead got Wentworth."

"So you think they were trying to kill Chef Wright when they poisoned Chef Butterbottom and his assistants?"

"Maybe," I said as I mixed the cakes. I was making chocolate, strawberry, and vanilla cakes to make Neapolitan petit fours. "I suppose it could also be different killers with different motives."

"You found the body." She picked up a towel to dry the dishes. "Did you see a gunshot wound?"

"No."

"Was his head bashed in?"

I shook my head and poured the chocolate cake into the long, thin jelly roll pan. "I didn't see any wounds to his head.

In fact, I didn't see any signs of blood loss. But he was really blue. We thought he might just have hypothermia. So I placed towels on him to help slowly warm him until the ambulance techs arrived."

"But he was dead," she said.

"Yes." I put the pan into the oven and set the timer. "They think he was dead at least an hour before we found him. I guess it was hard to tell because the freezer slowed down the post-mortem process."

"Yikes," Agnes said. "To think they had a dead man among all the food in the freezer. I don't think they can use any of that to feed the public now. I mean, yuck. Right?"

"Right," I said with a sigh. I hadn't thought about all the frozen foods and juices that were stored in the walk-in freezer. But I imagine they would have to clean the freezer out and start over like I did with my kitchen garden once Mr. Deems body was taken out.

I poured strawberry cake into a second jelly roll pan and placed it in the oven. "I wonder how you die with no marks on your body if you aren't poisoned?"

"Maybe there were marks you didn't see," Agnes pointed out. "Did you move him?"

"No. I didn't want to hurt him or contaminate the scene."

"Well, then he might have been shot or hit over the head or stabbed in the ribs or something."

"But wouldn't there have been blood?"

"You were in a freezer, right?"

"Yes."

"Maybe it was cold enough to stop the flow."

I winced. "I didn't think about that."

"Well, see, there you go. It most likely was something like

that. Did you ask the Detective Chief Inspector how Chef died?"

"Gosh, no, I doubt he would tell me. I mean there are things about Wentworth's death they didn't tell me. As far as Detective Chief Inspector Garrote and Security Chief Gordon are concerned, I don't have a need to know such details."

My phone rang. It was Nigel. I sighed and answered. "This is Chef Cole."

"Chef Cole," Nigel's voice was strong. "How are you?"

"I'm fine. I'm working."

"I understand," he said. "I heard you found Chef Wright's body in the Orangery. I'd love to have your take on the story."

"There's not much to say," I hedged.

"I suppose I can always run with the story of a lover's spat killing the man. I might mention your name and use the pictures of you and Chef Wright that Wentworth sold me."

"You would not!" I said. I hated to be blackmailed. And this was blackmail.

"I'm a tabloid journalist," Nigel said. "I go with whatever story I can get my hands on."

"Fine, I'm working until nine PM."

"Great, I'll meet you at Nags Head Pub at nine-thirty."

"All right," I said. "Do I need to bring a lawyer?"

"What do you need a solicitor for? We're friends, aren't we?"

"Not particularly," I said.

He laughed. "Oh, come on, it's not personal you know. It's just business."

"Right," I muttered. "See you then."

Chapter 22

I arrived at the Nag's Head Pub at nine-fifteen PM. It didn't take long to find Nigel. He sat near the windows on the right. "Hello, Nigel," I said as I approached.

"Hello, Chef." He stood to shake my hand. "I hope it's all right that I ordered you a pint."

I shook his hand then broke off and took a seat. "I'm tired, Nigel," I said. "What can I do to make this quick."

"Look, I'm sorry I had to threaten blackmail to get you to talk to me. I wouldn't really do it, you know."

"I don't know that," I said. "It's why I'm here. I don't want anyone—let alone *Fake News*—to suggest that I had anything to do with Chef Wright's murder."

"So he was murdered," Nigel said as he sat down. "I'm going to record this if that's all right with you."

"I'd prefer if you didn't."

"Okay. I'll take notes." He pulled a small notepad out of his coat pocket and started writing. "Chef Wright was murdered. Do you know how he was killed?"

"No," I said. "CID isn't disclosing that information."

"But you found the body. You saw him. What did you see?"

"I saw a man who looked frozen. His skin was blue and his eyes closed."

"I heard you found him in the freezer. Is that correct? Was he sitting, standing, stuffed in a corner?"

"Yes, I found him in the Orangery's walk-in freezer. He was lying on the floor. I didn't see any blood. There was no evidence that he'd been hurt other than he was blue and cold to the touch. We tried to warm him with towels while we waited for the ambulance techs to arrive."

"How long did it take for them to arrive?"

"I'm not sure," I said. "But when they came, they pronounced him dead. After that I was shuffled off. That's all I know." I put my elbows on the table. "It's hardly worth blackmailing me for the interview."

"Yeah, so that was probably an overstatement on my part. Look, I needed an insider to interview."

"And you know me."

"Exactly." He sat back. "You haven't touched your pint."

"I'm not thirsty," I said. "Is there anything else you want to know?"

"Sure, I'd love to know if you have any idea who might have done it. Who killed Chef Wright? Was it one of his girlfriends? Or maybe his wife?"

"I don't know," I said. "I won't speculate, either, Nigel. Is there anything else you need from me? I need to get to bed. I get up pretty early to feed the family."

"Do you think that Chef Wright's death is connected to Wentworth Uleman's death? Or the poisoning of Chef Butterbottom?"

"I can't speculate," I said, falling back on the words I'd heard so many times on procedural cop shows.

"Do you think it's a palace security issue? Or is there some-one on the inside committing these heinous crimes?"

"I have no idea." I leaned forward. "You really should inter-view Chief Gordon or Detective Chief Inspector Garrote. They are more up to date with the investigation than I am."

"What was it like?"

"What?"

"Finding another dead body?"

"It's heartbreaking, and I hope I never have to find another one my entire life."

"Oh, that's a great quote. Heartbreaking death of Chef Wright."

"Please don't write that," I said. "You make me sound like one of his women."

"Listen, I'm not trying to make you look bad . . ."

"No, you're trying to sell your tabloid."

"Yes," he said with a rueful smile. "But I also want to help you out. Clearly you are in the middle of something you had nothing to do with."

"Thank you . . ."

"I want to help. I have learned that all of the poisonings might be connected to Chef Wright."

"What do you mean?"

"I mean that you told me yourself that you left the pie for Chef Wright. Correct?"

"Yes, but that doesn't explain Chef Butterbottom and his staff getting sick."

"What if I told you that I have a source who confirms that Butterbottom was poisoned by using water from a bottle that was meant for Chef Wright?"

"Seriously?"

"Yes," Nigel said. "One of Butterbottom's assistants was told to get bottled water. You know how unreasonable Butterbottom can be."

"I do."

"Well, when the assistant said he couldn't find what Butterbottom wanted he was told to beg, borrow, and steal it if necessary."

"So he took it from Chef Wright's station?"

"He took it from Chef Wright's station. "Butterbottom's assistant used it to make tea and poisoned everyone at Butterbottom's station."

"That means that Wentworth's death might have been an accident."

"Yes," Nigel confirmed.

"The killer must have given up poisoning and simply done Chef Wright in themselves. But who? And how? I mean we found him in the walk-in freezer of a busy kitchen."

"Do you know if there is security footage of the inside of the kitchen?"

"No," I said with a frown. "No, I don't think they have cameras inside the kitchen. There really isn't any need."

"Who has access to the kitchen?"

"The staff, of course." I drummed my fingers on my chin. "I was able to get in fairly easily."

"Did they mention if anyone unusual was in the kitchen that day?"

"I didn't hear anything like that," I said. "But I can find out. Surely someone noticed people coming and going. I doubt a staff member would risk trying to poison Chef Wright. I mean, we all know how chaotic a kitchen can get."

"You don't think a member of his staff is responsible?"

"I highly doubt it." I drank a bit from the pint he had ordered for me. "Still . . ."

"What?"

I explained to Nigel about the meringue theory. "It means that the killer has to know something about cooking."

"At least how to make meringue that would fool a chef."

"Unless it didn't have to fool a chef," I said with a sigh. "People around here seem to believe that my cooking is second rate. The killer might have thought they could pass off bad presentation as mine."

"Which means they don't necessarily have to know how to do anything more than make rudimentary meringue."

"Yes," I said. "It could be anyone in Chef Wright's circle." I drew my eyebrows together. "Except maybe his wife. I have never met her. I don't recall anyone talking about her. I would think that a visit from her would be noticed by the staff."

"Especially since he had so many lovers on the palace grounds."

"I don't get that," I said. "I mean, the man was slimy. Not exactly lover material. I don't know what Rachel and Evie saw in him."

"Who are Rachel and Evie?"

I sat up straight. "I've said too much. Thank you for the drink and for not making up stories about me for your tabloid."

"Thank you for the interesting conversation," Nigel said and sent me a small two finger salute. "Until next time, *chérie*."

"No offense, but I hope there's not a next time."

He grinned. "No offense taken." He drank down the rest of my beer, then grabbed his own. "Cheers."

I left the pub in a thoughtful mood. What if someone had been out to kill Chef Wright all along? They finally succeeded. But who was it? How did they do it?

It probably wasn't the safest idea to walk from the pub back to the palace alone. But there was a cool, soft rain, and I was lost in my thoughts. There wasn't really a tube connection for the half a mile or so. I could have taken a car, I suppose, but I was glad for the walk.

I was about two blocks from the pub when I noticed the footsteps behind me. The streets were clear because it was late and raining. Trust me, no one walked in the rain unless they were a crazy American.

Shrugging deeper into my trench, I shoved my hands in my pockets and hurried along. The footsteps behind me seemed to match mine. I stopped and looked around. I didn't see anyone. But I suppose it would be easy to duck into a doorway. Maybe if I cut through the park I would be able to tell if someone really followed me or if I was being paranoid after everything that had been going on lately.

I hurried across the street and into the park. The large, still, mangled trees—twisted by the bombings from World War II—threw eerie shadows my way. The sound of footsteps echoed behind me, and I ducked into a brick building, which housed locked toilets. The footsteps stopped.

No one walked passed me. I bit my bottom lip and pulled out my phone.

"Hey, girl," Penny's familiar voice said. "Where are you? I came to your kitchen for tea and a biscuit and you weren't there."

"I had an appointment to see Nigel," I said.

"The tabloid reporter?"

"Yes," I said. "I'm walking home now from the Nag's Head Pub, and I thought I heard someone following me."

"Oh, that's not good," Penny said. "I just looked outside. It's raining. Are you crazy? Why didn't you take a car?"

"I like the rain," I said.

"Except that a murderer is out and about killing random palace chefs," Penny said. "Stay where you are. I'll come get you."

"No, that's silly," I said. "I'm not far."

"Where is not far?"

"I ducked into the rest area in the park."

"Are you seriously trying to get murdered?" Penny sounded genuinely scolding.

"I'm fine," I said.

"That's why you called me."

"Yes, see, I called you. I'm not stupid."

"What am I supposed to do if something happens while you're on the phone with me? I might as well be a million miles away."

"Now you're being dramatic," I said. "I'm stepping back out to head home."

"Chef Cole?"

I gasped at the sound of my name and turned nearly dropping my phone. "How do you know my name?"

"I didn't mean to startle you," the man said. "I'm Deputy Inspector Packman. I know you from your pictures in the tabloids."

"I'm on the phone with my friend," I said. "Penny, this man says he's Deputy Inspector Packman. He says he knows my name because of the tabloids."

"Oh my gosh!" Penny said. "I told you to wait for me. Take his picture."

I lifted my phone and took a flashing photo of the man. It was blurry and uncertain. "Stay away from me."

"Chef Cole," he raised his hands, "I'm going to reach inside my coat and get my ID."

"Sure you are." I took two steps back. "I've got people on the way. So if I were you, I'd get lost."

"Here is my ID." He held out a wallet with a badge on it.

"Are you the one who was following me?"

"Yes," he said. "I saw you talking to that tabloid reporter."

"So?"

"I am investigating the man for fraud and possible homicide."

"Wait, what? You're following Nigel?"

"Yes," he said. "I'd like to talk to you about your relationship with the man."

"Then call the palace in the morning and make an appointment," I said. "Don't scare the pants off me and my friends by following me late at night."

"Right," he said. He wore a black overcoat and his hair was dark. I'd gauge him to be in his early thirties.

"I'm on my way to you," Penny's voice said over the phone. "I'm bringing reinforcements."

"People are coming for me," I informed the DI. "I'd suggest you leave."

"I'd rather stay and see you get home safely," he said.

"Fine," I said. "But stay back. Do you understand?"

"Yes."

I walked backwards toward the palace keeping my attention on the man.

"You're going to get hurt walking that way," he said mildly.

"I'm not turning my back on you."

"Trust me, if I were going to harm you, I would have done it when there were dark alleys to pull you down. What are you doing walking in this area by yourself anyway?"

"I walked Chicago all the time," I said. "London is hardly more crime ridden than that."

"I see."

"I am a grown woman and can take care of myself."

"Right."

I rolled my eyes at the lack of conviction in his tone. "Why do you want to talk to me anyway? I barely know Nigel. In fact, I wouldn't have met with him at all if he didn't threaten to blackmail me."

"He threatened you? How so?"

"He said he might have to publish a story that I was a killer, if I didn't tell him what I knew about finding Chef Wright."

"And you took him seriously?"

"Yes, he writes for a tabloid. Who knows what they will say."

"But you trust him enough to go off on your own and meet with him, a supposed blackmailer."

"Look, believe what you want. Just stay away from me."

"Carrie Ann?"

I glanced over my shoulder to see Penny and Jasper rushing my way. "My friends are here. Please go away."

"Who the heck are you?" Jasper asked and put his arm around my shoulder. Jasper wore a sporty rain coat, jeans, and boots. "What are you doing scaring Carrie Ann?"

"I'm Deputy Inspector Packman," he pulled out his ID. Jasper took it and held up his cell phone flashlight to read the badge. "I'm investigating Nigel Bloom and saw Chef Cole speaking to him this evening."

"That gives you the right to follow her home?" Jasper asked.

"I didn't mean to scare her," he said. "I'll be in touch, Chef." He turned and left Jasper, Penny, and me on the sidewalk in Hyde Park.

"Well, that was interesting," I said.

"What are you thinking, walking home by yourself?" Jasper asked.

I made a face at him and Penny. "I was thinking it was rainy. I needed time to think, and I doubted that anyone was out on the streets."

"Lesson learned." Penny put her arm through mine and walked me toward the palace.

"I called you right away," I had to point out.

"Who's Nigel Bloom?" Jasper asked. "Do I have competition?"

"No," I said and laughed at the idea. "Nigel is a reporter for the tabloid *Fake News*. You were there when I met him, remember?"

"Oh, right, that Nigel. What did he want?"

"He heard I found Chef Wright's dead body and demanded an interview."

"How can he demand an interview?" Jasper asked.

"He threatened to make up an unfavorable story if I didn't come and give him my version of events."

"You shouldn't give in to threats," Penny said. "You work at Kensington Palace now. People need to know you are incorruptible."

"I am incorruptible," I said. "I was tired of people thinking I've come to London to kill people. It really didn't take much of a threat to get me to come tell my story."

"You really need to be careful of who you talk to," Jasper said.

"Well, it's definitely not going to be Nigel. Now that I know he is under investigation, I'm not going to talk to him anymore."

"Even if the headlines turn against you?" Penny asked.

"Even then." I hoped Nigel would keep me out of his headlines altogether.

Chapter 23

I laid in bed that night staring at the ceiling. Jasper and Penny were right. I should not have allowed Nigel's threat to influence me. Ugh. There was only one way to get to the bottom of this, and that was to find the killer once and for all.

But how?

Something was bothering me. It was as if I should know who did it but the thought was just out of reach. Why should I know? That was the biggest question.

The alarm went off at five AM, and my eyes felt filled with gravel from lack of sleep. I showered, put on my usual work clothes, and went down to the kitchen to work up the day's menus.

Feeling lost, I turned on the light and made a pot of hot water for my French roast coffee.

It was embarrassing to have to call Penny and have her and Jasper come get me from the park. I made a vow to myself to take a taxi or a car from now on. That is, if there was a now on. There was an email in my palace inbox from Mrs. Worth. She wanted to see me in her office after breakfast. Great.

Agnes showed up in time to pull out today's breakfast rolls, scoop the oatmeal porridge into a serving bowl, and plate the sliced seasonal fruits. The duke was out this morning, and the duchess had asked for a simple breakfast for her and the children.

"Whatever does Mrs. Worth want to see you for?" Agnes asked as she headed toward the door with the pushcart serving tray.

"I guess I'll find that out," I said. "Lunch menu is on the board. Tomato soup, grilled cheese sandwiches, and chocolate pudding for desert."

"Sounds good," Agnes said with a smile. "Good luck with Mrs. Worth"

"Thanks." I hung up my apron and put on a clean chef's coat before heading out of the kitchen, down the hall, and up the stairs. I could take the elevator but the walk helped soothe my nerves.

"Come in," Mrs. Worth's new secretary, Mrs. Hunter, said when I knocked on the door. "Ah, yes, Chef Cole. I'll let Mrs. know you are here."

I waited in the tiny office and glanced out the window. She had a view of the parking lot as well. Then the top of the Orangery. I imagined the views of the lush grounds were left for the royals who lived here.

"She will see you now." Mrs. Hunter pointed the way to the office door. Pointing wasn't necessary. The office was rather small, but I suppose it was polite. Mrs. Hunter seemed very polite.

"Thanks," I said and entered Mrs. Worth's office. Mrs. Worth sat behind a massive old desk. Behind her was a large window letting in bright light. There was an old fern on a stand soaking up the light. "You asked to see me?"

Mrs. Worth was no nonsense from head to toe. She led the household and, if anything or anyone was out of place, it was up to her to see that it got back into its place as quickly as possible.

"Yes, Chef Cole." She waved me in. "Please have a seat."

I sat in the small chair in front of her massive desk. I imagined the desk was over one hundred years old and was adapted to having a computer screen placed on it. The palace staff might live in history, but we were fully versed in the modern century.

I sat and waited for her to address me. She studied me for a moment and then let out a long sigh.

"Have I disappointed the duchess somehow?" I asked, my own insecurities shining through. I bit the inside of my cheek to keep from saying anything more.

"I understand that you have had quite a lot of trouble," Mrs. Worth said. "First with Wentworth Uleman's death and the subsequent searching of your kitchen. Now with Chef Wright's death, you must be . . . overwhelmed."

"I didn't know either very well," I said. "But it is sad and kind of scary."

"Have you been investigating these deaths?"

Okay, that was to the point. I sat back. "In my own way," I admitted. "I don't like it when people point fingers at me for crimes I didn't commit. I have no motive and certainly no means to poison or kill anyone. I'd much rather be coming up with new recipes for the duke and duchess."

"Good," she said with a nod of her head. "Good. I like to hear that you would prefer to do your job and let security do theirs."

"Mrs. Worth, is the duchess not happy with my performance?"

"The duke and duchess are satisfied with your work," she admitted.

"And they know that I had nothing to do with any of the crimes going on here."

"No one has said that you do," she said, tilting her head. "Why are you worried about that?"

"I've heard rumors that the duke and duchess might not want a chef who has stumbled over two deaths in a matter of months. I'm worried that my job is on the line."

"Is that why you are talking to tabloid reporters?"

"Oh, boy," I said. It was my turn to sigh. "He said if I didn't give him my story he would make one up about having a murderous cook in the duke and duchess's kitchen."

"And you thought you should handle this problem on your own?"

I drew my eyebrows together. "Should I have come to you about it?"

"Yes," she said. "Your employee handbook has an entire section on how to handle such nonsense. I recommend you go back to your rooms and reread the handbook. As an employee at Kensington Palace there will be many people attempting to blackmail you—whether true or false—into giving them what they want. Do not let this happen. We have an entire protocol on how to handle such things. Meeting said reporters after hours in seedy pubs is not acceptable."

I swallowed hard. "I didn't know."

"That is most likely my fault. I skipped some common training sessions with you due to the urgency to place a proper chef in your position. Let me rectify that. Starting this evening, you will be assigned an orientation class that meets twice a week for four weeks. The class covers all the salient points of the employee handbook and takes you through role playing on how to handle such things as threats from tabloids."

"Yes, ma'am."

"You will start with the other new employees tonight from six PM until nine PM."

"But the family's dinner is at that time," I protested.

"The duchess is aware of your training and will handle dinners for her family on appropriate dates."

"What will she do if she has a meeting or event? I've heard they sometimes will order takeout—but I—"

"We'll let the duchess figure out what is best for her family," Mrs. Worth said. "Having a properly trained staff is paramount to safety and security."

"Right," I said.

"Now, Mrs. Hunter has your schedule for the next month mapped out along with the proper materials. Let her know if you have any further questions."

"Yes, ma'am," I said as I stood up. "Thank you."

"There is also a formal process that happens if and when an employee is let go from the family. Learn this process," she said. "It should ease your mind a bit."

"Thank you." I left her office. I wasn't sure if it would ease my mind or make me worry more. I decided I would let it ease my mind.

* * *

"Agnes."

"Yes, Chef," the older woman said as she plated the sandwiches for lunch.

"How long have you worked in the palace?"

"I'd say my entire adult life, Chef," she said. "I started off as a part-time waitress in the Orangery. I've made my way throughout the various kitchen staffs here at the palace."

"I see."

"Why do you ask?"

"I have to go to a formal employee handbook training that will take up two nights a week for the next four weeks. Did you go through the training?"

"Yes, Chef, and all of the employees go through yearly update trainings. The royal family likes to have the best-trained staff available and the only way to do that is to train them."

"I see," I said.

"When does your training start?"

"Tonight." I winced. "Dinner has been cancelled. The duchess will be cooking, or the staff will bring in takeout."

"Takeout? I certainly hope they have a taster on hand to ensure the family's safety."

"I'm sure they will," I said. "It does break my heart that the duke and duchess would get takeout Thai food. I have this amazing peanut sauce recipe. I've been waiting for the children to outgrow the allergy stage to serve it."

"I'm sure they aren't giving it to the kids," Agnes said. "I guess this is good news for me." She smiled. "Shorter work days this month."

"Right."

"I'll take lunch up now," she said. "We're still making tea, right?"

"Yes," I said.

"Don't worry, Chef," she said and patted my shoulder. "Training is better than being let go. Right?"

"Right."

When Agnes left, I picked up my phone and texted Jasper. "Hi, how are you?" I hoped I could break it to him easy that I couldn't make our date tonight.

"Good," he texted back. "What's up?"

"I have to cancel tonight," I typed and then deleted. It was better to start with the reason. "Just got back from a meeting with Mrs. Worth."

"Is everything okay?"

"She is sending me to employee handbook training starting tonight." I hit send and waited, holding my breath.

"Ah, so no drinks."

"Right," I texted. "Can I have a rain check?"

"No worries," he texted back. "We'll figure it out."

"Thanks."

"See you soon."

I certainly hoped so.

* * *

The conference room was full. It seemed I wasn't the only one who needed a full month of training. I saw Evie and squeezed through the crowd to take the seat next to her. "Hi, Evie."

"Chef," she said in acknowledgement. Evie was all dolled up with picture-perfect makeup that included black cat-eye eyeliner and bright red lipstick. She wore a pale green shift dress. Her hair was done in soft waves around her face. Even her nails were spotless. I'm certain she had the more expensive acrylics. Next to her I looked like a working stiff with no-nonsense makeup and hair. My nails were trimmed short and plain. That way I could keep them clean.

"Call me Carrie Ann," I said. "Why are you here?"

She frowned. "Someone thinks I need a refresher."

"Why?"

She shrugged. "Who knows. Here it's all drama, drama, drama."

"Is it because you were fighting with Rachel in the parking lot? What was that all about anyway?"

"I don't want to talk about Rachel," she said. "I hate her." Her eyes flashed. "Don was mine. That girl tried to take him, but he showed her. He didn't fall for her seduction. He told me I was all he ever wanted. He was going to leave his wife and we were going to be together forever. Rachel just had to get over that."

"Ladies and Gentlemen," the instructor shouted to get our attention. "Let us settle down and begin. Tonight's subject is how to properly handle the press, from bloggers to the tabloids to national news media. Open your handbooks to page thirty-four. Let's begin."

I didn't have any more time to talk to Evie, as the training took two hours. All I could think was that Penny was right. Evie and Rachel were fighting over Chef Wright. I wondered what Chef's wife thought about it all. Unfortunately, the trainer made it perfectly clear that we were all supposed to stay away from news happenings that did not directly involve us.

No matter how much I felt involved in Chef Wright's death, I could not link myself to it directly.

At the end of class, I stood and turned to Evie. "Do you want to go get a glass of wine? I need to get out after sitting so much."

"No drinks for me," Evie said and put her hand on her stomach. "I'm pregnant."

"Oh my gosh, congratulations," I said. "Is it?"

"Yes, it's Don's child." Tears welled up in her eyes. "Now my baby is fatherless." She glanced at me. "He was going to leave his wife and take care of us. We had plans to move to the country and open a bed-and-breakfast. It was all going to be so beautiful."

"I'm so sorry for your loss," I said, patting her arm.

She sent me a watery nod. "Thank you. No one even thinks of me when they go on about how Don died. How he left three children, when in fact he left four children." She pulled me aside. "I'm going to sue for child support."

"Sue who?"

"Don's wife, of course. She is getting a large insurance settlement. I've talked to my lawyer. I know my rights. By rights my child should get a quarter of that money."

"Have you talked to Mrs. Wright?"

"I don't need to talk to the old bag," she said. "I have my solicitor doing it." She leaned back and patted her stomach. "We're going to be rich. Aren't we, baby?"

"I'm so sorry for your loss," was the only thing I could think to say at that moment.

Her eyes welled up with tears again. "It's terrible, isn't it? I told the cops that there's a good chance Don's wife is responsible for his death."

"She is? How so?" I tilted my head, considering.

"She had the most to gain. He had just told her about us. He was going to leave her. She would have gotten nothing." She looked at me with round eyes. "I might have done the same thing in her circumstances. I mean, you believe a man when he tells you that you are his one true love. That's why Rachel had to know that I wasn't going to stand for her sniffing around my man."

"Does Rachel know you're pregnant?"

Evie grinned. "I told her that day in the parking lot. That's when she attacked me. If you ask me, she should have gotten fired. But all they did was give her a stern warning and a write-up on her record."

"Oh," I said. "A write-up is bad."

She shrugged. "It takes three substantiated incidences before they can start procedures to fire you. I'm not concerned. Rachel, on the other hand, should be. This was her second write up."

"It was?"

"Oh yes, and if I have it my way she'll get another and be gone soon."

"Wow, you really don't like her."

"Not only did she try to take my man, but she's also on my list of possible killers."

"Why?"

"Because I saw her coming out of the Orangery the afternoon Don was killed," Evie said.

"Did you tell CID about this?"

"Not yet," Evie said. "First, I want her to lose her job, then she can lose her freedom."

"Right," I said, suddenly beyond my ability to put up with such venom. "Look, I've got to go."

"Sure, see you at the next class," Evie said.

I blew out a breath and took the long way around the building. The sun was just setting, and I needed to feel the cool, damp air on my face. I could not believe Evie. She was really messed up. Someone needed to tell CID about Evie seeing Rachel that day. I frowned. Rachel deserved to know that Evie had it out for her.

But I didn't know where Rachel was or even what her first write up was for. Maybe Evie was right. Maybe Rachel was the killer. In that case, I needed to stay as far away as possible.

Chapter 24

I ran into Penny and Rachel in the hallway outside Penny's room. "Oh, hello," I said. "Are you two going out?" Both women were dressed for clubbing. I blinked at Penny. "What happened to the vicar?"

"He said I was a little too fast for him. I wasn't fast," Penny said and I could tell she'd been drinking already. "I'll show him fast. We're going to the club. Want to come?"

"I thought I might want to get a glass of wine, but now I've got a headache," I said, which was actually true. I'd just spent two hours in a room full of people. I needed some space to clear my head.

"You know what they say will cure that?" Penny grinned at me.

"What?"

"A good shag," Rachel said with a laugh. She was as well-lit as Penny.

"Right," I said. "Not tonight, I'm afraid. I've got a date with my pillow."

"Too bad for you then," Rachel said. "Come on Penny, I'm in need of forgetting."

I grabbed Penny's arm as Rachel headed down the hall.

"What are you doing?" she asked.

"Be careful with Rachel," I said. "She has a reputation for getting in trouble with the staff."

"Rachel? She's harmless."

"Her fight with Evie was her second write up," I said. "One more and she's gone."

"Hey, what's the hold up?" Rachel called from the top of the stairs.

"Nothing," Penny called. "I'll be right there." She turned to me. "Maybe you should come with me to keep me out of trouble."

"No, thanks," I said, letting her go. "Go have fun. Just be careful, okay?"

"Sure," Penny said. "Careful to have a good time." She blew me a kiss and hurried down the hall. She put her arm through Rachel's and they laughed as they danced out of sight.

I sighed and went to my room. I really liked Penny and didn't want to see her getting mixed up with the wrong set. I don't know what I'd do if she got fired. Penny really was my best friend in London. The vicar's rejection must have really hurt her. If I were a better friend I'd go out with her and ensure she was safe.

Instead I put on and the kettle to make a cup of tea. I put on comfy pajama's and brought my tea to curl up on the sofa in my living room. It was just me and my employee handbook.

An hour later there was a knock at my door. I got up and checked the peephole before I opened it. "Hi," I said as I held the door open a crack.

"Sorry to bother you so late," Ian said. He looked every kind of dashing standing in the hall. I wanted to open the door and invite him in, but I was in my pajamas. And he had a girlfriend.

"What's up?" I asked and leaned against the doorframe.

"I thought you might want to know the latest on Chef Wright."

"Oh, yes, sure." I opened the door. "Sorry, I was getting ready for bed." I tugged on the edges of my bathrobe.

"Looks like you were studying your employee handbook." He nudged his chin in the direction of the book and my empty teacup on the coffee table. "Learn anything?"

"Yeah," I said, scratching my head. "I learned not to talk to the press."

He leaned against my doorframe and smiled at me. "That is always a good idea. They have a whole department for handling matters of the press. You should let those people do their job."

"You should have told me that when I talked to Nigel Bloom the first time."

"Who's Nigel Bloom?"

"He's a reporter for *Fake News*.

"You talked to him?"

"Yes, but it didn't go that well."

"And if I had told you earlier not to talk to him, would you have listened?"

"Well, you have me there," I said. "What is the update on Chef Wright?"

"He was stabbed."

"But I didn't see any blood," I said and frowned.

"It was too cold for the blood to pool outside the body," Ian said.

"Why are you telling me this now?" I asked. "Won't it get you in trouble with DCI Garrote?"

"No," Ian said. "I told you I would let you know what was happening when I learned details."

"What did the murderer stab him with? How many times?" Ian smiled at me wryly.

"Oh, right, no further details and such," I said.

"Exactly," Ian said.

"So, um, how have you been? I haven't seen you in a few days."

"I've been busy with security issues," he said. "I heard a rumor that you had an encounter with a tabloid journalist that wasn't so pleasant."

"Yes, he did threaten to make up a story about me and Chef Wright," I admitted. "But once I got there, the interview itself wasn't so bad. He thinks that all the murders and chef Butterbottom's poisoning are connected. He says someone in the kitchen wanted Chef Wright dead and accidently killed Wentworth."

"That's an interesting theory," Ian said.

"So no comment?"

"I told you what I can," he said. "I need you to be patient with me and let the Inspector and I do our jobs."

"Evie told me she saw Rachel leaving the Orangery about the time that Chef Wright was murdered."

"Rachel?"

"Yes, they say that poison is used mostly by female killers. Do you think that Rachel was trying to kill Chef Wright all along?"

"You think she's a jilted lover," he stated.

"Evie is pregnant with Chef Wright's child," I said. "She claims he was going to leave his wife and start a new life with her. Rachel was upset over Evie and Chef Wright's affair."

"Or Evie was upset over Rachel and Chef Wright's affair," Ian said thoughtfully.

"Do you think Evie would kill the father of her child?"

"It's amazing what people will do when affairs of the heart are involved."

I looked at him, trying to figure out if that statement had two meanings. A blush rushed up my cheeks. I could feel the heat of it and turned away from him. "Maybe you should check out Rachel's alibi."

"I will," he said and it was nice to be acknowledged.

"Oh," I turned to him. "Evie also said that Mrs. Wright got a very large insurance settlement. That means Chef's wife had a motive for his murder as well. He might have told her he was leaving her for Evie, and she stabbed him."

"We looked into Mrs. Wright," Ian said. "There is no record of her being on palace grounds that day. We keep a pretty tight eye on guests."

"There's no way that she could have gotten on the grounds without security knowing?"

"I certainly hope not," he said. "That would mean I have a giant hole in my security."

"But Wentworth was able to sneak around and take unauthorized pictures. Who's to say someone didn't sneak Mrs. Wright into the Orangery."

"Wentworth had authorization to be on the premises. I admit he misused that trust, but we were able to track his movements the day he died."

"Then you could track the movements of anyone who might have been with him?"

"You know as well as I do that people come and go out of

215

doors without swiping their cards. Especially if they are with another person with a badge."

"So Mrs. Wright could have done the same," I pointed out.

Ian frowned. "No, we have security at the gates. Mrs. Wright could not have gotten on the grounds without going through a checkpoint."

"Oh." I sighed. "Well, that's a suspect we can scratch off the list. But is it true that Chef Butterbottom and his crew were accidently poisoned with water that was meant for Chef Wright?"

"I can't say," he said.

"Right. Then that's most probably true," I tapped my fingers on my chin. "The thing that keeps bothering me is that whoever killed Wentworth tried to pin the deed on me. They used my pie. I don't know Mrs. Wright at all, but I do know Rachel and Evie. The last time I saw Rachel was the day Chef Wright was murdered. She passed me in the hall while I was talking to Chef Wright. She did give me a pretty nasty stink eye at the time."

"Maybe she believed the rumors that you were Chef Wright's next conquest."

I laughed and not in a good way. "Those were purely rumors. I really found the guy too urbane for my taste."

"Right."

Tilting my head, I looked at him. "Why do I feel as if my love life matters to you?"

He looked me in the eye. "Maybe because—"

"Chief Gordon!" Penny called in a loud, soused voice. "What brings you to our little hallway?" She walked up to him and flung her arm around him. "Talking to my friend again, I see. You know she didn't hurt anyone. She wouldn't hurt a fly. Isn't that right, Carrie Ann?"

"That's right."

"See? Now why don't you leave her alone? Hmm?"

"I see you've been out clubbing." Ian checked his watch. "What brings you in before the crack of dawn?"

She shrugged and leaned against the wall to help hold herself up. "Rachel ditched me. I thought I'd come back and see if Carrie Ann won't go out with me. Come on, Carrie Ann. Help a friend drown her misery."

"Misery?" Ian raised an eyebrow in my direction.

"Man trouble," I said and grabbed my key. "How about we get you off to bed?"

"No, I don't want to go to bed. I want to go out and drink until I'm blind. Blind, I tell you."

"Come on then." I put my arm under hers and let her rest against me.

"Are you going out like that?" She looked at my cotton pajamas and my old striped bathrobe. "Color suits you at least."

They were pink-and-white striped.

"Give me your key," Ian said.

"Why?" Penny said, grinning lasciviously at him. "Do you want to put me to bed?" She patted his chest. "Everyone knows you have a girl in Brighton. I don't spend time with other girl's guys. Sorry handsome." She patted his cheek.

"Right," he said. "Key." He held out his hand and she opened her pocketbook and fumbled inside it.

"Can't find it," she said, continuing to grin at him. "I'm just going to have to stay in your quarters."

"Oh no you don't." I handed her to Ian. Rummaging around in her purse, I found her key card. "Got it!" I opened her door and stepped aside so that Ian could help Penny into her rooms.

"Don't mind the mess," she said as Ian urged her to her random-stuff-covered couch. "I like a lived-in look. Just stay out of the bedroom." She sent him an exaggerated wink. "Or don't. Your choice, handsome." She ran her hand along his jaw again.

I grabbed her hand and moved it away. "I've got this. Thanks for the update."

"Right, okay." He left and closed Penny's door behind him.

"Okay, then." I filled Penny's teapot. "Let's get some tea into you."

"You mean coffee." Penny rested her head on the couch. "Don't they give drunks coffee? I don't have any coffee."

"Anything with caffeine will do," I said.

"Sorry to get between you and the big guy." She curled up on the couch and closed her eyes. "It's for the best. Men. You can't trust them."

I went over and removed her shoes and covered her with a pink knitted blanket that was on the back of the couch. "I'm sorry about the vicar."

She didn't answer. Instead I heard her snoring softly. I suppose I should have insisted she drink some water or tea. She was surely going to be dehydrated in the morning and feel every bit of her party state. But I didn't have the heart to wake her.

Instead I turned off the kettle and placed a small pink trash can beside her in case she got sick. I could hear her in my mind tell me it wasn't a trash can. It was a dust bin. I turned on her bathroom light and left the doors open so that she could find her way if she needed to. Then I left. Sometimes the only way to get through pain was to sleep it off.

Back in my own much sparser room, I picked up my cup and put it in the kitchen. What was Ian going to say? Did it make any difference? He had a beautiful girlfriend. Wasn't I pretty much seeing Jasper? I hated these tricky situations. I enjoyed both men's friendship. The last thing I wanted was to lose one because of the other.

Some things were out of my control.

*　*　*

The next morning, Penny wandered into my kitchen. "Do you have anything for a hangover?" Her eyes were puffy, and she squinted against the light. Her hair, although pulled back, stood up on one side and there was a pattern pressed into her cheek from the couch. At least she was dressed in a tidy blouse, simple skirt, and flats.

"Water and aspirin to start." I set down a glass and two tablets. She sat at the table in the kitchen.

"Look what the cat dragged in," Agnes said with a laugh.

"Oh, my head, please don't laugh. It's not funny," Penny put her head in her hands.

"Drink the water," I said. "I'll make you some tea and dry toast."

"Sounds nasty," Penny grumbled but did what I told her to do.

"Out late last night, were we?" Agnes asked as she cleared the breakfast tray. She put away leftovers and rinsed and stacked the dishes ready to put them in the dishwasher.

"I guess so," Penny said, squinting at me. "I vaguely remember you helping me into my room."

"Ian was there," I said.

"Ugh," she moaned. "I didn't need for him to see me at my lowest."

I hid my grin. I decided not to tell her that she practically threw herself at him last night. I placed a steaming cup of tea in front of her and pushed milk and sugar toward her. "You told me that Rachel dumped you."

Penny opened on eye and studied me. "Right."

"Why?"

"I got a text from Evie," Penny said. "Rachel didn't want anything to do with me after that."

"Did Rachel make sure you got home safely?"

"No," Penny said. "She just left me."

"What did you do? Did you have a driver?"

"Rachel was driving. I think the bartender called me a cab." She opened her eyes wide. "I hope I paid the guy."

"You don't remember?" I felt nervous in my heart. How sad that she was alone and vulnerable. This was worse than my walking home alone. "You should have called me from the club. I would have come and gotten you."

"With what? You don't have a car and you certainly haven't driven in London."

"It doesn't mean I can't get a taxi and come get you and see you safely home. We have to stick together."

"She's right, you know," Agnes said.

"Right. Fine." Penny sipped her tea. "Do you have any toast?"

I smiled and popped some into the toaster oven. "It's nearly ready. Security must have let you into the palace. Did anyone walk you to our hall?"

"It's kind of sad, but I don't really remember. Ow, my pounding head!"

I placed a plate of dry toast in front of her. "I bet someone helped you in. Chief Gordon tells me that security has its eyes on things these days."

"Like that science fiction book about big brother watching you," Agnes said. "Sad to say that life has come to being under surveillance at all times and yet still they can't figure out who killed Wentworth Uleman and Chef Wright."

"I heard Wentworth was poisoned with cyanide." She shuddered. "I searched it. There are articles on suicide and cyanide."

I made a face. "Do you think Wentworth committed suicide?"

"Why else bake it into the meringue of your pie?" Agnes asked. "Too complicated. If he was committing suicide, he'd just ingest the stuff."

"There are several how-tos on the internet for suicide by cyanide," Penny said morbidly and bit into her toast.

"I'm sorry I asked," I said. "But it does seem as if using that as a poison was rather difficult to do."

"I agree." Penny made a face and sipped her tea. "No more toast, thanks."

"Feeling queasy?" I asked. "I put a dust bin beside your couch last night in case you felt sick."

"Yes, I saw it. Thanks, but I wasn't that drunk. Not that I didn't try."

"Are you working today?" I glanced at the time.

"I begged off for the day," she said.

"Well, good. You need some time to take care of yourself."

She gave me a wry smile. "How was class last night?"

"I learned all kinds of interesting things about the employee handbook," I said. I was making rolls for the family's lunch. The dough had already risen twice, and now I was hand rolling the dough into individual balls to rise one more time before they were placed in the oven and baked.

"You said Ian helped me into my suite," Penny said. "Why was he there?"

"He stopped by to let me know how Chef Wright died."

"It was kind of late for him to be stopping by," she teased. "I bet it could have waited until morning."

"He must have been walking by and saw my light was on."

"It seems to me he wanted to do a little more than let you know how Chef died."

"Like what?"

"Like see you in your pajamas."

"Stop it. The man has a girlfriend."

"I heard he was stabbed," Agnes said. "With a kitchen knife most likely."

"Who was stabbed? Ian?"

"Chef Wright," Agnes said.

"Oh, yes, that's right," I said. "He was stabbed, but I didn't hear what with or how."

"Well, as long as they don't shut down your kitchen to search for blood on your knives, you'll be fine." Penny sipped her tea again. "Seriously, can you get the room to stop spinning?"

"Do you really think they will shut us down again?" Agnes asked. There was a worry wrinkle in her forehead.

"No," I said. "No, Ian—Chief Gordon—would have said so last night when he stopped by my rooms. Penny, do you know that Evie thinks it was Rachel who killed Chef Wright?"

"What?" Penny eyed me. "Why would she think that?" Penny raised her hand. "Wait, I know why. Evie is as vindictive as can be. I learned that last night."

"What do you mean?"

"Evie texted me that she heard I was out with Rachel. She swore she was going to do me in if I didn't cut ties with her."

"Ouch," I said. "I think Evie has gotten a little hormonal. She told you she was pregnant, right?"

"Yes."

"What?" Agnes said. "Seriously? What is that girl going to do now that her lover is dead?"

"She told me she was suing Mrs. Wright for a quarter of the insurance settlement. She patted her stomach and said she was going to be rich."

"Oh boy," Penny said. "She really has gone off the deep end."

"You don't think that Rachel really killed Chef Wright, do you?" I asked.

"I don't think that Wentworth's death is even connected to Chef Wright's death," Penny said. "We really haven't looked that deep into Lord Heavington and his recipe book. I'm telling you, the man could have hired someone to kill Wentworth so that he would stop blackmailing him."

"The only way to know for sure is to see if anyone in the Orangery kitchen needed the money enough to poison Wentworth. I mean, I've been told that only palace employees could have possible been in that kitchen that night. It is highly unlikely that a hit man would have stolen my pie, replaced the meringue with one laced with cyanide, and somehow forced Wentworth to eat it."

"That's the key," Agnes said. "Don't you think?"

"What is?" I asked.

"Whoever did it convinced that boy to eat the pie. Who could convince a young man to eat dessert?"

I laughed. "It doesn't take much convincing with most young men. He could have been working late and wanted a snack."

"But why would he eat that particular pie on that particular night if he wasn't with someone who encouraged him to eat it?" Agnes asked.

"That's true," Penny said.

"But there wasn't any evidence that there was anyone else in the kitchen. Wouldn't there have been two plates and such had someone snitched the pie with him?"

"A killer might have served up two plates of pie and then gotten rid of the evidence. It really doesn't take a lot of work to put a piece of pie back in the pie plate and wash the dishes."

"All the while, Wentworth was sitting there dead? That's morbid, isn't it?"

"Cold-blooded, I'd say," Agnes said, "but not beyond consideration."

"True, they did just murder someone," Penny said. She was reading her cell phone. "Eww, murder by cyanide poisoning is not pretty."

"I have to believe that the murderer did not accidently poison Wentworth like some believe, but specifically targeted him."

"I think you're right," Penny said. "Why poison a pie and leave it for whoever comes along if you have a specific target in mind."

"That means we are back to finding the link between Wentworth and Chef Wright."

"Not necessarily," Penny said. "What if the poisoner and whoever stabbed Chef Wright are two different people. What if Chef Wright's killer used the opportunity to kill him?"

"That sounds too planned," I said. "Think about it. Poisoning takes planning, but stabbing someone is more spur of the moment."

"So we have two different killers with possibly two different motives," Agnes said.

"That means no one on staff is above consideration," I said.

"Speak for yourself." Penny took another bite of toast. "Agnes and I didn't kill anyone. Did we, Agnes?"

Agnes nodded. "Too much work in that."

"Murder is a lot of work, isn't it? Who has time for that?"

Chapter 25

Who has the time to plan a poisoning and then stay hidden? That was the question going through my mind. I had just sent Agnes up to the family with lunch. Today was fish, chips, and mushy peas. The children liked the basics.

My thoughts turned to Lord Heavington. If he was the one who killed Wentworth, then he had to have hired someone who had the time to create cyanide—since buying it was nearly impossible—and put it in the pie. Someone who had the time to look for an opportunity—like me leaving the pie—and taking advantage of it. Someone who worked in and around the kitchen on a regular basis and needed money enough to commit murder for it.

Maybe Chef Wright figured out who it was and that's why he was killed with a knife.

That means we should be looking at people who worked in the Orangery. Maybe I would have a talk with Sandy.

"I'm going out for a moment," I said to Agnes when she got back. "We're making strawberry tarts and scones for tea. I have the dough chilling in the fridge."

"Then I'll take my lunch."

"Sounds good." I stepped out into the gray light of a rainy day in London. The parking lot was filled with puddles and dark cars as people ducked in and out of vehicles. I had an umbrella, but it was nice to feel the rain on my face.

Inside the Orangery was warm and bright. Soft music played and people talked in low tones. There was the clink of teacups and dishes. I made my way to the back kitchen, waving at the staff along the way. By now everyone knew who I was. Even the new hires because they took the handbook training class with me.

"Chef, what brings you to the Orangery?" Peter Chadsbury, the new day manager, said when I walked into the kitchen.

"I'm looking for Sandy."

"Right, well, she's in the office." He pointed toward the tiny office at the far end of the kitchen.

"Thanks." I maneuvered around the busy workers, making a bee-line to the office. "Chef," I said as I knocked on the open doorjamb.

"Oh, hello." Sandy sat back from her work. "What can I do for you Chef Cole?"

"Carrie Ann," I said and entered the room.

"Yes," she said.

"I wondered how things were since we last saw each other," I said. "May I?" I pointed at the stack of cookbooks and note-books on the chair across from the desk. The office was a very small place with next to no shelving.

"Yes, please, have a seat," she said and put her elbows on the desk. "Things have been crazy here. I've been temporarily placed in charge of the kitchen while they interview new chefs to take the job."

I winced. "They didn't just give the job to you?"

"No," she said with a shake of her head. "I have to interview and go through the same process as the other candidates." She sat back. "I prefer it actually. I don't want anyone to get the idea that I might have been the one to off Chef Wright."

"Motive," I said. "It never crossed my mind that anyone would think that you killed him."

"It's okay, I didn't kill him. I have witnesses."

"Whew!" I smiled. "There is some thought that Wentworth's killer might have been paid to poison him."

"Why?"

"The tabloid pictures he took. He was blackmailing Lord Heavington. I suspect Lord Heavington wasn't the only one."

"You think one of my staff was responsible for the poisoning?"

"It had to be someone who had the time to make the poison, then cook it into the meringue."

"So someone off the street couldn't have done it."

"Nor anyone who doesn't know their way around the kitchen."

"That's the thing," Sandy said. "My staff weren't the only people in Chef Wright's kitchen. He used to bring in his mistresses and show off by cooking for them."

I winced. "What about his wife? I hear she got a big insurance settlement."

"She hasn't been seen on the palace grounds in years," Sandy said. "I've been here for five years and I haven't seen her since I first started."

"Yes," I said, sitting back. "That matches what Chief Gordon told me. He said only staff were on the premises that night."

"That means it had to be one of my staff members," Sandy sighed.

"Most likely, yes," I said. "I think they might have been targeting Chef Wright at the bake-off and Chef Butterbottom interfered."

"I was one of the assistants for Chef Wright that day in the park. I don't remember having packed water."

"You were? I thought you were left in charge of the Orangery."

"Yeah, no," she said. "Chef Wright asked me to come at the last minute. Chef Lancaster was the one who stayed behind and ran things."

"Wow, why don't I remember you being there?"

She sent me a short smile. "No one remembers assistants. They are practically invisible."

"Practically invisible," I repeated. "That's why Chef Wright was able to have so many mistresses. He kept his attention on assistants like Evie and Rachel."

"Because they are practically invisible in the palace," Sandy said. "Yes, they came and went in the kitchen and no one questioned them."

"Who else could come and go like that? I mean, someone with baking skills. Someone who could make the meringue."

"There is Vladimir Rischek. He is an assistant pastry chef. And Geoff Theilman, the Orangery pastry chef," she said. "Both men could come and go at any time without anyone thinking it was unusual."

"Do they need money? I'm thinking of motive."

"I don't know. I haven't heard anything about their needing money. That said, Chef Theilman doesn't like you at all," she said. "I'm speaking of motive to use your pie. That man does nothing but grouse about how you catered the bridal shower in his kitchen."

"Chef Wright was okay with it," I said.

"Chef Wright wanted to add you to his list of conquests," Sandy said. "He would have let you take over his kitchen for a week. Chef Theilman hated Wright for that."

"So he had means and motive to kill Chef Wright and frame me. Where is he now?"

"He's in the kitchen," Sandy said. "We can't just accuse him. He's interviewing for the head chef spot same as me."

I winced. "So people would think it was you trying to get him out of the running."

"Let's not give them anything to think."

"Right. What about this Vladimir person? Is he around?"

"He has been on leave ever since the competition. The gossip is that he got sick like Butterbottom and his crew, but while they came back to work, he didn't."

"So Vladimir might have poisoned Wentworth and then poisoned Butterbottom to throw the police off his trail."

"And accidently poisoned himself."

"Except," I said, "they say poison is a female murder weapon."

"I think that's a bunch of hogwash. I think a guy is more likely to figure out how to make cyanide. They like screwing around with chemistry and making bad stuff."

"True." I stood. "Thanks for the talk."

"What are you going to do?" Sandy asked.

"I'm going to tell Chief Gordon about Geoff and Vlad. Maybe get this mystery solved."

"It's bugging you, isn't it?" Sandy said.

"Yes," I said. "I'm worried that there is at least one, if not two killers out there. They seem to be trying to frame me. I'd rather not have to worry about my kitchen or the royal family. You know?"

"Yeah, I get it."

We exchanged phone numbers and made a promise to get drinks sometime. I needed more friends. Sandy seemed like someone who would understand the new world I lived in.

* * *

"Hi." I had decided to stop by Ian's office. He was inside doing paperwork. It was a relief to find him alone. "Your secretary let me in."

"This is a nice surprise." He stood. "Come in, sit down. What can I do for you?"

"I . . . we sort of got interrupted." I took the offered seat in front of his desk.

"Probably for the best," he said. "How's Jasper?"

"Good, I guess," I said. "I haven't seen him in a while."

"Are you two not dating?"

"I think we're dating," I said. "Sort of, anyway. It's weird because he thinks you have a thing for me."

"Huh."

"Look, I know you have a girlfriend. I didn't really come to talk about that." I leaned forward. "I've been thinking about Wentworth's murder."

"Oh boy."

"Please hear me out," I said. "His death had to be deliberate. I mean, no one would go through all the trouble of finding or making cyanide, put it in a pie and let someone—not the intended victim—eat it. It just doesn't make sense. Do you know how hard it is to get your hands on cyanide?"

"It's not an easy substance to come by," he agreed. He sat behind his desk with his hands folded on top, looking at me intently.

"You can try to make it with apple seeds, but that's nuts."

"Or seeds."

"I'm being serious," I leaned toward him. "I was speaking to Sandy about it."

"Sandy?"

"Chef Wright's sous-chef."

"Right."

"Listen we think that whoever poisoned the pie had to be someone like an assistant. Someone who can come and go from the kitchen and no one pays very much attention to—"

"Do you have a suspect in mind?"

"We're thinking Vladimir Rischek or Geoff Theilman. Both men had access to the kitchen and the skills to make the meringue."

"Men don't usually use poison," he said, pointing out the obvious.

"Check into their backgrounds," I said. "I've heard that Geoff didn't like me catering the bridal shower. He had access to the kitchen and my pie. I also found out that Vladimir has been out sick since Chef Butterbottom was poisoned. Maybe Vladimir accidentally poisoned himself. Either man could have been paid to do the deed. You should look into who might need the money. Lord Heavington could have paid them."

"Sounds like a stretch, but I'll look into it."

"Thank you." I stood. "I understand it's pretty hard to find, buy, or make cyanide."

"We have the chemical formula for the poison that killed Wentworth. We know how it was produced."

"How?"

"It wasn't apple seeds," he said firmly. "Why do you still care about this? I told you we weren't investigating you."

"You might have ruled me out, but my coworkers and the press haven't. I need to help you until this is solved. I need to protect myself and my staff."

He studied me a moment. "Why don't you let me do that?"

"I'm not a victim. I can't sit and wait to be rescued."

"Right."

"What?" I asked and put my hands on my hips.

"Wondering when you're going to learn to trust me."

"Maybe the day you start accepting my help. People tell me things, you know. Things they might not tell security or the cops. I can help."

"And I can make a mean egg salad," he said. "But it doesn't mean you want me in your kitchen."

I pursed my lips. "Point taken."

"But it's not going to stop you from investigating, is it?" He crossed his arms over his chest.

"Nope," I said. "Not until my name is cleared."

"I figured. How about we make a deal?"

"What kind of deal?"

"You don't go talking to dangerous people, and I'll listen when you bring me your ideas."

"Who do you consider dangerous?"

"Anyone who might hurt you."

I laughed. "I'll try to stay clear of people with weapons. Fair?"

"Fair enough."

Chapter 26

"I'm glad you didn't have to take the entire day off. It's better to keep busy when your heart is broken."

"Work did help," Penny admitted.

"I still can't believe Rachel just left you at a club alone because Evie texted you," I said. It was after dinner and Penny and I were in the kitchen. Penny had finally gone into work after lunch. She worked late, and I had made us both ham and cheese sandwiches, sliced pickles, and cups of tea.

"I think she's gone a bit bonkers about Evie," Penny said and chewed a bite of pickle. "She told me that Chef Wright had promised her that Evie was out of the picture. Can you believe that?"

"I think he was playing them both. Evie told me that Chef Wright was leaving his wife for her and her unborn baby."

"The joke's on them both." Penny picked up half of her sandwich. "I heard that he had a new girl on the line."

"A new girl?"

"Yes, according to the kitchen staff Chef Wright was planning a private demonstration. He only did those when the girls were still in the first impression stage. I hear Chef Wright would bring them into the kitchen late and give a cooking lesson. His whole staff knew about these lessons. No one said anything because they were afraid they'd be fired."

"Oh, how awful," I said. "Do they know who his latest girl was?"

"There was some thought it might be you."

"What? No, I don't need cooking lessons from anyone. Besides, ew."

"That's what I said," Penny said. "It had to be someone else."

"And no one knew who?"

"It had to be someone who wasn't part of the kitchen staff. I'll give him this, he didn't mess around in his own kitchen."

"That's true, Evie and Rachel belong to the admin staff." I chewed my sandwich thoughtfully. "It most likely was a woman on the administration staff. What about Beth?"

"Beth?"

"You know," I waved my sandwich. "The one who was selling secret recipes to Lord Heavington. She might know more admins. She might know who Chef Wright had his eye on. Or she started flirting with Chef Wright herself to get access to more recipes."

"Now that would be something," Penny said with a laugh. "She would be out maneuvering the slick old man."

"We can ask her," I said. "She was pretty forthcoming about her involvement with Lord Heavington. I bet she's the type to laugh about putting one over Chef Wright."

"Yikes, that has to make Evie and Rachel insane."

"I don't think we should be the ones to tell them either," I said. "Those two will chew us up and spit us out for dinner."

"Beth Branch," she said thoughtfully. "Did you ever rule

her out as Wentworth's killer? I mean, she stood to be as embarrassed by the photos of her with Lord Heavington as Lord Heavington would be."

"You know that Ian and I both spoke to Beth," I said. "She didn't seem bothered by the photos. It's strange. Do you know if anything came of her transgression? I mean did the palace do anything about her selling recipe secrets? If she didn't think anything of selling recipes what other secrets would she sell?"

"Maybe Wentworth knew," Penny said. "I'll look more into Beth. It seems like she should have been severely reprimanded at best and fired at worst."

"I haven't heard of anyone being fired since I got here," I said. "The employee handbook says that you get three warnings before they fire you—unless you commit a true crime."

"Like selling state secrets." Penny wiggled her eyebrows. "Wentworth could have had pictures of Beth selling more than recipes."

"And if she had access to Chef Wright's kitchen, she could have killed Wentworth."

"We should go see her," I said. "Is she living in the city?"

"I think she lives just outside of the city," Penny said. She mentioned something about taking the tube."

"I wonder what Rachel and Evie will do when the news comes out that they were both being dumped for a new girl."

"Probably lose it," Penny said. "Evie's pregnant, right?"

"Yes," I said and shook my head. "Not good."

"I've known both of those girls for the last year," Penny said. "They aren't people to mess around with. Although why Rachel would go after Chef Wright is beyond me. I thought she was dating another guy in security. I think his name was Richard something."

"But you told me that she was flirting with a new guy and wanted to keep it secret. Remember? She must have broken up with Richard. Maybe you just can't remember that."

"Hmm," Penny said. "Maybe Rachel will talk to you. You aren't exactly on Evie's best friend list."

"Evie sat with me at the employee handbook training," I said. "People are going to know that."

"Maybe Rachel doesn't," Penny pointed out.

"I can't," I said. "I'm still mad at her for leaving you alone like that. Something really bad could have happened to you."

"Thanks." Penny sipped her tea. "But nothing happened. At least nothing I noticed." She winked at me.

"There are a lot of women working at the palace," I said thoughtfully. "What if Beth wasn't the one?"

"Don't worry." Penny patted my hand. "We'll figure it out."

"I certainly hope so."

* * *

The next day I was on my way to class when I ran into Rachel. "Rachel," I called out and she turned around.

"Yes?"

"What were you thinking abandoning Penny like that?"

"I beg your pardon?" Rachel stopped short and frowned. She wore a tweed skirt and navy sweater.

"Penny told me about the other night. You and she were out at the clubs and you just left her to find her way home. Something bad could have happened to her. I mean something really bad."

"I don't know what the big deal is," Rachel said. "She was texting Evie. I asked her to stop and spend time with me. She refused, so I left."

"She was drunk," I said. "She had to get a bartender to call her a cab."

"Look, I don't want anything to do with anyone who talks to Evie Green." She narrowed her eyes. "That woman is a menace. I wouldn't be surprised if she was the one who killed Don."

"You think Evie killed Chef Wright?"

"Why not? He got her pregnant and moved on to me."

"I heard he moved on from you." I crossed my arms. "Maybe you had cause to kill him."

"Oh, I wanted to kill him," Rachel said. "But I realized soon enough that he wasn't worth it." She shook her head and sighed. "You're right. He did move on from me and pretty quickly. I tried to warn Evie, but she dished me bad. It's why we got into a fight the other day. That woman was serious about Chef Sleaze. As far as I'm concerned, she got what she deserved."

"You didn't have to take it out on Penny," I said. "We girls have to stick together."

"Yeah, I'm sorry. I shouldn't have done that."

"Good," I said. "You should tell Penny."

"I will." Rachel winced. "I've been a bit of a jerk lately. Can't help it. Seems so weird that Don is dead. He might have been a skank, but you kind of know that going in."

"So why'd you do it?"

She shrugged. "Evie was talking about how he was going to leave his wife for her. I wanted to prove to Evie that the man wouldn't leave his wife for anyone. That if he two-times his wife, he'd two-time anyone. But Evie didn't believe it. So I started flirting with him. Then one thing led to another. The guy was really good at making you feel like you were the only girl in the entire world, you know?"

"I guess not," I said. "I've never been in that situation."

"You're lucky," Rachel said.

"There is a rumor that Chef Wright had moved on to a new girl. Do you have any idea who that was?"

Rachel laughed. "No, and I don't want to know. Maybe the new girl is the one who killed him?"

"Why?"

"Because the man could make you crazy."

I spotted Evie going into the lecture hall. "I have to go to class. Listen, call me before you leave Penny on her own next time. Okay?"

"Oh, I doubt there will be a next time," Rachel said with one raised eyebrow.

"Fine, whatever." I made my way into class and took a seat beside Evie.

"Was that Rachel you were talking to?" Evie asked. Her eyebrows were drawn down and her mouth a thin line.

"Yes."

"What did she want?"

"Actually, I flagged her down," I said. "I wanted to find out why she left Penny drunk and alone."

"She did what?" Evie turned toward me. "That witch. Wait, what was Penny doing going out with Rachel?"

Oh boy.

"She knows that Rachel and I are on the outs. Serves Penny right to get left alone. I warned her Rachel was a back stabber." She crossed her arms over her chest.

"Funny, Rachel just told me that she started to see Chef Wright to prove to you that the man was still on the prowl."

"A likely story," Evie said. "Rachel can't stand it when I have even the tiniest bit of good luck. She seduced my Don. Lucky for her, he put an end to her schemes and plans."

"He did?" That was not the story I got from Rachel and Penny.

"He did, and he told me so himself. She lured him into a closet in the kitchen. Then Rachel wrapped herself around my Don, but he was true to me. He pushed her off and told her to stay away from him."

"Huh," I said.

"Like I said," Evie went on. "It wouldn't surprise me if Rachel killed him. He humiliated her in front of half the kitchen staff."

"Like who?" I asked.

"Talk to Chef Theilman or that Sandy chick. Don told me that they saw him tell Rachel to leave him alone. In fact, he told me he put in a complaint to security to keep Rachel out of his kitchen."

"Huh," I said again. "No one mentioned that to me before."

"Well, I know why Rachel wouldn't mention it. How humiliating. Serves her right if you ask me."

Class started and I was left to wonder if Rachel had lied to me or if Evie lied. Or maybe Chef Wright had deluded them both.

Chapter 27

"I haven't seen you in a while," Jasper said. He stepped into my kitchen from the greenhouse. "Are you okay?"

"Yes, fine," I said. It was five-thirty in the morning. I was up early making yeast dough for breakfast rolls and the supper meal. "I thought you were avoiding me."

"Why would you think that?" He leaned against the closed door to the greenhouse. Jasper looked gorgeous in the morning. He wore blue jeans and a dark brown T-shirt that outlined his well-muscled chest. As always, his feet were encased in rugged work boots. His hair was a bit shaggy, but his face was chiseled and clean-shaven. Why hadn't we gone on a third date yet?

"The last time I saw you we made a date to get some quick drinks. But then I had to cancel and after that you disappeared."

"Oh, come now, it's hard for a man my size to disappear."

"I know." I washed my hands then put on the kettle. "That can only mean one thing."

"What's that?"

"You're avoiding me."

"Why would I avoid a beautiful woman?" He asked.

"I don't know. Why don't you come on in, sit down, and have some tea?" I asked. "You can spin me a tale of where you've been."

He laughed a hearty laugh and came in, taking a seat at the kitchen table. He made the chair look small. I didn't think men had so many muscles in real life.

"How do you like your tea?" I asked as I filled the teapot with hot water to steep. I paused and looked at him. "I don't even know how you like your tea."

"Let's remedy that," he said. "I like it hot and sweet."

"No milk?"

"No milk." His blue gaze was bright and filled with life. My heart flip-flopped in my chest.

"Care for breakfast?"

"No, thanks, I ate an hour ago."

I winced. "You ate at four-thirty? When do you get up in the morning? Three-thirty?"

"Four usually," he said as I placed a mug in front of him along with a sugar bowl filled with cubes. "I like to get a head start on things."

I poured his tea, then I poured my own and sat down across the table from him. "That means you're a morning person."

"Yes, aren't you? I see you here at five-thirty every morning."

"You do? Wait, are you stalking me?" I teased.

"I know your routine." He grinned. "I like to think of it as paying attention—not stalking." He stirred sugar into his mug.

"I must be boringly predictable." I sipped my own tea. It was Earl Grey, and I preferred it hot and plain.

"There's nothing boring about you, darling." He winked at me.

I felt the heat of a blush rush over my cheeks. "If you know my schedule, why have you been missing? I thought we were supposed to get drinks."

He shrugged. "There was a problem with blight in the roses and I'm working with the master gardener of the grounds to put in some new trees."

"I thought you're supposed to plant trees in the fall."

"Depends on the tree." He sipped his drink. "And the financing, of course."

"Of course." I leaned my elbows on the table. "So you've been too busy to swing by."

He studied me a moment. "I'm here now. Do you want to go out tonight?"

"Do you have a girlfriend?"

"What?"

"A wife? A mistress or lover tucked away somewhere?"

"Why would you ask that?"

"I've learned a lot about sexy men in the last few days."

"What? Wait, are you saying I'm sexy?" His grin widened.

"You're evading the question."

"No, I don't have a wife, a girlfriend, or a lover at the moment," he said, lifting one eyebrow. "I'm hoping that will change soon."

I felt my hands tremble and put my cup down. "A few quick drinks do not a date make," I said.

"Good," he said. "Then let's go out to dinner, maybe some dancing."

"Seriously?"

"Seriously," he said. "And to make it a proper—Carrie Ann will you go out with me on Saturday night?"

"I work until nine."

"Perfect." He stood. "I'll pick you up at nine-thirty. Wear something lovely."

"Like what?" I asked as he headed toward the door.

"Whatever makes you feel lovely," he said. "Just leave the granny panties in your drawer." With that he walked into the greenhouse garden.

"How do you know I have anything other than granny panties?" I called after him.

Agnes bustled in. "What's that chef?"

"Nothing," I said, blushing.

"Was that Jasper?" She pointed with her chin toward the garden as she took off her black jacket and hung it on the hooks by the kitchen door.

"Yes. I have a date tomorrow night."

"Good for you!" She tied her apron around her waist. "It's about time."

* * *

"The Orangery staff is having a memorial for Chef Wright," I said to Agnes. It was after lunch and before tea. "I'm going. Do you want to come along?"

"I didn't know the man," Agnes said. "But I have friends who work in the Orangery. So yes, give me a minute to spruce up."

"Sure." I looked in the mirror by the door to ensure my face was flour-free. I'd been making piecrusts, and flour had a tendency to stick to my skin. I fluffed my hair and straightened my white shirt.

"Where's the memorial being held?" Agnes asked as she slipped on a gray sweater.

"In the garden," I said. "I heard they set up chairs and a place for a preacher to come and run the ceremony. Mostly I think it's a way for everyone to express their loss."

"Good for the palace to think of that."

"Do you think the duke and duchess will come?" I asked.

"I doubt it," Agnes said as we left the palace and walked across the parking lot toward the garden area. "They know if they show up the photogs will follow, and it will be quite the mess."

"Oh, right." I noticed several small groups of people heading across the parking area to the garden. In a small semiprivate garden was a fountain. In front of the fountain were rows of folding chairs, an easel with a picture of Chef Wright on it, and lush pots of flowers beside the picture.

A preacher was talking to a woman in a slim black suit. She wore a wide-brimmed black hat and held the hand of a small child also in black. Beside her stood two more children dressed in black. They all appeared to be between the ages of four and ten.

My heart hurt for them. This must be Mrs. Wright and her children. How terrible to lose your father at such a young age. I wondered if the killer realized that they were leaving a widow and small children.

We took our seats near the back and watched the Orangery kitchen staff enter. Mrs. Wright and her children took their seats on the front right. Sandy and two men took their seats near the front on the left.

"Who are the guys?" I asked Agnes.

"That's Chef Theilman in the middle and Chef Rischek on the end. I noted that all three were also dressed in black. A departure from the white chef's coats they normally wore.

The seats were filing up when I noticed Evie. She was

dressed in all black. Her slinky midi-length dress showed off a thin frame and slight baby bump. She wore a black hat with a veil over her face. Her lips were drenched in crimson. She walked with her head up to the front of the chairs and sat down boldly in the same row as Mrs. Wright.

There was an audible gasp from the small gathering. Mrs. Wright stiffened and pulled her children toward her.

"That girl has some nerve," Agnes whispered.

The preacher went over and had a whispered conversation with Evie, but it was clear that she wasn't about to budge.

"Oh, boy," I said. Everyone at the gathering was tense waiting for a fight to break out.

The preacher nervously adjusted his collar and started the service.

I looked around to see who else was here. I recognized the waitstaff from the Orangery. There was also staff from Butterbottom's kitchen. I was surprised to see that Butterbottom himself didn't come. Was he in some kind of feud with Chef Wright? Could that have been why he and his staff was poisoned? Or was it all accidental, as Ian thought?

"Do you know where Butterbottom is?" I whispered to Agnes as the preacher droned on about friends and family and the nature of death.

"The two didn't get on," Agnes whispered back.

"I'm not the only one Butterbottom doesn't like?"

"Hardly," Agnes said. "Those two had a feud for the last ten years."

"Maybe it was Chef Wright who poisoned Butterbottom," I said.

"Shh," a woman in front of us said.

I pressed my lips together. Sandy stood at the front of the gathering and talked about Chef Wright. I glanced around to see if Rachel had come. I caught sight of her to the far right. She sat in the last row as if ready to escape but still drawn to come.

There were a couple of other women there who were not associated with the Orangery or the other kitchens. I noticed they were all crying. Would it be safe to assume they had all been Chef Wright's mistresses at some point?

The man in front of me moved to the left and revealed another person I knew—Beth Branch. Beth didn't work with Chef Wright. Leaning in, I noticed her raise a tissue to her eyes. Were we right? Had Beth been one of Chef Wright's mistresses?

What was wrong with all these girls that they could have an affair with a man they knew would move on to another?

Chef Theilman spoke next and then Vladimir. Each man gave thoughtful and charming examples of why they enjoyed working with Chef Wright.

The preacher then asked that anyone who wanted to say something about Chef Wright to come up. Evie stood and walked to the front. You could have heard a pin drop as the entire crowd held its breath.

She turned dramatically to the crowd and stopped to dab at her wet eyes. "Chef Wright—Don—and I had a special and profound relationship." She patted her tummy.

Mrs. Wright's back got stiffer. She gathered her children around her as if to protect them from Evie. I knew I wasn't the only one who thought Evie didn't have any right to speak—not in front of his family.

"I first met Don last year. He catered a small party for Princess Anne's staff. I found him to be charming, witty, and caring.

We fell in love over the next few months." Her voice broke and tears ran down her cheeks. She addressed Mrs. Wright. "I—we—have lost a good man, a thoughtful lover, a wonderful father."

Mrs. Wright stood, grabbed her children's hands, and walked down the aisle to leave.

"As we all know, Don was in a terrible marriage. Trapped because he felt it was his duty to take care of his children. But our happy love affair produced a new child," Evie went on. "My child. And Don swore he would leave his wife for me. None of this is new, not to you or to Mrs. Wright." Evie pointed at the woman who pulled her children out of hearing range. "I know there are others here who loved Don. He was that kind of guy—big hearted. He promised me that his days of taking lovers were over. He told me I was the love of his life."

She broke down into sobs. "We were going to be a family."

The preacher put his arm around Evie and drew her back to her seat in the now empty first row. He didn't ask for any more memories. Instead he hastily went on with the program.

We all sat stunned for a moment. It must have taken Evie a lot of nerve to get up like that. After bundling her children into a car, Mrs. Wright walked back up the aisle with her chin in the air. She sat down, and the preacher finished the service.

There was a sense of us all on the edges of our seats to see what happened next. Mrs. Wright got up after the closing ceremony. She went to the podium.

"Thank you all for coming today and honoring my husband." It was all she said before she walked back down the aisle and got into her car.

"Wow," Agnes said. "What a classy lady."

Evie moved down the aisle, dabbing at her eyes with a white handkerchief like she was in a bad drama. She stood at the end, waiting for people to hug her and give their condolences. Only a handful of people went to her. The majority escaped out the sides of the garden, carefully avoiding a scene.

Agnes and I skirted around the edge, careful to keep from making eye contact with Evie. I didn't want to get dragged into any palace politics. It was clear that most people felt like I did: embarrassed for Evie.

I realized that Mrs. Wright handled the situation with grace I wasn't sure I would have had. It was clear to me that she was a woman doing her best to shield her children from the transgressions of their father. My heart went out to her. In sticky situations like the one Evie presented, it was easy for adults to forget about the children. Mrs. Wright just proved she didn't forget about hers.

Chapter 28

"I heard Mrs. Wright was icy cold at the memorial," Penny said. It was after tea and before dinner. Penny had come into my kitchen to have tea and biscuits. She grabbed one of the macaroons I had made for tea and took a bite. "Yum. Okay, spill. Was it nuts?"

"It was the most cringe-worthy moment of my life." I poured tea into my mug. "Evie has some nerve. She acted as if we were there to support her in her loss. Meanwhile, Mrs. Wright had her children there."

"Wow, I wish I could have been there."

"No, you don't," Agnes said as she finished the dishes. "It was embarrassing for both women. No one should do that to children, ever."

"Evie will be lucky Mrs. Wright doesn't sue her."

"You can't sue for embarrassment," I pointed out.

"But you can sue for harassment," Penny pointed out. "I would say that Evie crossed a line."

"I heard Evie is barred from the family funeral," Agnes said.

"There's to be a funeral?" I asked. "I thought the memorial was all there was."

"Oh, no," Agnes said. "I heard that they still have to release the body. When they do that, Mrs. Wright is having a family-only funeral."

"Do you think that Evie will try to come?" Penny asked.

"Chef Wright's family members will see that she doesn't," Agnes said. "Some of the kitchen staff have said they would be at the cemetery as well to ensure there isn't a repeat of the memorial service. They want to honor Chef Wright's children."

"I do feel sorry for his kids," I said. "They are too young to be dragged into whatever it is that Evie is doing."

"So Evie just acted as if she was the weeping widow?" Penny asked.

"Yes."

"That's nuts."

"Rachel was there," I said. "She wasn't the only one from administration. Beth Branch was there, too."

"Oh," Penny's eyes lit up. "We thought Beth might have been one of Chef Wright's conquests."

"I'll ask Sandy if they knew she was or not. Maybe Beth was the next in line."

"Maybe Beth was trying to get recipes out of Chef Wright," Penny said.

"What if Chef Wright found out? They could have fought," I said.

"You think Beth may have stabbed Chef Wright?"

"Maybe," I said. "She certainly is a person who would be easy to overlook."

"If she killed him, why show up at his memorial?" Agnes asked.

"Killers often like to be involved in investigations. Maybe she wanted to see what happened at his memorial service."

"I can talk to Beth," Penny said.

"She isn't going to admit out of the blue that she killed him."

"You don't know that," Penny said. "She admitted that she was selling secrets pretty easily."

"Let's just see what Sandy knows first," I said. "I'll make a dinner date with her."

"Speaking of dinner dates," Agnes said. "What are you going to wear to yours?"

"You have a dinner date?" Penny pinned me down with her gaze.

"Yes," I said and raised my chin. "Jasper asked me out."

"Not just quick drinks?"

"No, a real dinner date," I said.

"Sounds like things are getting serious," Penny said. Her gaze lit up. "Good for you. I've seen your closet. You have nothing to wear. Let's get you something from my closet." Penny took my hand. "We'll be back in time to get dinner going," she said to Agnes.

"Oh boy," I muttered. Nothing like being dragged to my doom. Although, really, I was glad that Penny could help. I really didn't have anything of interest in my closet.

Penny opened her apartment doors and sunlight and colors hit me. "How can you live in this chaos?" I asked as she pulled me through her colorful living space into her equally colorful, overstuffed bedroom.

"Messiness is a sign of intelligence," Penny said with a laugh. "Come on, I know right what you should wear."

I reluctantly pushed clothes aside and sat on the bed. "Yes, but do you know where to find it?"

Penny laughed. "Of course, I know exactly where everything

is. Got my own filing system right here." She pointed to her temple. Then she dug around in the back of her closet. "So, Jasper, huh? I thought you had a thing for Ian."

"Ian introduced me to his girlfriend," I said with a sigh. "Unlike Evie and Rachel, I don't mess with guys who are in a relationship."

Penny stuck her head out of the open wardrobe. "Jasper's a real keeper, you know." She reached into her wardrobe and pulled out a sapphire-blue wrap dress with long sleeves and a fit and flare skirt. "Here you go, say thank you."

"Oh, thank you!" I said, taking the dress from her. "It's gorgeous."

"Now for shoes," Penny reached into her closet and pulled out two pairs. One pair were a matching sapphire blue with four-inch heels and an open toe. The second pair were silver sandals with a tiny kitten heel.

"Silver," I said and took the shoes.

"I thought so," Penny said. "Now for the icing."

"Icing?"

"You know, bling, rings, bracelets, necklace, earrings, and a pretty belt." As she spoke she grabbed a bag and placed each piece inside. "There you go. You will look amazing. How are you doing your hair?"

I touched my pulled back ponytail. "Loose?"

"Perfect." Penny disappeared into her bathroom and came out with a wand curler. "Use this to make soft waves all around your head. Do you have makeup?"

"Of course I have makeup," I said. "I like to keep it light."

"Do your eyes in a smoky gray," she said. "It will really make the blue pop."

"Smoky eyes," I said. "Right."

"And eyelash extensions and a bright red mouth to accent your pale skin."

"No," I said. "No eyelash extensions. I tried them once and they got stuck to my fingers."

"Hmmm." Penny put her hands on her hips. Her mouth was a thin tight line. "I can put them on for you."

"No, thanks," I said. "I prefer to look like myself. He asked me out with me dressed like this." I pointed to my plain face, white polo, and black slacks.

"Yes, but if you want sex, you need to turn up the volume." The heat of a blush rushed up my cheeks. "Men are not allowed in our rooms."

"Doesn't mean he doesn't have a room of his own," Penny said, waggling her eyebrows. "You need to be prepared. Do you have a condom?"

"Okay." I picked up the dress and shoes. "Thanks for loaning me your outfit."

Penny's face brightened as she followed me to the door. "You're welcome. I'm a girl on her own these days. I need to live vicariously through you." She clasped her hands in front of her.

"We need to fix that," I said.

"Give it time," she said, her expression falling. "I need time to get over things."

I gave her a quick hug. "You really liked him, didn't you?"

"Yes," she said softly. "Now, I expect a full report after the date."

"I'll share as much as a lady should."

Penny wrinkled her nose. "Details," she said. "I want all the details."

I shook my head. "Don't get your hopes up. I don't know if there will be anything to tell."

"Oh, there will be something," she said. "I've seen how Jasper looks at you."

"Right."

*   *   *

After hanging up Penny's things in my room, I decided to make a custard but we were low on eggs. I left the kitchen prep work to Agnes and headed to the market. It was a lovely spring evening. Flowers were blooming everywhere. The British really had a way with gardens. Where I grew up, grass was the main plant grown. But here the yards were smaller and flowers sprang from every nook and corner, brightening the gray skies and buildings.

I ran into the sanctioned local grocery. You couldn't get food for the future kings from just any source. The duchess liked fresh, organic, grass fed, and free range. Most of the time the food came from the family farms. But in a pinch, I could stop at a local market.

"Hello, Chef," Sally, the cashier, said. "What brings you in today? Looking for a poison?"

"Stop," I said. "Why would you say such a thing?"

"Just teasing," she said. "I've had a look at the tabloids and there's some speculation about all the killings going on up there near the palace."

She pointed at the rack of tabloids. There was a picture of the duchess looking distressed and the headline read "American Chef Poisons Competition."

"Oh, good lord." I pointed at the papers. "This one says there are werewolves in London. This one leads with aliens spotted in Hyde Park."

She laughed. "I know they're ridiculous, but that don't mean there isn't a kernel of truth in them somewhere."

"Only if you're selling poisoned eggs." I headed down the aisle toward the dairy section. A quick scan to find the grass-fed, free-range chicken eggs and a quick look to see that none were broken and I made my way back to the cashier. "That's all I need. A few eggs for dessert."

"What are ya making?"

"Egg custard," I said. "An old family recipe."

"Ooh, that is a good spring pudding," Sally cooed. "Would you share your recipe with me?"

I laughed. "No. I won't share." I tapped my head. "It's up here and won't be written down."

Paying for the eggs, I put them in my tote and headed toward the door. Just outside I ran into two men I recognized from the memorial.

"Chef Cole," The smaller red-headed man said.

"Yes?"

"Chef Theilman," he said, holding out his hand.

"Chef Theilman?" I shook his hand. "Carrie Ann."

"I know," he said. "Vlad and I are stalking you." He pointed to the taller black-haired man with blue eyes. Vlad was also thin. Both men wore white shirts and white pants as if they had come straight from their kitchen.

"Stalking me?" I asked. "Why?"

"Let's get a tea," Chef Theilman said, pointing to a coffee shop on the corner.

"I don't know." I took a step back.

"We are who we say we are." Vlad took out his palace security badge and showed it to me. "We met at the baking competition. Remember?"

Wow, Vlad was the second assistant I hadn't paid attention to at the competition. I must have really been focused on keeping my food safe. "Okay," I said. "Let me text my assistant and let her know where I'll be."

"Sure."

I let them lead me to the coffee shop. We ordered drinks and took a seat in the far corner.

"This is good," Chef Theilman said. "Far from the door. We don't need to attract any more attention."

"More attention?" I echoed. Placing the tote with eggs on the windowsill behind me, I sat down.

"The tabloids are absolutely bonkers these days," Chef Theilman said. "They'd have a field day if they got word that three palace chefs were sitting together to have tea."

"Listen, we wanted to have a word with you," Vlad said, leaning in toward me. "Rumor has it that you suspect Geoff and me of killing Wentworth and Chef Wright."

"Oh." I glanced around for exit signs. "Right."

"Don't worry, we aren't angry about it," Vlad said.

"Speak for yourself." Geoff took a sip of his tea.

"We want to set the record straight," Vlad went on. "Tell us why you sent security to question us."

I wiggled in my chair. "I didn't kill Wentworth or Chef Wright. But someone is trying—not very successfully—to make it appear that I did."

"We didn't kill them, either," Geoff said. "In fact, no one even thought that we might have done it until you put a bug in Gordon's ear."

"So we have to ask why you were pointing fingers in our direction?"

I swallowed hard. "You make it sound like we're in grade school."

Neither man replied, making the silence nearly unbearable.

"Look, I didn't mean to upset either of you. I apologize if that has happened."

"What the hell did you tell Chief Gordon?"

"I was told that you, Chef Theilman—"

"Geoff."

"Geoff, I was told that you were upset that I catered the bridal shower. Someone said they heard you saying my pies weren't professional."

He made a dismissive motion with his hand. "That was bluster."

"And Vlad, you were not happy with me either."

"So you pointed a finger at us for killing Chef Wright?"

"Whoever killed Wentworth used my pie to do it. That means they most likely were trying to pin that murder on me. It had to be someone with access to the kitchen."

"So you suspect us?"

"Geoff, you are applying for the position that opened after Chef Wright's was killed."

"So is Sandy, and you didn't tell Chief Gordon to look into her."

"That's because he already questioned her like he questioned me." I wrapped my hands around my paper mug and warmed my chilled hands.

"For the record, I was at the pub with twenty witnesses the night Wentworth was murdered," Geoff said.

"I was catering a family affair, also with witnesses," Vlad said.

"Then neither of you has anything to worry about," I pointed out.

"Except my being questioned by Chief Gordon is putting a kink in my chances to get Chef Wright's job."

"How so?" I narrowed my eyebrows.

"They are considering an outsider with no connections to the staff politics," he said bitterly. "So even your precious Sandy is not likely to get the position."

"I'm sorry to hear that."

"Are you?"

"Look, I don't have a problem with either of you," I said and raised my hands. "Do either of you have any idea who killed Wentworth or Chef Wright? Do you think they're connected?"

"I think Wentworth was the only target," Vlad said. "That death took planning. Chef Wright's death was more impulsive."

"We think there are two killers," Geoff said. "We told Gordon that as well."

"Did either of you see anything suspicious the day Chef Wright was murdered?"

"I wasn't there," Geoff said. "I was at a day conference on the making of gluten-free pastries."

"I was at a job interview," Vlad said.

"Job interview? But you have a job." I wiggled in my seat.

"I was interviewing for a place in Buckingham Palace. Better pay and better hours."

"Any idea who Chef Wright was seeing? Sandy said that he was planning on bringing around a new girl."

"You think his new girl did this?" Geoff drew his eyebrows together. "Why?"

"Maybe not his new girl, but maybe his old one," Vlad said.

"Rachel?" I said. "You think she did?"

"Not Rachel," Vlad said. "That monster who hijacked the memorial service."

"Evie? Why would she kill Chef Wright? She said he was leaving his wife for her."

"No, he wasn't," Geoff said. "What made you say he was?"

"Evie told me."

"That woman is crazy," Vlad said. "Chef Wright loved his wife. He would never leave her."

"But the mistresses . . ." I said.

"Chef loved the thrill of the hunt. But he never would have compromised his children," Geoff said.

"But the women . . ."

"All knew," Geoff said. "He told them straight up."

"It doesn't make any sense."

"What doesn't make sense?" Vlad asked.

"Why would anyone want to be his mistress? Why would his wife allow him to have so many mistresses?"

"Oh, you are so American in your thinking," Vlad said with a sad shake of his head. "They had what you would call an open marriage. Mrs. Wright accepted her husband's 'entertainments' as part of him. But those two were fiercely devoted to each other."

"Then why was Evie allowed to take over the memorial?"

"It was an open service," Geoff said with a shrug. "No one was prepared for that woman's antics."

"I don't know," I said with a shake of my head. "I'm pretty sure he promised Evie that he would leave his wife for her. Evie's pregnant."

"Not sure whose kid it is," Geoff said.

"What do you mean?"

"Everyone knows Chef had surgery right after his last kid was born."

"What?"

"He was shooting blanks," Vlad said.

"Did Evie know this?" I asked with my eyebrows drawn. The woman was more insane than I'd ever imagined.

"Everyone knows it," Geoff said.

"Wow." I sat back. "Just wow."

"Changes things a bit, now doesn't it?" Vlad said.

"Yes," I said. "Does Ian know about this?"

"He's aware," Geoff said. "We thought you should be aware before you point any more fingers at people."

"Thanks." I stood. "This has been very enlightening."

"You're welcome," Vlad said. "We hoped it would be."

I left the two chefs at the coffee shop and hurried back to my kitchen. Could I have been sitting next to Chef Wright's killer at class all along? The idea made me shudder. The next question was what did Evie have against Wentworth that would maker her kill him and why try to pin the death on me?

Unless Evie wasn't the only one who wanted Wentworth dead.

Chapter 29

"I can't believe the chefs confronted you," Penny said. It was after dinner, and I had sent Agnes home. Penny sat in her usual spot in the kitchen.

"I feel stupid," I said. "They both had solid alibies for Chef Wright's killing and even Wentworth's murder. Chef Theilman was really mad. He said that my questioning him and other people on the staff meant that the most likely person to replace Chef Wright would be an outsider."

Penny winced. "I suppose I could see that."

"You're a friend of Evie's, right?"

"Sure, at least I think so. Why?"

"Did you know that Chef Wright was no longer able to have children?"

"What?"

"Yes, I guess it's rather common knowledge that he had a vasectomy. It must be why Mrs. Wright isn't beside herself with anger at Evie. She must figure that a paternity suit will soon enough prove Evie's claim to be false."

"You think all she has to do is wait for the baby to come and the lawsuit will go away?"

"That would be my guess. It's why she seemed so calm at the memorial. She must think Evie is off her rocker."

"Maybe Evie is." Penny widened her eyes. "Do you think Evie is fake pregnant?"

"What?"

"You know, fake pregnant. Where it's all in the woman's head. There is no baby but they have all the symptoms."

"Now you're just being silly," I said with a tsk. "That doesn't really happen, does it?"

"Yes, it does," Penny said. "It's a mental disorder."

"Well, after the memorial service, I can believe that Evie has some kind of mental disorder. Who does that?"

"Do you think they'll suspend her from work?" Penny asked.

"I don't know. Did she really do anything wrong?"

"Hmm, I suppose not," Penny said. "Unless she actually did kill someone."

"Why would she want to kill the man she claims she's in love with?"

"Maybe because he didn't love her back," Penny suggested.

I remained skeptical. "She doesn't have any motive to kill Wentworth or poison Butterbottom."

"We may have two killers."

"The chefs have iron-clad alibies. That leaves Lord Heavington. But he has an alibi."

"Unless he hired a hit man." I rubbed my head. We seemed to be going round and round.

"Why would a hitman kill someone with poison? I mean, I suppose they could have made him bite a cyanide capsule, but those don't exist anymore, and why would they put poison in the pie?"

"I think we'll never solve this thing. What we have is one murder by poison, one attempted poisoning, and one murder by stabbing, which is not the same. If we had two killers, who would they be? We've cleared everyone."

"Don't they have video footage from inside the kitchen?" Penny asked.

"No," I said. "They didn't think they needed it. Everyone with access to the kitchen has to use their palace ID. The electronic ID log only shows Wentworth going into the kitchen by himself that night."

"He had to let someone in," Penny said. "So it was someone he knew and trusted."

"Someone who had regular access to the kitchen so that they could put poison in the meringue and pass it off as mine."

"Maybe it was someone who had access to your kitchen and the Orangery kitchen," Penny suggested.

"No," I said with a frown. "That would only be me. Agnes had the day off."

"Right," Penny stood and stretched. "Come on then, let's off to bed. Tomorrow is your big date and you want to get some sleep so that you look your best."

Penny was right. I did want to look my best. After our last date, I wanted to put my best foot forward.

* * *

"I heard the chefs had a talk with you," Agnes said as we made breakfast the next morning.

"Wow, information gets around fast," I said as I made fruit salad. Today's breakfast was eggs, beans, muffins, and fruit salad.

Agnes laughed. "It's a small community. How do you think they knew you suspected them of the murders?"

"I didn't think I told anyone but Ian."

"And Penny and I were here. People talk, dear."

"Then someone should know who killed Wentworth and who killed Chef Wright. Chef Wright was murdered in a freezer while people worked all around him, for goodness sakes. Someone saw something."

"People tend to live in their own little bubble," Agnes advised. "We all have our own drama."

That got my attention. "What drama do you have?" I realized I didn't know that much about Agnes. "Is your granddaughter okay?"

"Yes, my granddaughter is doing fine, thank you for thinking of her. But my son has been diagnosed with bone cancer."

"What? No!" I stopped what I was doing and went to hug her. "Is there anything I can do? Do you need time off? Are you okay?"

"I've put in my notice," Agnes said. "Emailed it to the office this morning." She hugged me back. "I thought you should hear it from me. I enjoyed working with you these last few weeks, but my children and grandchildren come first, you see."

"No, I fully understand. When did this happen? How long have you known?"

"He hasn't been feeling well for the last six months. The doctors were stumped. They kept doing all kinds of tests. Finally, last night they called my son and his wife in to discuss the results."

I swallowed hard. "What is the plan of care? Can they cure him?"

Tears welled up in her eyes. "They said it would be a battle. I'm going to move in with them and watch the kids. That way they can make appointments and emergency doctor's visits and all the things that go with the diagnoses."

I grabbed a tissue from the box near the sink and handed it to her. "Please sit down. Let me get you some tea."

"But the breakfast—"

"Is done. I'll run it up to the family." I poured tea into her cup. "Please sit here and take a moment. I'll be right back down and we can talk about this."

"Thank you, Chef," Agnes said. "I didn't realize how heavily it was weighing on me."

I grabbed the tissue box and placed it beside her. "Please, stay here. I'll be back shortly."

I loaded up the warming dishes and the food onto a mobile tray and took it up to the family's dining room. It was hard not to berate myself the entire time. Agnes was right. I had been caught up in my own little world. I didn't even know her son was sick. I barely knew she had children. It was an assumption on my part since she had asked for an early evening to go see her grand-daughter's class program.

Kicking myself for not paying closer attention to my coworker, I realized that Agnes was right. It was easy to over-look someone you worked with side by side every day.

That opened a whole world of possibilities when it came to the killer. After all, Wentworth and Chef Wright worked with the same people.

I set up breakfast and went back to the kitchen. Agnes sipped her tea. Her eyes were puffy and her face thoughtful. "I'm sorry, chef," she said when I entered the kitchen. "I shouldn't bring my private life into the kitchen."

"Why ever not?" I asked. "My goodness, I spend more time with you than anyone. I should know about your life."

"Is that so that you don't feel guilty?" she asked with knowing eyes. "It's all right. You don't have to know about me."

"Yes, I do." I laid my hand on hers. "I need to apologize for being so myopic. Is your son your only child?"

"I have a daughter as well. She is in York working as a marketing manager for some internet company. She's going to get married next year." Her eyes sparkled with tears. "My son is here in London. He is going to try to work through all the treatments. His wife also works for a financial corporation. She has built up holiday time, but they really need an extra hand. The doctors told them there would be times when things might not go as planned through the treatment. So they asked me to help them out."

"Of course, I'm glad that you are able to do that. How are you today?"

"I'm shaken, I suppose. I don't know what will happen. I know that I will lose my income because I need to stop working and be there for the children, but that isn't important. What is important is getting my son well."

"Is there anything I can do?"

She smiled wistfully. "Will you be a good reference when I return to work?"

"Of course, of course," I said, and I meant it. "You are an excellent chef. Can we be friends? Will you keep in touch and let me know about your son and your grandchildren?"

"I can do that."

"Thank you," I said. "I know you gave two-week's notice, but I think you should take that time to do what your family needs to prepare for this big change. I can handle things here."

"Thanks, but I need my pay."

"Then let's keep your hours to a minimum," I said. "We'll have you go home after lunch. Is that okay?"

"Thank you, Chef," she said. "You are a good friend."

"If not a bit selfish," I gave her a big hug. Here I was concerned about my big date and the investigation to clear my name, but it seemed so small compared to what Agnes was facing.

"Well, enough self-pity." Agnes brushed away her tears. "Let's start on lunch. I'll pick the vegetables from the garden and have them prepped and ready."

"Thanks," I said. "You are amazing."

"Stop it. I'm just doing my job while I have it."

"It will be here when you are ready to come back," I said.

"Oh no, you will find someone else to work with, but that is fine. I know I'll always have a place in one kitchen or another at the palace."

Her years of working at the palace told me she was right.

Chapter 30

After dinner, I headed back to my room earlier than usual to get ready for my date. I had showered, put on Penny's dress, and was in the process of curling my hair when there was a knock at my door. "Just a second," I called, glancing at the bedroom clock. It was a half an hour before my date. Jasper shouldn't be here this early. I winced because half my hair was curled and I had no makeup on and no shoes.

The knock came again and I hurried to the door. A quick glance through the peephole and I opened the door. "Rachel," I said. "Hi, what brings you by?" I glanced up and down the empty hall. "If you're looking for Penny, I haven't seen her."

"Hello, Chef," she said with an odd look in her eyes. "I need you to come with me." She grabbed a hold of my arm and pulled me into the hallway.

"I'm sorry, I'm getting ready for a date," I said as she pulled me down the hall. "What is this about? Surely it can wait until morning."

"It's Evie," she said. "She needs you."

"Is it an emergency? Because I can go get my phone and call for help."

269

"Calling won't help," Rachel said. "She needs you now."

We hit the end of the hall and I forcefully yanked my arm away from her. "This is ridiculous. I don't even have my shoes on. Let me get my phone."

"No," Rachel said. She raised her hand and I blinked. She had a gun.

"Is that a gun?" I know it was a stupid thing to say, but I'd never been near a person with a gun. This is England, not America.

She took my wrist. "Come with me, now!"

"Okay, okay." I raised my spare hand. "I don't have my shoes."

"You don't need shoes." She pulled me down the stairs, beyond my kitchen, and down into the cellars below the palace. I had never been down here. It was cold and smelled of mold and dampness.

"How did you get a gun?" I asked. I guess it was a strange question to ask when one was being kidnapped but handguns were prohibited in England. Even police officers rarely had them—although I'd seen Ian and his guards pull them out in emergencies. "Is that one of security's weapons?"

"Shut up and come on," Rachel said.

"You know they have cameras in the halls, right? So they saw you force me down the hall."

"I said shut up." Rachel dragged me down another set of stairs into darker reaches. This area was built out of stone and had to be hundreds of years old.

"Fine." I pushed through the damp darkness. It was clear these were all storage areas. There were lights, but they were not close together. The area might have been used as bomb shelters during World War II. "Is Evie down here?"

"Go up these stairs," she said as she pushed me up. We

climbed two flights and I opened the door at the top to come out in the exterior hallway of the administration area.

"Huh," I said. "How did you know about this route?"

"You'd be surprised what administration has access to." She stuck the gun barrel into my side. "Now out we go."

I opened the door and found myself out in the parking area. "To the Orangery," she whispered in my ear.

"Cameras will see us," I felt the need to point out. "You can shoot me here but people will know it's you."

"I know the camera guy," Rachel said with a gleam in her eye. "He and I go way back."

I walked with more confidence than I felt. I knew from school that the chances of a rescue dropped when you moved away from where they expect you to be. Thankfully, she didn't seem to be forcing me into a car. We walked quietly around the building to the rear of the Orangery. The back door to the kitchen was open.

"Inside you go." She waved the pistol at me.

I stepped into the kitchen to find Evie standing near the walk-in freezer. The door to the freezer was open and condensation filled the air shrouding her in a mist.

"Hello, Carrie Ann," Evie said.

"Evie," I said. "I thought you and Rachel were feuding."

"We did a good job of fooling everyone, didn't we?" Rachel said and closed the door behind me.

"Yes," I said. "You did. Nice touch, by the way, abandoning Penny that night."

"She is a gossip and a do-gooder," Rachel sneered. "She needed to know what it felt like to be abandoned."

"Why am I here?" I asked.

"Shut up and sit down," Evie said. She grabbed me by the

arm and put me in a chair inside the freezer. It was icy inside and my bare feet stuck to the floor. I lifted them up but the circulating air was not much warmer.

"You don't have to know why you're here," Evie said. She raised her hand and I could make out the outline of a knife.

"If I'm going to die, I think I should know why."

The only light in the kitchen was the light inside the freezer. I could see my breath and a shiver struck, me running down my spine.

"You have returned to the scene of the crime," Evie said.

"What crime?" I hedged. They hadn't tied me to the chair yet. But Rachel held the gun steady on me, and Evie had a knife. It was a sure bet one would do me in before I could run very far. I tried to move so that I sat on my feet.

"Stop wiggling!" Evie commanded, putting the knife to my throat. I felt a burning sensation and a pull tug. It was the same quick feeling you get when you accidently cut your finger while chopping vegetables. I'd only done it a few times when I first started cooking, but it was a feeling you didn't forget.

I slowly, carefully put my feet down to where they hovered over the cold floor not quiet touching it. "What crime scene?" I asked again. "Wentworth Uleman's or Chef Wright?"

"You don't fool us with the Chef Wright business. We know you were sleeping with him."

I swallowed carefully. "I can assure you I wasn't sleeping with Wentworth."

"Of course you weren't sleeping with that strange little man," Evie said with disgust. "We are talking about Don. We're all grown women here. You can admit that you and Don were lovers."

"I have no idea what you are talking about."

"Don't you?" Rachel said. "He told Evie that you were sleeping with him."

"What? No, I'm dating Jasper."

"Jasper doesn't date," Evie said. "He has a wife."

"What? Jasper told me he was single." It all seemed pre-posterous. I'd met his family members. Surely they would have said something about his showing up with another woman in tow.

"See?" Evie said. "You are no different than we are. When a man shows interest we go for it. It has nothing to do with the women he left behind."

"Evie, why did you kill Wentworth?" I searched for anything to get her to slow down.

Evie chuckled. "I didn't kill Wentworth. Rachel did." She looked at Rachel with pride in her eyes.

I licked my lips and tried to smile at Rachel. "That was very clever. How did you do it?"

"You made it so easy by leaving the pie for me."

I sent a small smile her way. "Did you put the poison in the meringue?"

"That would have been clever," she said. "But too much work. He drank it, actually. After he was gone, I sprinkled some on the pie to divert attention. The rest was a matter of cleanup. Do a few dishes and, poof, no more evidence."

"How did you get the poison?"

"Aren't you full of questions?" Evie said. "Why is that so important?"

"It was all so clever," I said. "I did some research and cyanide is near to impossible to purchase."

"I didn't need to purchase it," Rachel said. "I have a degree in chemistry. It wasn't cyanide, exactly, although it had the same effect. It was acetonitrile from my acrylic nail remover. Drink it and wait."

I frowned. "How long did you wait?"

"Long enough to enjoy a piece of pie," she said with a smile.

My stomach lurched. "Why? What did Wentworth do to you?"

"He tried to blackmail me. He threatened to tell Evie I was sleeping with Don."

"But she knows." I looked from one woman to another and fought the shivering in my chest. It was incredibly cold in the freezer. My feet had started to go numb along with my fingers.

"Of course she knows," Rachel said with a sigh. "I told you I slept with Don to show Evie how fickle he was."

"That Wentworth boy thought he could extort money from my friend. He was wrong to do it. Something had to be done," Evie said. Then she shrugged. "So we did it."

"And Chef Butterbottom's poisoning?"

"Purely accidental," Rachel said. "I was trying to make Don sick."

"Why?" I shivered hard, my back teeth clanking. "I thought you loved him."

"I didn't love him. Evie did." Rachel waved the gun around. "Don needed to learn a lesson," Evie said. She stood tall. "He told me I was his one true love. He promised me that he would leave that evil witch of a wife of his for me when I got pregnant."

"But he had a vasectomy," I said. "You couldn't get pregnant."

"See, that's where everyone has it wrong," Evie said her voice rising. "I can get pregnant and I did. He promised to leave her. He promised."

"You told him you were pregnant that day didn't you?"

I felt pity for her. "He laughed at you and told you there was no way it could be his."

"He said he would leave her for me if I got pregnant," Evie said. "Then he ridiculed me. He said I was nothing to him." She patted her tummy. "But you see, I got pregnant for him."

"How?" I whispered.

"Fertility clinics are so expensive," she said. "But he should have been happy to pay. I was giving him what he wanted."

"You picked up a knife and killed him." I calculated whether I would make it to the door. My numb feet wouldn't take me far. But if I could get out into the parking area . . . If I could get under the cameras . . . At the very least they might figure out who killed me.

"I didn't kill him, but I wanted to. He laughed at me. He told me I was stupid. He said he had moved on to a new girl—someone who understood him better." She pushed the knife under my chin. "You."

"Not me," I said. "It was clearly someone else."

"Who?" Rachel asked. "It was you. Everyone knows he was interested. We watched him kiss your hand. We watched him hover over you at the competition."

"Why did Sandy say Chef Wright was prepping the kitchen to cook for a new mistress? I don't need anyone to cook for me."

"You're reaching," Evie said. "We're done arguing with you."

"Chef Wright is dead," I said. "Why kill me?"

"Why indeed," Evie said. "Because we want the investigation to be over. I didn't kill Don, but I did try to poison him. I'm pregnant and I refuse to go to jail. Instead, you are going to admit to everyone you are the killer."

"What? Why?"

"You deserve to die for taking my man," Evie said.

"That's crazy. I didn't take him from anyone."

"You see this camera over here?" Rachel moved to a tripod just outside the freezer door. "I'm going to turn it on and you are going to tell everyone that you killed Don and Wentworth. Tell them that you can't live with the guilt anymore."

"Why would I do that?" I asked and shivered again. "You're going to kill me anyway. Why would I admit to something I didn't do?"

"Because we can make you suffer first," Evie said. She grabbed me by the hair and yanked my head back until tears filled my eyes. She squeezed my numb hand around the knife and raised it as if to plunge it into my thigh.

"Wait!" I said. "I'll do it. I'll say it."

"See, now wasn't that easy?" Rachel said. "Remember, I have a gun on you." Evie stepped out of the freezer and turned on the camera.

"I want to get something off my chest," I said.

She turned off the camera. "What are you doing? Say it."

Evie hit me with the back of the knife and my head snapped back. I could feel pain blossom through my skull.

"Okay." I held my face. "Okay. I'll say it."

Evie walked out of the freezer and Rachel turned the recorder back on. She pointed at me.

"Evie Green tried to poison Chef Wright," I blurted. "She told me she did it."

"Liar!" Evie rushed into the freezer with anger in her eyes and the knife raised high. I jumped up and put the chair between us. My body didn't work was well as it should. I was half-frozen and my bare feet stuck to the freezer floor.

She rushed me again, and I picked up the chair and put it between us.

"Shoot her," Evie shouted to Rachel.

I tried to keep Evie between me and Rachel.

"Get out of the way," Rachel ordered.

Evie ducked. I ducked and a bullet went hot over my head. I might have screamed. I think I cursed. I rushed Evie with the chair and pushed her to the ground. I heard another gunshot. Grabbing the knife from Evie I flung it into the depths of the freezer. My hand was too cold to properly grasp it.

I pushed the chair into the downed Evie and hit her as hard as I could. Another bullet zinged by. I had to get out of the freezer. I had to get away. I rolled off Evie and hit the ground running. My feet felt like wooden stumps. I rushed Rachel daring her to shoot me. For some reason, she dropped the gun and stared. I leapt on her like a madwoman, pulling her hair, biting, and hitting.

Someone was on my back yanking me. I fought as if my life depended on it and it did.

Hard arms surrounded me. "Stop!" I heard a shout in my ear. "I've got you." I kicked and wriggled and head-butted. Someone cursed. The lights came on, bright and blinding. "Stop!" My brain registered that I was fighting a man—a man with a familiar voice, who held my back to his chest and lifted me up off the ground. My heart pounded and I shook my head. "Carrie Ann, I've got you."

The man was Ian. All the fight went out of me. "Ian?"

"Yes," he said. "Yes, we've got you. You're safe."

My vision cleared. Security guards had both Evie and Rachel on the ground. They were cuffing them. The chair was in splinters. I tried to breathe. It felt like I'd just run a marathon.

"You're safe now," Ian said. He turned me so that I could see his face. His eyes were bright and fierce. "It's okay. We got them."

I tried to stand but my feet were numb. He helped me to a stool. Time moved quickly and slowly at the same time. It was as if everyone moved in slow motion, but before I could think, an ambulance crew was there. Evie and Rachel were hauled off. The ambulance techs were warming my feet. There was a long furrow cut into my arm where a bullet grazed me.

My hands tingled with that uncomfortable sensation you got when blood returned to warm your extremities.

"Carrie Ann!" I looked up to see Jasper coming my way. He wore dark-wash jeans, a pale blue dress shirt, and a blazer made of black velvet. "Are you all right?"

"Jasper?"

He glanced from me to the ambulance tech. "Is she all right?"

"We're going to take her to hospital for overnight observation."

"I'm fine," I said.

"It's a precaution," the tech said.

Tears ran nonstop down my face. "I guess I won't be able to make our date."

"It's okay" He sent me a sunny smile. "Can I go with you?"

"Sure." I looked at the ambulance tech who nodded in agreement.

"I need to interview her," Ian said.

"You can do that at the hospital," the tech said. "Her feet are in bad shape and she needs stitches for that arm."

"My head feels funny," I said as my vision blurred. It all came crashing down around me.

Chapter 31

The next thing I knew, I was in a hospital room. My hands were in some kind of warm mitts. My feet were bandaged and raised slightly by a pillow under them. I was in a hospital gown and my arm was throbbing and also bandaged.

"Welcome back," Jasper said. He sat beside me. "Do you need anything?"

"Water?" I said, wincing.

"Sure thing." He opened a bottle of water. I tried to take it before I gave up. The mitts were still warming my numb hands and too big to hold anything.

"I can't."

"Here, I'll help." He put his arm around my shoulders and lifted the bottle to my lips. I drank a few sips before he took it away. "Okay, that's enough for now. How are you feeling?"

"Pain." I closed my eyes. "What—" I licked my lips. "What happened?"

"I came to pick you up and your room was wide open. You were nowhere to be seen so I called Gordon. He took a look at the camera footage. It didn't take long before we figured out where you were. By then we'd heard gunshots."

"Rachel and Evie tried to kill me."

"Yes." He tucked my blankets around me. "Gordon tells me when they arrived on the scene you were kicking the heck out of Rachel. Evie was down for the count with a chair busted over her."

"Evie had a knife and Rachel had a gun," I said. "They were both crazy." I licked my parched lips and tried to curl my fingers. Relief washed over me as I discovered my fingers moved just fine. But my feet were still numb. "They forced me into the freezer. They wanted me to confess to killing Chef Wright and then make it look like I killed myself out of remorse."

"It's okay," he said, patting my shoulder. "You're safe."

"I need to talk to her," Ian said as he strode into the tiny room. The room was filled with the two important men in my life. Both were handsome and strong. Both looked grave. It made me fear that I looked really bad at the moment. I tried to lighten the mood.

"I'm not exactly wearing an interview outfit."

Ian's expression softened. "Why don't you go tell the nurses she's awake," he said to Jasper.

"Sure," Jasper planted a quick kiss on my forehead. "Be right back."

"How are you feeling?" Ian asked. His tone had softened somewhat.

"Things hurt a bit," I said. "But I suspect they will hurt more tomorrow."

"You have a nice black eye."

I placed my fingers on my cheekbone and found one eye was twice as puffy as the other. "Great, no need to wear eye shadow. I'll just make my own."

"What happened?" he asked.

"There was a knock on my door. I thought it was Jasper come early for our date. I glanced out and saw Rachel so I opened the door."

"We saw in the hall video that she grabbed you and pulled you down the hall, but then we lost you."

"She took me through the cellar and out another door. Then we crossed a garden and went in the back of the Orangery."

"That's what took us so long. We didn't know if you were in the apartments of the palace or someplace else. I sent security down all the public areas. We finally saw her take you into the Orangery. By that time there were gunshots heard."

"Thankfully, the Orangery closes at four PM and no one was there," I said.

"Except you were there," he said. "It looks like you were gazed by a bullet."

"I had no idea," I said. "I just knew I had to do something. Evie had a knife and I went for her first. Then, Rachel. I'm sorry if I hurt you. I didn't know it was you and I was just trying to survive."

"I'm fine." He touched a black and blue spot on his chin. "You have a heck of a punch."

"Who knew?" I laughed. "Rachel killed Wentworth. She said she poisoned him with artificial nail remover. Wentworth was trying to blackmail her and Evie."

"Neither woman is talking," Ian said. "Detective Chief Inspector Garrote will be in to talk to you. Right now we have them on kidnapping and assault."

I shook my head. "Evie told me she killed Chef Wright. She really thought if she got pregnant he was going to leave his wife for her. I think she might have gone through a sperm donor to get pregnant."

"Chef Wright made it well known he wasn't having any more children."

"She killed him when he told her he wasn't going to leave his wife. She had gone through so much to please him."

"Did you get any of this on tape? Or is there any way to confirm this?"

"No," I said. "My phone was in my room. I didn't even have my shoes on."

"It's okay. I'm certain the Inspector will work it out. The information you gave will help us to find clues that support your allegation."

"That's nuts," I said with a shake of my head. "They confessed to me."

"Without proof of that, it will be your word against theirs," Ian said.

"Well that stinks." I closed my eyes. I was suddenly very tired.

"Carrie Ann, are you okay?" Penny said.

I opened my eyes to see her and Jasper at the door to the hospital room. "I'm alive," I said with a small smile. "A little banged up is all."

"Thanks for talking to me," Ian said. "We'll do some looking into the basement area you spoke of so that this won't happen again."

Ian left with a nod to Jasper.

"You look terrible." Penny gave me a quick hug that hurt my arm. I sucked in a sharp breath. "Oh, sorry," she said, grabbing a seat next to me. "I got home to see security all over the hallways and blocking your open door. I about had a heart attack. What happened?"

I gave her a quick outline of Rachel and Evie's plan.

"Yikes," Penny said. "That's crazy."

"What's really crazy is that Ian thinks the police won't be able to charge them with anything more than kidnapping and attempted murder."

"But you said they admitted to killing Wentworth and Chef Wright."

"It will be my word against theirs."

"Well, shoot," Penny said. She held onto my hand. "I'm sorry I got you mixed up with them. If they were in this together, why did Rachel get mad at me for texting Evie?"

"I don't know," I said with a shake of my head. "I think they're crazy."

"Maybe they are bonkers," Jasper said. He stood beside Penny with a tall cup of ice water with a straw. "Here, drink some of this."

I took the cup from him and sipped. It felt good. My throat was rawer than I thought.

"I'm sorry I ever introduced you to those two," Penny said.

"At least we know who the killers are," I said. "So the tabloids should leave my reputation alone."

"Yes, my guess is that by tomorrow no one will even know your name," Penny said.

* * *

The next morning, I was discharged with stitches on my arm and my feet wrapped and in slippers because of minor frostbite. Lucky for me, Penny brought me one of her fit-and-flare dresses. There was no way I would have gotten my bandaged feet into a pair of my slacks.

Penny pushed my wheelchair out into a mob of reporters. I blinked at the flashing of the cameras. "Chef Cole! Chef Cole!"

It was as if a mob called my name. I didn't know where to look. Penny brightened at the attention and I didn't blame her. She looked gorgeous, with her hair in an effortless updo and her perfectly done cat-eye makeup. I hadn't done more than put mascara on my eyelashes in case Jasper showed up. I'm pretty sure I looked wan, and I didn't want to think about the fact that I'd only brushed my hair and pulled it into a low pony.

"Chef Cole, how are you?"

"What was it like to be kidnapped?"

"Did you know your kidnappers?"

"Where did they take you?"

"Did you really run toward the gunwoman?"

"What kind of gun did she have?"

"Did you tackle Evie Green with a chair?"

"Why are your feet bandaged?"

The hospital administrator came out and leaned toward me. "Do you want to make a statement?"

"Why are they here?" I asked, perplexed.

"You're a hero," the administrator said with a smile. "They are calling you the American cowboy chef because you took on two killers—one with a gun!"

"Oh, boy," I said under my breath.

"Come on, Carrie Ann, say something," Penny encouraged me while she smiled and preened for the camera like a pro.

"Hello," I said as the cameras flashed and video cameras rolled. "I would like to thank Kensington Palace security for coming to my rescue and to the doctors and staff of the hospital for taking such good care of me."

I paused and the questions flooded back to me. I felt like a deer in the headlights. "That's all, thank you." With a quick wave, Penny rolled me away from the cameras and toward a car. Jasper stood beside the open back door.

I smiled as he helped me inside. A second quick wave to the paparazzi and Jasper drove Penny and me off.

"Wahoo, did you see that?" Penny asked with a happy smile. "We're famous." She glanced in the side mirror of the car. "I hope I looked good."

"You look amazing," I said. "Did you know that was going to happen?"

"I had no clue," Penny said. "Or I would have worn something super wow."

"Wish I knew what they wanted me to say." I drummed my fingers.

"You did a great job," Jasper said, winking at me from the driver's seat.

I put my head in my hands. "I'm going to be on all the tabloids. It's the opposite of what I thought. What will the duchess say? What will Mrs. Worth say? It's the opposite of everything they were teaching us in the employee handbook class."

"They will be worried for your health, of course," Penny said.

"I'm afraid they will be worried for the family's health," I said. "Things haven't exactly been calm since I've been on staff."

"They love you," Penny said. "Everyone loves you. Isn't that right, Jasper?"

"Yes," Jasper said with another wink and I felt the heat of a blush rush up my cheeks.

"Oh my gosh, Agnes!" I said as we pulled up to the palace. "I forgot Agnes. She needs to go be with her family. Please tell me she has not been in charge of the kitchen this whole time."

"Actually, the duchess has been cooking for her family while you were in hospital," Jasper said.

"How do you know?" I asked.

"She had me bring her veggies from the garden."

"What if she decides she doesn't need me?" I pressed my hands to my face as we parked in the parking lot across from the kitchen door.

Jasper opened my car door and helped me out. "She needs you. She loves your work. It's going to be okay."

"I can barely walk," I said. "The cold blistered my feet."

"It will be fine," Jasper said. He put his hand around my waist and practically carried me to my kitchen. It was nice to be snug up against all those muscles. I barely felt the ground beneath my slippered feet.

"You can cook in slippers," Penny said with a giggle. "We'll get you some pink bunny slippers."

"No!" I felt horror at the idea of pink bunny slippers in my kitchen.

"Just kidding," Penny said as she followed us up the hallway to my apartment. "Really, you have no sense of humor."

I opened my door to see my place exactly as I left it. There were borrowed shoes near the door. My phone was on the counter. My bedroom was wide open with clothes in a small pile near the bath. My bathroom light was left on.

"Let me take care of your bed," Penny said.

"No, don't," I said. "I'd rather be in the living area. I'm okay, really. It's just my feet."

"No," Jasper said. "The doctor said you should be in bed for at least another day. So off you go."

"But!"

"No means no." He picked me up and held me against him with one hand and used the other to whip the covers back. Then he plopped me in the bed. Penny pushed pillows behind me so that I could sit up.

The things that were on the bed tumbled to the floor, and I blushed again at the thought of Jasper manhandling me so well.

Penny took one look at my face and said, "I'll go make tea." And she was gone.

I was alone in my bedroom with Jasper. He sort of filled the room with male muscle. "Well." I put my hands in my lap. "I'm sorry I ruined our date."

He put his hands on his hips and let out a laugh that made me giggle as well. "You were busy engaging in hand-to-hand combat staving off a knife-wielding crazy woman and a live shooter, and all you can say is that you're sorry about missing our date? Who are you, James Bond?"

"I'm glad you aren't upset." I chewed on my bottom lip. "I do have one question."

"What?" He took my hand.

"Evie told me you were married. She said I wasn't any better than she was because you are married. Is that true?"

"Would I ask you on a date if I were married?" His gaze turned serious.

"I hope not," I said. "Are you married?"

"No wife, no kids to spring on you," he said.

"Why would Evie say that?"

"Maybe to get you questioning yourself," he said. "Who knows?"

"And you've never been married?"

"Once, a long time ago, but it's been over for a very long time."

"And you are divorced?"

"I'm divorced. Do you feel better now?"

"I do," I said. "Will you ever ask me out again?"

"We'll go once your feet are healed."

"It could be a couple of weeks," I said with sadness.

"You're worth the wait," he squeezed my hand. "I'm going to go now so you can rest." He planted a kiss on my forehead and walked out. I closed my eyes. What a crazy life.

* * *

The next day I was called into the security offices to speak to Detective Chief Inspector Garrote.

"Chef Cole," he said, shaking my hand as I walked in. Today I wore a denim skirt and a white pullover. On my feet I had gel-soled soft slippers. "Thanks for seeing me today."

"I'm happy to help when I can," I said. "You know that."

"Yes," he said with a nod. "Please sit. I was hoping to go over the details of your kidnapping."

"Okay." We went over what happened.

"You're telling me Rachel admitted to killing Wentworth Uleman?"

"Yes," I said with a nod. "She said she poisoned him with artificial nail remover."

"Indeed." He looked at his notes. "I did some research into artificial nail remover. It seems that it can turn into cyanide in the body."

"Oh," I said. "That's why the cause of death was—"

"Not immediate," he said. "It can take a few hours after ingestion for that to happen."

"So how did she ensure it killed him?"

"That's a question we don't have answers to yet," he said. "Evie told you she killed Chef Wright?"

"Yes, she said they had an argument. She wanted him to leave his wife for her. He said he would if she got pregnant. But he had a vasectomy years ago."

"She wasn't going to get pregnant."

"No," I shook my head. "She wasn't going to get pregnant, but then she took matters into her own hands. She thought it would cement their relationship."

"He didn't agree."

"She said he laughed at her."

"So she killed him."

"She told me she was suing Mrs. Wright for part of the insurance money to support her and her child."

"Did she say how she killed him?"

"She had a knife." I drew my eyebrows together. "I assumed she stabbed him in the back."

"The knife she used on you was not the murder weapon," he said. "Thank you for coming down and giving me your story."

"Ian—Chief Gordon—tells me that you can't charge them with murder even though they confessed to me."

"Right now it's hearsay," he said. I do have one more question for you."

"Sure."

"Why do you think they kidnapped you?"

"They told me they wanted me to confess to the murders and then they would make my death look like a suicide."

"I see. Why you?"

"The tabloids suspected I was having an affair with Chef Wright."

"Were you?"

"No," I said. "I wasn't, and I had no intention of doing that. I'm here to create good, home-cooked meals for the family."

"You're not dating anyone?"

"I'm seeing Jasper Fedman."

"And how long have you been dating?"

"We had a few quick drinks," I said. "Saturday was to be our first fancy date."

"A young, vibrant woman like you has not been dating anyone?"

"I just broke up with a long-term boyfriend," I said. "I don't see what any of this has to do with what happened."

"Just trying to flesh out details, Chef Cole."

"That's all I know," I said. "Can I go?"

"Yes, of course."

I stood and carefully walked toward the door, then paused. "What will it take to bring justice for the murdered men?"

"Leave that to me," he said with confidence.

"Right," I muttered and went to push the door open when he stopped me.

"Chef Cole," he said.

"Yes?"

"I will bring your attackers to justice, too."

"Thanks."

*　*　*

Later that afternoon, right before tea, I had an appointment to see Mrs. Worth. I arrived early. I was getting used to moving around on my blistered feet. The bandages and slippers helped. It was still a bit strange to wear slippers in such a proper place as the household offices. But it was all I could wear for the next week.

"Mrs. Worth will see you now," the secretary said.

"Thanks," I said and made my way down the short hall to the office door. I knocked.

"Come in," she said. "Ah, Chef Cole. Please take a seat. How are you doing?"

"I'm a bit sore, but good," I said. "I'm looking forward to getting back to my kitchen."

Mrs. Worth's brown hair was pulled back. She wore only the smallest amount of makeup. Her proper suit was of brown tweed.

"Good," she said. "The duchess has asked about you. I am happy to report that she is looking forward to your return as well."

"Oh, good," I said with relief.

"I'm sorry you had to go through such an ordeal. The necessary parties have been dismissed and I have tasked security with ensuring even more stringent background checks so that we don't have these issues in the future."

"Great," I said.

"You are new to the palace and therefore don't have much vacation or personal time built up."

"No, but I can get back to work tonight," I said.

"With slippers on your feet?" She gave me a pointed look.

"I'll find shoes."

"You can find shoes tomorrow. The duchess and I want to know that you are well and healthy. It will extend to your work."

"Yes, ma'am." I tried not to be too disappointed. "Thank

you for believing in me enough to keep me as the family's chef during this trying time."

"It wasn't my choice," she said sternly. "The duchess loves your work and believes in you. Don't let her down."

"I won't," I said. Getting up, I made my way to the door. The first thing on my list was to get a comfortable pair of kitchen appropriate shoes. That meant I needed to go shopping. Not my favorite thing to do in the world, but sometimes it had to be done. This was one of those times.

* * *

"What are you doing?" Penny asked. She popped into my kitchen just after tea.

"I'm shopping online for shoes that are comfortable, yet kitchen appropriate. I need them if I'm going to go back to work tomorrow."

"Why don't you go with me? I'll take you shopping. I know this great shoe store."

I bit my lower lip. "Do you think that we can get there without any paparazzi? The last thing I need is more exposure in the tabloids. The one thing I got out of the first two employee handbook trainings is that we aren't supposed to draw attention to ourselves. Mrs. Worth let me know that she didn't approve of me."

"Really?"

"She said I was lucky the duchess liked my work or I wouldn't be working here."

"Ouch," Penny said.

"You work with the duchess," I said. "Does she blame me for having to cook for herself the last two days?"

"Oh, no," Penny said. "Kate loves you. Trust me. With her

schedule she is so glad to have someone she trusts feeding her family."

"Oh, good," I said.

"Come on," Penny said. "I get off in an hour. Come out shopping with me."

"All I've got for my feet is slippers," I said and raised my feet to show off the soft, fluffy footwear.

"No one will notice," Penny said with a wave of her hand. "Trust me, there are people wearing worse out there."

"Okay," I said. "I'll meet you at the parking area in an hour."

"Yay!" Penny clapped her hands. "I can't wait to show you my secret shoe shop."

I met Penny in the parking lot at the designated time.

"Normally I would walk," she said. "But with your wounded feet, I asked Cameron to drive us." She opened a car door and I slid inside.

"Hello, ladies," Cameron said. "Welcome. Where are we going?"

"Cameron is a driver for Prince Harry," Penny said. She blew him a kiss. "He had a free hour and will take us to the shop. It's on High Street."

"Thank you for taking us," I said. "Are you sure you won't get in trouble?"

"It's all good," he said with a quick grin as he drove us out into the street. "It's really only five minutes, and I'm not scheduled until after dinner."

"Yay!" Penny clapped her hands again. "Look, we're here." She pointed out the window. It felt like we only went a few blocks. Cameron pulled to the side and got out to let us out of the car.

"I'll be back in thirty minutes," Cameron said. "Be ready."

Penny threw her hands around his neck and gave him a big kiss on the cheek. "You're the best."

He grinned and stepped back into the car and was gone.

"This is my favorite shoe shop in London." Penny put her arm through mine. We walked into Burks.

"How fun," I said. "My first London shop." We went in. I was fitted and out in no time with a pair of nice black shoes that cradled my bandaged feet.

We stepped out onto the street. It was a busy evening. We looked up and down for Cameron. A car pulled up and the window rolled down. It was Beth Branch. I found myself taking a visceral step back. Penny was bent down to see who was in the car. After I recognized Beth, I saw the gun in her hand.

"Penny!" I grabbed Penny, pushing her to the ground and out of the way.

The sound of a gunshot filled the air. People all around ducked. I felt my heart rate spike. Anger surged through me. "No!" I tore the door open and reached in, startling Beth. I grabbed the lapel of her dress and yanked her out of the car and into the street. The car lurched forward hitting the car stopped in front of it.

People stopped and stared. Some people took video with their phones. I must have surprised Beth. She was half in and half out of the car. I kicked her hand that was holding the gun so that the weapon spun into the gutter. Beth grabbed my pant leg and pulled me to the ground. I could feel her trying to pull me into the car. I kicked and screamed.

Men came running. Suddenly arms grabbed me and yanked me from her grasp. Other people held Beth down. Police sirens rang out. "Why did you tell Ian to question me?

Everything was going as planned. Evie and Rachel should have been the primary suspects. Everything was going as planned until you. I should have killed you first," Beth shouted. "I should have sliced you like I did Don."

"Wait, you killed Chef Wright?" I asked. "But Evie told me—"

"Don't be a fool," Beth seethed. "Evie didn't admit to anything. She wouldn't kill Wright. She was in love with him."

"But, if you killed Chef Wright, why?"

"He found out I was stealing recipes. He threatened to have me fired." Her eyes flashed. "He threatened me." She lunged at me and the men pulled her back.

"Don't let her near anyone," I said.

"You should have never pushed Ian Gordon to question me," she sneered. "Who do you think you are? They had Evie cold for this case until you got involved."

After those words, it seemed like everything happened so fast. The police came and took control of Beth. The crowds were roped off. Penny and I were sitting in the shop doorway hugging each other.

Cameron called Penny. She put the call on speakerphone. "I can't get to you with the traffic," he said. "I'm sorry but I have to take the boss out to a state dinner."

"No problem," Penny said. "We're kind of in the middle of things here. We'll get a taxi home."

"Okay," Cameron said. "Are you okay?"

"We're safe," Penny said.

I saw Detective Chief Inspector Garrote walking toward us. He had on a fancy overcoat and was dressed as if he had a dinner date. "What happened?"

Tears came to my eyes. "We went shopping and Beth

Branch . . . I'm sorry," I said. Penny pulled a tissue out of her purse and I dabbed the tears in my eyes.

"We have it on video," Penny said with more calm than I felt. "We came out of the shoe store and Beth pulled up beside us. I didn't realize what was going on. She rolled down the window and called out so I went over."

"I saw the gun and pushed Penny out of the way," I said. "I don't really remember what all happened after that."

"Carrie Ann grabbed her and knocked the gun out of her hand," Penny said. "The crowd got involved."

"Did anyone get hurt?" Detective Chief Inspector Garrote asked. He was taking notes.

"I don't think so," I said. "Some bruises but that's it."

"There was some sort of traffic incident?" He asked as he looked at the cars.

"I pulled Beth from the car to knock the gun out of her hand and the car lurched forward."

"I see."

"What I want to know is why." Penny hugged me tight. "This is the second time someone tried to kill Carrie Ann. Why is this allowed to go on?"

"We were close to an arrest," he said. "I didn't expect her to lash out."

"She said she wished she had killed me like she killed Chef Wright," I said. "We have witnesses and I think some people got it on their phones."

"Our techs are reviewing all the video footage now," he said. "The most important thing is that you are all right."

"Can we go home now?" I asked.

"Yes," He said. "But I may need to speak to you tomorrow. Do you have a ride?"

"Our ride couldn't get here," Penny said.

"I'll have a constable take you," he waved over a police officer. "See these ladies get home safely."

"Yes, sir."

We rode in silence back to the palace. Penny clung to my arm as if I was going to keep her safe. Or maybe she was afraid I was going to disappear.

We showed our badges at the gates and got into the palace before tears started running down my cheeks. I guess the adrenaline had worn off. Penny hugged me.

Ian met us at the palace door. "I heard what happened. Are you all right?"

Jasper came running up. "I've been going crazy. Are you okay?" He put his arms around me, and I melted into his warmth as the sobs started.

"Beth Branch almost killed us," Penny said. "It was horrible, but Carrie Ann was amazing. She pushed me out of the way and opened the door. Beth was surprised. Next thing I know Carrie Ann had Beth halfway out of the car and kicked the gun out of her hand. People were videoing and others got involved. It was chaos."

"We didn't know if shots were fired or not," Jasper said. "There were rumors that one or more of you were dead."

"Come on," Ian said. "Let's get you inside away from prying eyes."

He opened the door and ushered us into the hall. I glanced over my shoulder to see that the press had gathered outside the gates and were snapping pictures.

"Beth said she killed Chef Wright. She screamed it in front of the crowd. People have it on video."

"I really thought Evie killed Chef Wright," I said with a

shiver. "I guess she never really admitted to murdering Chef Wright. I just assumed. I should never assume."

"It's easy to make assumptions when faced with a killer," Ian said. "Don't beat yourself up."

"I think Evie and Beth have done enough of that already." We laughed and walked up to our apartments. "Why don't you all come to my place," I said. "I'll make tea."

I opened my door and they settled in while I started the electric kettle.

"You're bleeding," Ian said. He stood by the counter and pointed to my arm.

"I might have pulled out my stitches." I touched the spot where the stitches were. It was seeping. "I'll go put on another shirt."

"I'll go with you and check it out," Penny said.

We ducked into my bathroom. I had indeed popped a few stitches.

"Darn," I said.

"Looks like you need to go to the clinic," Penny said.

"I'll take her," Jasper said outside the door.

"Good," Penny said. She helped me get into a short sleeve shirt. "Off you go."

"But we were going to have tea."

"No worries. I'm exhausted. I'll head off to bed."

"But it's early." I pointed to the clock, which read nine-thirty PM.

"I'm fine. I think a little quiet will be nice for me."

"I'll let you know when I get back," I said. "You can stay with me if you need anything."

Penny smiled. "You can stay with me, too."

"It's pretty bad when a girl can't even go shoe shopping safely," I said.

"Oh, you do have your shoes, right?"

"I have my shoes," I said, pointing to the shopping bag near the door. "I managed to keep a hold of it." It was important to me that I would be able to go back to work in the morning—busted stitches and all.

Jasper walked me out to the car and drove me to the clinic.

"I'm surprised they didn't check you out at the scene," he said as he pulled into the now quiet streets.

"The officers asked, but we thought we were fine."

"Well, you aren't fine." He held my hand. "I'm sorry this is happening to you, Carrie Ann."

"There's never a dull day in the palace," I said. "I guess it can't all be glamour."

He laughed a loud hearty laugh. "I guess not."

Chapter 32

I was back in my kitchen at five-thirty the next morning. I was so happy to be there making coffee and sticky buns for the family breakfast. Baked beans, sausage, and eggs were on the menu.

My arm was freshly stitched and bandaged. The throbbing was kept at a minimum by pain killers. The doctor at the clinic had insisted on checking out my feet. I had torn up the scabs from the blisters in my struggle with Beth. He gave me some salve to put on with instructions to apply every four hours.

My new shoes were as comfortable as slippers.

"You are alive!" Agnes said as she entered the kitchen.

"Of course I'm alive," I said with a smile and returned the hug she gave me.

"The news have video of you pulling that woman out of her car and kicking the gun away. Everyone is calling you the cowboy chef. There's talk of making you a superhero costume."

I felt the heat of a blush rush up my cheeks and into my hair. "That's a bit dramatic, don't you think?"

"Have you seen the video?" Agnes asked. "That was one crazy brave thing you did."

"I haven't seen the video," I said. "I don't want to see the video. I want to go back to being the best chef for the family—quiet and behind the scenes."

"It's a little late for that," Agnes said. She washed her hands and got to work.

We worked that morning in warmth and laughter. I knew my time with Agnes would be over soon. She told me about her son and the challenges he would face.

After lunch, Penny popped into the kitchen. "Hello, my hero," she said with a smile.

"You look good," I said. "Did you find any bruises this morning? Because I woke up sore in places I didn't know could get sore."

Penny laughed. "I have a few scrapes and bruises. One on my bum where I fell after you pushed me."

"Oh, I'm so sorry." I put my hand to my mouth. "Is it too bad?"

She laughed. "I'll live, thanks to you. Who knew you were so strong?"

"Adrenaline," I said.

"So, seriously, the duchess sent me down to get you."

"To get me?" I placed my hand on my chest.

"Yes, she wants to see you."

"Oh boy." I pulled off my working chef's coat, grabbed my clean one, and pulled it on. "How's my face? Do I have anything on it?"

"You look fine," Penny said. "Oh wait," she pulled out a tissue and rubbed at something on my cheek. "Now you look perfect."

"Thank goodness," I said with a grin. We went up to the duchess's study. Penny knocked on the door and stepped inside. I waited nervously outside until Penny came to get me.

"The duchess will see you now," Penny said as she opened the door.

The duchess was dressed in a casual sheath dress. Her perfect hair was pulled back in a low ponytail. The little prince was chatting with her. He wore a school uniform. His backpack sat on the floor beside him. A nanny played blocks with the little princess in the sunlight from a tall window. My heart warmed.

"Come in, do come in," the duchess said.

"Are you the cowboy chef?" the little prince asked.

"Oh, no," I said. "I'm just your chef."

"Will you make me chocolate biscuit cake?" His expression was very serious.

"It would be my pleasure," I said.

"Please come in and have a seat." The duchess waved to a pair of chairs in front of her desk.

"Thank you," I said and took a seat.

"I'm going to speak to Chef now," the duchess said to the little prince. "Why don't you help Nanny get your sister down for a nap?"

"Okay." He picked up his backpack. "Goodbye, Chef. Don't forget my cake."

"Goodbye, sir," I said with seriousness. "I won't forget."

We waited a moment as the nanny ushered the children out of the study. My hands were in my lap and I tried not to wiggle nervously.

The duchess turned to me with a gentle smile. "How are you, Chef Cole? I understand you've been through quiet a lot in the last few days."

"I'm a bit bruised, but nothing that will keep me from making cake for the prince."

"He loves your cakes," she said. "Penny tells me you saved her life last night."

"I—"

"No need to be humble," she said, raising her hand in a "stop" fashion. "We've all seen the video. The duke teased that perhaps we should hire you on the security staff. You have the makings of a great bodyguard."

I felt the blush at my cheeks. "Thank you, but I do prefer to cook."

"Good," she said. "Because we all love your cooking. It's been good and bad the last few days. My family loves me, but my cooking isn't exactly at your level." She laughed. "No, don't tell me that you bet I'm good at it. It's why we're so thin."

I smiled.

"I asked you here today to let you know that we are glad you are a part of our household. You are doing a wonderful job, and we hope you continue to make more of your fresh meals."

"Thank you," I said. "It means a lot."

"We thought you should know how much we appreciate you. Now," she said, "for a bit of business. We will be taking a week's trip to the country. We want you to come with us. Is that possible? I know you might need to rest—"

"I would love to come," I said. "I'm looking forward to continuing on with my work as your personal chef."

"Good," she said. "Oh, yes and one last thing—"

"Yes, ma'am?"

"Good job on the pie competition. The duke said he would love to taste the peanut butter pie. Can you make one?"

"It would be my pleasure." I stood.

"Wonderful, Penny will help you with the details on the country holiday."

"Thanks again," I said.

"Good day." The duchess turned to work on her computer.

Penny showed me to the door and closed it behind us in the hall.

"A country holiday?"

"Yes, the end of the month," Penny said. "I'll get together with you to fill in all the details."

"Wonderful," I said. "I'm always up to seeing more of England. Especially a part without any murderers."

Penny laughed. "We can hope."

I gave her a quick hug and went back to my kitchen. I had a pie and a chocolate biscuit cake to make for the family. With the killers properly locked up, my life was finally back on track.

Basic Pie Crust

Ingredients

3 cups all purpose flour
2 tablespoons sugar
1 teaspoons salt
1 cup plus 2 tablespoons (2¼ sticks) chilled unsalted butter,
    cut into ½-inch cubes
8 tablespoons ice water
1½ teaspoons apple cider vinegar

Stir flour, sugar, and salt in medium sized bowl. Add butter; cut with pastry cutter until it resembles a fine meal or pea sized. Add 8 tablespoons ice water and cider vinegar; stir with a wooden spoon until moist clumps form, adding more ice water by teaspoonful if dough is dry. Gather dough together. Turn dough out onto work surface; divide dough in half. Form each half into ball and flatten into disk. Wrap disks separately in plastic; refrigerate at least 1 hour.

Makes two 9 inch pie crusts.

Rum Banoffee Pie

Ingredients

1 9 inch pie crust from basic pie crust recipe
4 ripe bananas—peeled and sliced
1 tbs butter
1 tbs sugar
1 12.25 oz can of caramel sauce-reserve 2 tbls
11 oz dark chocolate
1¼ cups cream
2 tbs caramel
3 tbs dark rum
1 tbs sugar

Roll out the pastry on a lightly floured surface until big enough to line a pie pan. Chill for 30 mins.

Heat oven to 400 degrees F. Line the pastry with baking parchment, fill with baking beans, and bake for 15 mins until the sides are firm and turning golden. Remove the beans and parchment, and cook for another 15 mins until browned.

Meanwhile, fry the bananas, butter and sugar in a wide frying pan until golden and caramelized. In a saucepan, bubble the caramel for 5 mins until slightly thickened.

Melt 1 oz of the chocolate, brush over the base of the tart case and set aside to harden. Once the bananas are cool, and the chocolate has set, arrange the bananas over the base. Top with the caramel, then chill while you make the topping.

Put the remaining chocolate, the cream, 2 tbsp caramel, the rum and sugar in a heatproof bowl over a pan of barely simmering water and melt until smooth and combined. Pour the mix over the bananas, then chill for at least 4 hrs. Top with whip cream if desired. Slice and serve.

Seville Meringue Pie

Ingredients

½ basic pie crust recipe
¾ full-fat milk
¼ c cornstarch
1 cup sugar
zest and juice 3 medium oranges
    (about 1 cup juice)
¼ cup thin-cut Seville orange marmalade
¾ cup unsalted butter
4 large egg yolks
For the meringue
4 large egg whites
1 cup golden caster sugar
1 tsp cream of tarter

Using a little flour to dust the surface, thinly roll out the pastry and place in a loose-bottomed tart tin. Leave the excess over-hanging and prick the base with a fork. Chill for 30 mins until firm. Heat oven to 400 degrees F. Put the tart tin on a baking sheet, then line the pastry with foil and fill with baking beans. Bake for 15 mins or until the pastry is firm and dry, then remove the beans and foil. Bake for 20 mins more or until the pastry is golden brown and biscuity. Leave to cool.

Pour the milk into a pan and bring to a simmer. In a large mixing bowl, whisk together the cornstarch, sugar, orange zest, juice and marmalade. Pour the warm milk into the bowl, whisking constantly. Put the mixture in a clean pan and cook over a low heat, stirring all the time, until simmering and thickened. The custard might look a bit lumpy at first, but keep stirring and it will come together. Take off the heat and beat in the butter, followed by the egg yolks.

For the meringue, beat the egg whites to stiff peaks in a large bowl. Add the sugar in four additions, beating back to stiff peaks after each, to make a thick meringue. Whisk in the cream of tarter.

Trim the edges of the pastry case with a small serrated knife. Warm the orange filling until it bubbles, stirring occasionally. Spoon the filling into the case and smooth the top. Carefully spoon the meringue on top of the hot filling, starting at the edge and working towards the middle to prevent the meringue from sinking. Gently swirl the meringue down to meet the pastry all around the edge of the tart.

Bake for 15–20 mins or until the meringue is pale golden brown. Cool for at least 1 hr, then remove from the tin and serve.

Acknowledgments

Special thanks goes out to my family for their love and support. The only way to get a book written is with a lot of help and patience.

Thank you to the team at Crooked Lane. You all are awesome.

And always, special thanks to my agent, Paige Wheeler.